Town Justice

"Get your lousy hands up!" Eddie Pangman rammed the muzzle of his rifle into the man's belly.

Tommy Hemus grinned and kicked him in the groin. He fell down with a scream, clawing at his middle. Dave Hemus picked him up and pinned him against the truck.

Burney Hackett brought out a muddy calf halter and slipped it over the suspect's head.

"Nobody goin' to shoot you, killer," he assured. "Not for a while, anyway."

More Suspense from SIGNET

The Glass Village

Ellery Queen

A SIGNET BOOK from
NEW AMERICAN LIBRARY
TIMES MIRROR

Cast of Characters

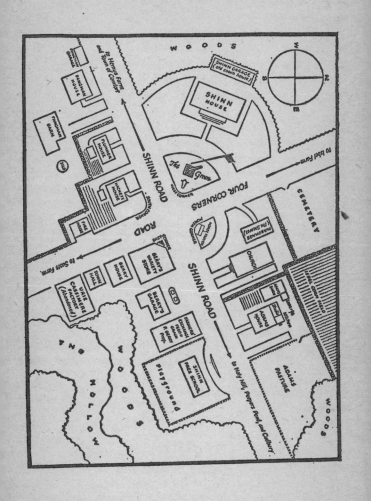

One

❖━━━━━━━━━━━━━━━━━❖

"Now you take murder," said Superior Court Judge Lewis Shinn, putting down the novel his house guest had left lying on the porch. "Murder in New England is not the simple matter you furriners from New York and such places hold it to be. No back-country Yank would have reacted like this criminal."

"Fellow who wrote this, for your information," said Johnny, "was born twenty-eight miles from here."

Judge Shinn snorted, "Oh, you mean Cudbury!" as if the bench he had occupied there for the past thirty-two years had never raised the calluses he was currently sitting upon. "Anyway, he couldn't have been. I'd know him."

"He moved away at the ripe old age of eleven."

"And that makes him an authority, I suppose! Not that you've damaged my thesis." The Judge leaned over and dropped the book gingerly into his guest's lap. "I know Cudbury people who are as ignorant of the real New England as this fellow. Or you, for that matter."

Johnny settled back in one of the Judge's rush-bottomed rockers with a grin. The early July sun in his face was smoothing the wrinkles around his eyes, as the Judge had promised, and Millie Pangman's breakfast—consisting chiefly of their Peepers Pond catch of the day before— had accomplished the same feat for his stomach. He brought his feet up to the porch railing, sending a brittle paintfall to the warped floorboards.

"Cudbury," Judge Shinn was sneering. "Yes, Cudbury is twenty-eight miles northeast of Shinn Corners as the pesky crows fly—look at 'em over yonder in Mert Isbel's corn!—and just about ten thousand miles away from the Puritan spirit. What would you expect from a county seat? It's practically a metropolis. You'll never learn about the back-country Yankee from Cudbury."

In the week Johnny had hung about Cudbury waiting

9

for the Judge to clear his docket he had heard Shinn
Corners referred to with snickers, like a vaudeville
joke—Cudbury asserting its cultural superiority, the Judge
had said. Johnny had grasped the reason on the drive
down Wednesday evening. They had taken a chewed-up
blacktop road out of Cudbury, bearing southwest. The
road ran through flat tobacco farmland for a few miles,
worsening as low hills appeared and the farms petered
out. Then they were in scrubby, burned-over-looking
country. The boy at the wheel of the Judge's old Packard,
Russell Bailey, had spat repeatedly out his window . . .
not very tactfully, Johnny had thought, but Judge Shinn
had seemed not to notice. Or perhaps the Judge was used
to it. While court was in session he lived in Cudbury, in
Bessie Brooks's boarding house next to the County Lawyers' Block and within a hundred yards of the County
Court House. But on occasional weekends he had Russ
Bailey drive him down to Shinn Corners, where Millie
Pangman would open the old Shinn house, air the beds
and dust the ancient furniture, and cook his meals as if
the Pangman farm across the road had no connection
with her at all. Perhaps—Johnny remembered thinking—
the fact that the road Millie Pangman had to cross to reach
the Judge's house was named Shinn had something to do
with it. Not to mention the Shinn Free School, which had
graduated her Merritt and her Eddie, and which little
Deborah was to attend in the fall. Powerful name, Shinn.
In Shinn Corners.

Twenty miles out of Cudbury the scrub had changed
to second-growth timber as the hills thickened, to degenerate a few miles on into a land of marsh and bogs. Then
at the twenty-five mile mark they had skirted Peepers
Pond with its orchestra of bull fiddles, and suddenly
they had topped the hill named Holy and seen Shinn
Corners in the wrinkled valley a mile below, looking
like a cluster of boils on an old man's neck. Everything
in the shifty dusk had seemed poor—the untidy land, the
dried-up bed of what his kinsman said had once been
a prosperous river, the huddle of once-white buildings.
When Russ Bailey deposited them in the heart of the
village on the uncut lawn of the Shinn house and drove
the Judge's Packard away to be garaged in Cudbury at
'Lias Wurley's for the week of their stay, Johnny had
felt an absurd sinking of the heart. It was different from

Cudbury, all right. And Cudbury had been bad enough. It was the last place in the world a man could find an answer to anything.

Johnny smiled at himself. All hope was not dead, then. The thought tickled him in a lazy sort of way.

"But you mentioned murder," Johnny said. "I suppose you're prepared with an impressive list of local homicide statistics?"

"Well, you've got me there," admitted the old man. "We had one gaudy case in 1739—infanticide by a seventeen-year-old girl who'd made the two-backed animal with a deacon of the church—that church there on the north corner, where your grandfather was baptized, married, and buried from. Then there was a regrettable corpse during the Civil War, the result of an argument between an Abolitionist and a Vallandigham Democrat. And we had a murder only about fifteen years ago. . . . I suppose you wouldn't say that three in two hundred and fifty-some years constitute much of a statistic, no. For which, by the way, the Lord be praised, and may He continue to stay the hand of Cain *ad finem*." And Judge Shinn glowed at his village, a panorama of sunny emptiness. "Where the dickens was I?"

"The complexity of murder *in re* the back-country Yank," Johnny said.

"Exactly. You have to understand that the Puritan spirit lies heavy within us, like gas on a troubled stomach. None of your New York or even Cudbury melting pots for us, to reduce us to some watery soup with a furrin handle. We're concentrated in our substance, and if you set your nose to the wind you'll get the whiff of us."

"Not me," said Johnny. "I'm all scattered to hell and gone."

"Who said anything about you?" demanded the Judge. "Your disease is about as close to Shinn Corners as Asiatic cholera. Don't let your name fool you, my boy. You're a heathen ignoramus, and it's historical fact I'm preaching. Let me tell you about the Puritan nature that's somehow been bred out of you. The Puritan nature boils down to just one thing—privacy. You let me be, neighbor, and I'll do likewise. Unless and until, of course, the community is threatened. That's a different pack of pickles. That's where the contradiction starts operating."

"Murder," reminded his New York kinsman.

"I'm getting there," said Judge Shinn, warming to it. "Murder to folks hereabout is more than a legal indiscretion. We've been taught with our mush that killing is forbidden by the Bible, and we're mighty set on it. But we're also all wrapped up in the sacred rights of the individual. Thou shalt not kill, but thou hast a powerful hankering sometimes, when your personal pinkytoe's been trod on. Murder being a crime that wantonly destroys a man's most precious piece of assessable property, we're pulled back and forth like Rebecca Hemus trying to decide between her waistline and that extra helping of gravy and potatoes. It makes us sure of one thing: it's got to be punished, and quick. Puritan justice doesn't delay.

"Take that case I mentioned a minute ago," said the Judge. "The one that happened just before the war—not the Korean business, but the big war."

"Funny thing about wars," said Johnny. "I was in both of them and I couldn't see much difference in scale. The one you're in is always the biggest one ever was."

"I s'pose," said the Judge. "Well, in those days Hubert Hemus's brother Laban helped work in the Hemus farm. Laban was a slowpoke, not too sha'p, mostly kept his mouth shut. But he never missed a town meeting or failed to vote right.

"The Hemuses employed a hired hand by the name of Joe, Joe Gonzoli, a cousin of 'Squale Gonzoli's of Cudbury. Joe made a real good hand for the farmers who didn't have modern equipment. Back on the farm in Italy, Joe used to say in his broken English, if you needed a new sickle or a hoe handle, why, you just made it. He had curly hair and black eyes like a woman's, and he always had a joke and a snatch of Italian opera song for the girls.

"Well," said the Judge, "Joe and Labe had trouble from the start. Labe would make out he couldn't understand Joe's English, and Joe would poke fun at Labe's slow ways. I guess Labe didn't like being outplowed and outworked; that Joe was a working fool. They got into quite a competition. Hube Hemus didn't mind. He had a real brisk farm in those days.

"Now Labe had never looked at a woman twice, far as any of us knew," continued Judge Shinn, "till Adaline Greave grew up to be a strapping fine women with the build of a Holstein. Then Labe took to taking baths regularly and hanging about the Town Hall square nights, or at church socials when Adaline would be helping out. She kind of led Labe on, too. At least Labe thought so, and everybody said it was working out to something. But one night Laban went looking for Adaline after a church supper, and he found her in the hayloft of the Farmers' Exchange Feed and Grain barn across from the church, that Peter Berry runs. She was lying in Joe Gonzoli's arms."

The Judge squinted through the V made by his shoes on the porch rail as if a gunsight. "There was a pitchfork sticking in a bale, and Labe went crazy mad. He plucked that fork out and made for Joe with a roar. But Joe was too quick for him. He rolled Adaline aside and like a cat came up under the fork with the knife he carried in his belt. There was a terrible fight. It ended with Joe's knife sinking up to the haft between Laban Hemus's ribs."

Through his pedal sight Judge Shinn fixed on the flagpole which stuck out of the wedge of village green fronting his property like an anniversary candle. "I'll never forget the hullabaloo that night on the green there. The men buzzed around the flagpole and cannon and your forebear Asahel Shinn's monument as if war'd been declared. Burney Hackett was constable then, too—that's the Hackett house across Shinn Road there, on the south corner—and Burney had quite a time getting Joe into his house, which he figured was the safest place to wait for the state police. Labe's brother Hubert tried to get at the prisoner with his bare hands. Hube is a skinny fellow, but that night he was all puffed out and vibrating like a frog. Earl Scott and Mr. Sheare, the minister, had to sit on him till Burn Hackett got Joe Gonzoli behind locked doors. Nor was Hube the only one het up. Everybody's sympathy was with the Hemuses. If this had been down South . . .

"But it was New England back-country, Johnny. Vengeance is mine, saith the minister, speaking for the Lord; but the Puritan's always torn between his sovereign individuality and the 'Thou shalt nots.' I don't deny it was a narrow squeak, but in the end we compromised. We signed over our personal interest in Joe Gonzoli to the community. And that's where we made our mistake."

"Mistake?" said Johnny, bewildered.

"Well, we'd liked Labe. But more important, he was one of us. He belonged to the town and the land, and no Papist furriner with tricky furrin ways and Italian songs had a right to come between a Shinn Corners Congregationalist Republican member of a founding family and the girl he was fixing to marry. Justice was what we wanted, meaning that if we couldn't light fires under Joe Gonzoli with our own hands, we could at least see to it he fried in that Chair up at the Williamston prison practically immediately.

"So we let the state police come, and they took Joe from Burney Hackett's custody, and they shot out of Shinn Corners followed by most of the village in cars and buggies going lickety-split, which is not the way your New England farmer usually goes. They just about got Joe safely locked up in the county jail. Judge Webster sat in the case, best fly-fisherman in Cudbury County. At least, he used to be. You remember, Johnny—I introduced you to Andy Webster last week."

"Hang Andy Webster," said Johnny. "What was the verdict?"

"With Adaline Greave to testify that it was Laban attacked Joe first with the pitchfork?" said Judge Shinn. "Why, that Cudbury jury never hesitated. Brought in an acquittal.

"And Shinn Corners," said the Judge, "never did get over that verdict, Johnny. We still slaver about it. It shook our Puritan sense of justice to the crosstrees. In our view Laban had been defending his hearth and our community from the dirty depredations of an opera-singing furriner. The fact that Labe Hemus didn't happen to have a hearth at the time he was defending it we dismissed as the puniest technicality; Adaline'd practically been promised. We made it so hot for the Greaves that Elmer Greave had to sell his place off and move downstate. Joe Gonzoli wisely never came back to pick up his satchel. He just ran, and to this day not even 'Squale Gonzoli's heard from him.

"That verdict," said the Judge, "taught us we were living in a hostile, new sort of world, a world which didn't understand beans about the rights of God-fearing, tax-paying Shinn Corners property owners. We'd been betrayed and corrupted and shamed. It was just about the last straw."

"I can understand that," said Johnny. "Maybe I'm not so much of a furriner as you think."

But Judge Shinn ignored that. " 'Cause things hadn't been going well with us for a long time. A hundred years ago Shinn Corners was bigger than Comfort is today. You can still see the ruins of houses and barns and mills on the Comfort road past the Hemus farm and up beyond the Isbel and Scott farms on Four Corners Road. That three-story red brick building across from the firehouse is the remains of the Urie Cassimere Factory—"

"The what kind of factory?" asked Johnny.

"Cassimere, what they used to call cashmere. Around 1850 the Urie factory employed over two hundred people, made as fine a line of woolens as you could find in New England. Then Comfort and Cudbury and other towns around drew off a lot of our working people with a spurt of new mills, eventually the river dried up, and what with one thing and another all that's gone. We're reduced to a total population of thirty-six."

"Thirty-six!"

"And that includes fifteen minors. Thirty-six, going to be thirty-seven in December—Emily Berry's fifth is on the way. Thirty-seven, that is, if nobody dies. Old Aunt Fanny is ninety-one. Earl Scott's father Seth is in his eighties . . . might just as well be dead, he has senile obesity and lives in a wheelchair. For that matter, so does Earl. He's helpless, too, had a stroke five-six years ago that left him paralyzed. Hosey Lemmon—nobody knows how old Hosey is. I'll tell you about old man Lemmon sometime; it's an interesting story.

"Twelve families," murmured Judge Shinn. "That's what we're down to. If you leave out the unattached ones—me, Prue Plummer, Aunt Fanny, Hosey, and Calvin Waters—there's only seven families.

"We're down to four producing herds, in an area that during the last century had some of the best dairy farms in this section of the state. Hemus, Isbel, Scott, Pangman. And there's a question how long they can keep going, with milk fetching eight cents a quart from the Association out of which they have to pay for cartage and rental of the cans.

"Only store left is Peter Berry's over there on the east corner, and the only reason Peter makes out is he gets the trade of the Comfort people who happen to live closer to Shinn Corners than to their own stores. . . . So you might say," said the Judge dryly, "we have nothing left but fond memories and a tradition. Let the rest of New England welcome the durn New Yorkers and the rest of the furriners. We want none of 'em."

"Except you," said his guest.

"Well, I'm sort of on the sidelines," grinned Judge Shinn. "Privileged character, I and Aunt Fanny, that is."

"That's the third time you've mentioned Aunt Fanny," said Johnny. "Just who is Aunt Fanny?"

"Aunt Fanny?" The Judge seemed surprised. "Aunt Fanny Adams. That's her house t'other side of the church. That hewn overhang, one of the few left in this part of the state."

"Fanny Adams . . ." Johnny sat up with a thump. "The painter of primitives?"

"Aya."

"Aunt Fanny Adams comes from Shinn Corners?"

"Born here. It's this valley most of her painting's about. Aunt Fanny's pretty good, I'm told."

"Good!" Johnny stared across Four Corners Road, past the little church. He could just make out the old New England house, with its flowering garden.

"Didn't start diddling around with paints till she was eighty, after her husband—Girshom Adams, he was her third cousin—died. Only kin Aunt Fanny's got left is Ferriss Adams from over Cudbury, her grandnephew, practices law there. She was kind of lonely, I guess."

"She's said to be a fabulous old lady. Could I possibly meet her?"

"Aunt Fanny?" Judge Shinn was astonished. "Couldn't miss her if you tried, 'specially when she hears your grandfather was Horace Shinn. Parade forms at her house, seeing she's the oldest resident outside the cemetery. You won't find her much different from any other old woman around here. They're all pa't and pa'cel of the land. Know every bulb in their gardens and every surveyor's description in their land deeds. They outlive their men and they're as indestructible, seems like, as the rocks in their fences."

"She lives alone?"

"All alone. Does her own housework, needlework, cooking, puts up her pickles and preserves—they're like ants, these old women; their routine is practically an instinct."

"Well, I'll be darned," said Johnny. "Who handles her business affairs?"

"Why, she does," chuckled the Judge. "She sold a painting last week for fifteen hundred dollars. 'I just paint what I see,' she says. 'And if folks are fool enough to pay for what they could have for nothin' if only they'd use the two eyes the Lord gave them, let 'em pay through the nose.' Ferriss Adams takes care of her contracts, but he'll be the first to tell you there isn't a word in them she doesn't know backwards and forwards. She's made a fortune out of her Christmas card, wallpaper, and textile designs alone. Minute some big city dealer tries to skin her, she sits him down with some of her apple pan dowdy and cream she separated with her own hands—she keeps a Jersey cow, milks it herself twice a day and gives most of the milk to the school—and before he knows it he's agreed to her terms."

"What does she do with all her money?"

"Invests some, gives the rest away. If not for her, Samuel Sheare would have had to look for another church years ago. His only income is what Aunt Fanny donates and his wife Elizabeth makes as our grade school teacher. And Aunt Fanny's made up most of our annual town deficit now for years. Used to be my chore," said the Judge wryly, "but my income isn't what it used to be. . . . And all that comes out of Aunt Fanny's diddling with paintbrushes." He shook his head. "Beats me. Most of her daubs look like a child could do 'em."

"You'd get a violent argument from the art critics." Johnny stared over at the Adams property. "I should think Shinn Corners would be proud of her."

"Proud?" said the Judge. "That old woman is Shinn Corners's one hitch to fame. She's about the only part of our corporate existence that's kept our self-respect from falling down around our ankles."

Judge Shinn rose from the rocker, brushing his pearl gray sharkskin suit and adjusting his Panama hat. He had dressed with care this morning for the Independence Day exercises; it was expected of him, he had chuckled. But Johnny had gathered that the old man took a deep pleasure in his annual role. He had delivered the Shinn Corners Fourth of July oration every year for the past thirty years.

"Lots of time yet," the Judge said, pulling out his big

gold watch on its black silk fob. "Parade's set for twelve noon, midway between milkings. . . . I see Peter Berry's opening his store. Rushed you off so fast after those fish yesterday, Johnny, you never did get a chance to see Shinn Corners. Let's walk off some of Millie's breakfast."

Where the thirty-five mile Cudbury-to-Comfort stretch of county highway ran through Shinn Corners, it was called Shinn Road. Shinn Road was intersected in the heart of the village by Four Corners Road. Squeezed around the intersection was all that survived of the village, in four segments like the quarters of a pie.

At each of the four corners of the intersection a curved granite marker had been sunk into the earth. The point of the Judge's quarter of the pie, which was occupied by the village green, was marked WEST CORNER, in letters worn down almost to the base.

Except for the green, which was village property, the entire west quarter belonged to the Judge. On it stood the Shinn mansion, built in 1761—the porch with its ivy-choked pillars, the Judge told Johnny, had been added after the Revolutionary War, when pillars became the architectural fashion—and behind the house stood a building, older than the mansion, that served as a garage. Before that it had been a coach house; and very long ago, said the Judge, it had been the slave quarters of a Colonial house occupying the site of the 1761 building.

"Slavery didn't last in New England not for moral reasons so much," remarked the Judge slyly, "as for climatic ones. Our winters killed off too many high-priced Negroes. And the Indian chattels were never a success."

The Judge's seven hundred acres had not been tilled for two generations; choked woods came to within yards of the garage. The gardens about the house were jungles in miniature. The house itself had a gray scaling skin, as if it were diseased, like most of the houses in the village.

"Where's my grandfather's house?" demanded Johnny, as they strolled across the arc of cracked blacktop before the Shinn property. "Don't ask me why, but I'd sort of like to see it."

"Oh, that went long ago," said the Judge. "When I was a young man. It used to be on Four Corners Road, beyond the Isbel place."

They stepped onto the village green. Here the grass was

healthy, the flagpole glittered with fresh paint, the flag floating aloft was spanking new, and the Revolutionary cannon and the shaft to Asahel Shinn on its three-step granite pedestal had been cleaned and hung with bunting.

"That's too bad," said Johnny, wondering why it should be.

"This is where I preach my sermon," said the Judge, setting his foot on the second step of the pedestal. "Old Asahel Shinn led an expedition from up north in 1654, massacred four hundred Indians, and then said a prayer for their immortal souls on this spot. . . . Morning, Calvin!"

A man was dragging a rusty lawnmower across the intersection. All Johnny could think of was a corpse he had once stumbled over in a North Korean rice paddy. The man was tall and thin and garmented in hopeless brown, topped with a brown hat that flopped lifelessly about his brown ears. Even his teeth were long and brown.

The man shambled toward them in sections, as if he were wired together.

He touched his hatbrim to Judge Shinn, jiggled the lawnmower over the west corner marker, and sent it clacking along the grass of the green.

The Judge glanced at Johnny and followed. Johnny tagged along.

"Calvin, I want you to meet a distant kinsman of mine. Johnny Shinn, Calvin Waters."

Calvin Waters stopped deliberately. He set the mower at a meticulous angle, slewed about, and looked at Johnny for the first time.

"How do," he said. And off he clacked again.

Johnny said, "Brrr."

"It's just our way," murmured the Judge, and he took Johnny's arm and steered him into the road. "Calvin's our maintenance department. Custodian of town property, janitor of the school and Town Hall and church, official gravedigger . . . Lives halfway up the hill there, past Aunt Fanny's. Waters house is one of the oldest around, built in 1721. Calvin's outhouse is a museum piece all by itself."

"So is Calvin," said Johnny.

"All alone in the world. Only thing Calvin owns is that old house and the clothes on his back—no car, not even a buggy or a goat cart. What we call around here a real poor man."

"Doesn't he smile?" asked Johnny. "I don't think I ever saw a face with such a total lack of expression outside a military burying ground."

"Guess Calvin thinks there isn't much to smile about," said the Judge. "Far back as I can remember, Shinn Corners youngsters have called him Laughing Waters. Fell out of a farm wagon when he was a baby and 's never been quite right since."

They crossed Shinn Road to the south corner. Burney Hackett, who owned the corner house, Judge Shinn explained, was not only the local constable, he was the fire chief, town clerk, tax collector, member of the school board, and the Judge didn't know what all. He also sold insurance.

"Burn has to keep hopping," said the Judge. "His wife Ella died giving birth to their youngest. His mother, Selina Hackett, keeps house for him, but Selina's pretty old and deaf now, and the three children have kind of brought themselves up. Hi, Joel!"

A stocky boy in jeans came slouching down Shinn Road toward the Hackett house, looking curiously at Johnny.

" 'Lo, Judge."

"Burney Hackett's eldest, Johnny—junior at Comfort High. Joel, this is Major Shinn."

"Major?" The boy left Johnny's hand in midair. "A real major?"

"A real ex-major," said Johnny, smiling.

"Oh." The Hackett boy turned away.

"Aren't you up kind of early, Joel, for a summer's morning?" asked Judge Shinn pleasantly. "Or was the thought of today's excitement too much for you?"

"That corn." Joel Hackett kicked the sagging picket gate. "I'd a lot rather take my twenty-two and go huntin' with Eddie Pangman. But Pop made me go over to ask Orville for a job. I'm startin' tomorrow—strippin' his darn-fool cows."

He went into the Hacket house and banged the door.

"You'll have to make quite a speech today to impress that boy," remarked Johnny. "What's that sign?"

The house next to Burney Hackett's was a redpainted clapboard with drawn white blinds, sitting primly in the sun. A sign on a wrought-iron stand in the front yard read PRUE PLUMMER—ANTIQUES AND OLD BUTTONS. Everything needed paint.

"Well, there's enterprise," said Johnny.

"Prue makes out. Sells an occasional piece in summer, when there's some traffic between Cudbury and Comfort, but mainly she does a small year-round mail order business in antique buttons. Prue's our intellectual, has some arty Cape Cod friends. She's tried to interest Aunt Fanny Adams in 'em with no luck. Aunt Fanny says she wouldn't know what to say to them, 'cause she doesn't know anything about art. It's just about killed Prue," chuckled the Judge, "having a national art celebrity as a lifelong neighbor and not being able to turn her into a profit. There's Orville Pangman."

"Judge, don't introduce me as Major Shinn."

"All right, Johnny," said the Judge quietly.

They had rounded the stone fence separating the Plummer lot from the Pangman farm and were trudging past the small farmhouse toward the big red barns. A huge perspiring man in bib overalls was in the barn doorway, wiping his face.

" 'Scuse my not shakin' hands," he said when the Judge introduced Johnny. "Been cleanin' out the manure troughs. Millie feedin' ye all right, is she, Judge?"

"Fine, fine, Orville," said the Judge. "What do you hear from Merritt?"

"Seems to like the Navy a lot more than he ever did farmin'," said Orville Pangman. "Raise two sons, one of 'em enlists in the Navy and the other's too lazy to scratch." He shouted, "Eddie, come 'ere!"

A tall skinny boy of seventeen with great red hands appeared from the interior of the barn.

"Eddie, this is the Judge's kin from N'York, Mr. Shinn." Johnny said hello.

"Hello," said Eddie Pangman. He kept looking sullenly at the ground.

"What are you going to do when you graduate next year, Eddie?" asked Judge Shinn.

"Dunno," said the Pangman boy, still studying the ground.

"Great talker, ain't he?" said his father. "He don't know. All he knows is he's unhappy. You finish cleanin' those milkin' machines, Eddie. I'll be right along."

"Hear we're due for a rain tomorrow, Orville," said the Judge as Eddie Pangman disappeared without a word.

"Aya. But the forecast for the summer's dry." The big farmer scowled at the cloudless sky. "Another dry summer'll just about finish us off. Last September we lost practic'ly the whole stand of feed corn; rains came too late. And there wasn't enough hay in the second cuttin' to see us through Christmas. Hay's been awful scarce. If it happens again . . ."

"Don't ever be a farmer, Johnny," said the Judge as they walked back toward Shinn Road. "Here's Orville, with the best farm around if you recognize degrees of indigence, good herd of Brown Swiss, Guernseys, and Holsteins, makes almost ten cans, and it's a question if he can hang on another year. Things are even sorrier for Hube Hemus, Mert Isbel, and the Scotts. We're withering on the vine, Johnny."

"You're really setting me up, Judge," complained Johnny. "For a time there I thought you had designs on me."

"Designs?" asked the Judge innocently.

"You know, getting me up here so you could talk to me like a Yank uncle, pump some blood into my veins. But you're worse than I am."

"Am I?" murmured the Judge.

"You almost make me revert to my ancient chauvinism. I want to twist your arm and tell you to look at that flag flying up there. That's not going to wither away, no matter what happens to you and me. Droughts are temporary—"

"Old age and wickedness," retorted Judge Shinn, "are permanent."

Millie Pangman was waddling across Shinn Road. She was almost as large as her husband, formidably feather-bedded fore and aft. The sun bounced off her gold-rimmed eyeglasses as she waved a powerful arm. "Made you some jiffy oatmeal bread, Judge," she called in passing. "I'll be back to fix your supper. . . . Deb-*bie?* Where are you?"

The Judge waved back at the farmer's wife with tenderness. But he repeated, "Permanent."

"You're a fraud," said Johnny.

"No, I mean it," said the Judge. "Oh, I make sma't rema'ks on and off, but that's only because a Yankee'd rather vote Democratic than make a public parade of his feelings. The fact is, Johnny, you're meandering along the main street of a hopeless case."

"And here I was, laboring under the delusion that you're a gentleman of great spiritual substance," grinned Johnny.

"Oh, I have faith," said Judge Shinn. "A lot more faith than you'll ever have, Johnny. I have faith in God, for instance, and in the Constitution of these United States, for another instance, and in the statutes of my sovereign state, and in the future of our country—Communism, hydrogen bombs, nerve gas, McCarthyism, and ex-majors of Army Intelligence to the contrary notwithstanding. But Johnny, I know Shinn Corners, too. As we get poorer, we get more frightened; the more frightened we get, the narrower and meaner and bitterer and less secure we are. . . . This is a fine preparation for a Fourth of July speech, I must say! Let's drop in on Peter Berry, cheeriest man in Shinn Corners."

The village's only store occupied the east corner of the intersection. A ramshackle building painted dirty tan, it was evidently a holdover from the nineteenth century. The entrance straddled the corner. A pyramid of creaking wooden steps led to a small porch cluttered with garden tools, baskets, pails, brooms, potted geraniums, and a hundred other items. Above the porch ran a faded red sign: BERRY'S VARIETY STORE.

As Johnny pulled back the screen door for the Judge, an oldfashioned bell tinkled and a rich whiff of vinegar, rubber, coffee, kerosene, and cheese surged up his nose.

"I could have used this smell once or five times," said Johnny, "in those stinking paddies."

"Too bad Peter didn't know that," said the Judge. "He'd have bottled it and sold it."

There was almost as much stock in midair as on the floor and shelves. They made their way through a forest of dangling merchandise, crowding past kegs of nails, barrels of potatoes and flour, sacks of onions, oil stoves, tractor parts, counters of housewares, drygoods, and sundries, cheap shoes, a wire-enclosed cubicle labeled U.S. POST OFFICE SUB-STATION—there was even a display rack of paper-backed books and comic books. Signs advertised charcoal and ice, developing and printing, laundry and dry-cleaning—there was no service, it seemed, that Peter Berry was not prepared to render.

"Is Berry's Garage next door on Shinn Road his, too?" asked Johnny, impressed.

"Yes," said the Judge.

"How does he take care of it all?"

"Well, Peter tries to do most of his car-tinkering nights, after he closes the store. Em helps out when she can. Dickie—he's ten—is big enough to handle the gas pump and run errands, and Calvin Waters makes deliveries in Peter's truck."

They edged along a narrow aisle toward the main counter of the grocery department, where the cash register stood. A large fat man with a head like William Jennings Bryan was stacking loaves of bread on the counter as he talked to a lanky teenage boy in jeans. There was something tense about the set of the boy's head, and Judge Shinn touched Johnny on the arm. "Let's wait," he said.

The boy at the counter said something at last in a low voice. Peter Berry smiled, shaking his head. He was about forty-five, with a jowly face that kept changing shape as its curves merged and dissolved. It was the kind of face that should have been rosy; instead, it was a disappointing gray. And where the blue eyes should have twinkled, they were lumpy and cold.

"Who's the boy?" murmured Johnny.

"Drakeley Scott, Earl and Mathilda Scott's eldest. He's seventeen."

"He seems distressed about something."

"Well, Drake's got his row to hoe. With Earl and Seth helpless, it's his farm to run. It's cut into his schooling." The Judge shrugged. "He's a full year behind. Don't suppose he'll ever finish. . . . Good morning, Drake."

Drakeley Scott shuffled toward them, eyes lowered. They were beautiful eyes with great welts under them. His thin face was pimpled and sore-looking.

"Mornin', Judge."

"Want you to meet a relative of mine."

The boy raised his eyes unseeingly. "How do," he said. "Judge, I got to get back to the barn—"

"Getting any help these days, Drakeley?" asked the Judge.

"Some. Old man Lemmon right now. Jed Willet from over Comfort—he's promised to cut the south lot and help

me get the hay in, but Jed can't come till next week."
The Scott boy pushed by them suddenly.

"See you at the exercises?"

"Dunno, Judge. Ma'll be there with Judy." Drakeley
Scott shuffled out rapidly, his meager shoulders drawn
in as if he expected a blow from behind.

"Mornin'," boomed Peter Berry. He was all overlapping
smiles. "Real fine day, Judge! Lookin' forward to your
speech today . . ." He kept glancing from Judge Shinn
to Johnny, his gray face shifting and changing as if it
were composed of seawater.

"Thank you, Peter." The Judge introduced Johnny.

"Real glad to meet you, Mr. Shinn! Judge's kin, hey?
Ever visited before?"

"No."

"That's too bad. How d'ye like our little community?"

"Nice solid sort of town," said Johnny tactfully. "Settled. Peaceful."

"That's a fact." Johnny wished that Berry's face would
stand still for a moment. "Visitin' long?"

"A week or so, Mr. Berry."

"Well, now, that's fine. Oh, Judge, Millie Pangman was
in t'other day chargin' some groceries to your account. Is
it all right?"

"Of course it's all right, Peter," said the Judge a bit
sharply.

"Darn fine woman, Millie. Credit to Shinn Corners—"

"We won't keep you, Peter," said the Judge. "I know
you're open only for a few hours this morning—"

"Judge."

"Yes?"

Peter Berry was leaning over his counter in a con-
fidential way.

"Had it in my mind to talk to you for quite a while
now . . ."

Johnny delicately drifted off to the book rack. But
Berry seemed to have forgotten him, and the booming
voice carried.

"It's about the Scotts."

"Oh?" said Judge Shinn. "What about the Scotts?"

"Well, now, you know I been carryin' the Scotts right
along . . ."

"Owe you a big bill, do they, Peter?"

"Well, yes. I was wonderin' what I could do about it. You bein' a lawyer and a judge—"

Judge Shinn's voice grew shrill. "You mean you want to take the Scotts to court?"

"Can't carry 'em forever, Judge. I like to oblige my neighbors, but—"

"Haven't they paid you anything?"

"Dribs and drabs."

"But they have been trying to pay."

"Well, yes, but the balance keeps gettin' bigger."

"Have you talked to Earl, Peter?"

"No use talkin' to *Earl*."

"No, I s'pose not," said the Judge, "Earl being tied down to that wheelchair."

"I've talked to Drakeley, but shucks! Drakeley's not half a man yet. Lettin' a boy run a farm! Seems to me what Earl ought to do is sell out—"

"What does Drakeley say, Peter?"

"He says he'll pay first chance he gets. I don't want to be hard on them, Judge—"

"But you're contemplating legal measures. Well, Peter, I'll tell you," said Judge Shinn. "I remember—a long time ago—when Nathan Berry was so deep in a hole he had the Sheriff peering down over the edge. You remember it, too—it was during the depression. Old Seth Scott was a man then, standing on his two feet, not a bag of mumbling lard whose legs won't support him, the way he is today. And between Seth and his son Earl, they'd weathered the storm. And your father, Nathan Berry, went to Seth and Earl Scott for help, and they saved his neck, Peter—yes, and yours, too. You wouldn't be standing behind this counter today if not for the Scotts!" And Judge Shinn's voice came to Johnny in a long thin line, like charging infantry. "If you had to carry those people for five years, Peter Berry, you ought to do it and be thankful for the chance! And while I'm riled up, Peter, I'm going to tell you what I think of your prices. I think you're a highway robber, that's what I think. Taking advantage of these folks you grew up with, who can't deal anywhere else 'cause there's nowhere else to deal! Sure you work hard. So did Ebenezer Scrooge. And so do they, only they haven't got anything to show for it, the way you have!"

"No call gettin' het up, Judge," said the other voice, still smily-boomy. "It was just a question."

"Oh, I'll answer your damned question! If the Scotts owe you less than a hundred dollars, you can file your claim in the Small Claims Court. If it's anything above that up to five hundred, you can go to the Court of Common Pleas—"

"It's a hundred ninety-one sixty-three," said Peter Berry.

"On second thought," said the Judge, "you can go to hell. Come along, Johnny!"

And as Johnny caught up with the old man, whose gnarled neck was as red as the flannel shirt swaying over his head, he heard the Judge mutter, "Trash!"

The Judge seemed ashamed of himself. He mumbled something about getting to be a crotchety old fool, losing his temper that way, after all Peter Berry was within his rights, what was the use of trying to keep people from drowning when the whole damned countryside was under water, and would Johnny excuse him, he'd go lie down for a while and think over his speech.

"You go right ahead," said Johnny. He watched the Judge head across the intersection for the Shinn house with his old man's stiffkneed bounce, wondering just what sort of speech Shinn Corners was going to hear that day.

Johnny Shinn wandered about the village of his paternal ancestors for a few minutes. He went up Four Corners Road past the Berry house with its droopy front-and-side porch and its ugly Victorian turret, stopped before the decayed box of a Town Hall with its flaking sign, examined the abandoned woolen factory beyond, windowless, its entrance doors gone, the ground floor caved in . . . stood on the rim of the ditch behind the factory building. It was choked with sickly birches and ground pine and underbrush—and, away to the south, tin cans and rubbish.

He trudged back to the intersection and crossed over to the north corner. He inspected the old horse trough with its leaking faucet and green slime, the church and the parsonage set in lawns overrun by crab grass, chickweed, and dandelions, the little parsonage strangling in the clutch of ivy and wistaria vines and evergreens set too close to the walls. . . .

Beyond the parsonage lay the cemetery, but Johnny suddenly did not feel like exploring the cemetery. He

suddenly felt that he had had enough of Shinn Corners
for one morning, and he crossed over to the west corner,
skirted the now-deserted green with its toy cannon and
its chipped monument and its mocking flagpole . . . set
foot on the Judge's precincts, achieved the shaky porch,
and sat down in the rocker and rocked.

"Lewis Shinn's a reprobate. The idea him not fetchin'
you to visit soon's you came," said Aunt Fanny Adams.
"I like young men. 'Specially young men with nice
eyes." She peered at him through her silver spectacles.
"Color of polished pewter," she decided. "Clean and
homey-lookin'. But I expect Lewis likes 'em, too. There's
no more selfish o' God's creatures than a cantankerous
old man. My Girshom was the most selfish man in Cudbury County. But he did have the nicest eyes." She
sighed. "Come set."

"I think," said Johnny, "you're beautiful."

"Do ye, now?" She patted the chair beside her, pleased.
It was a comb-backed hickory chair, an American Windsor that would have brought tears of avarice to the eyes
of an antique hunter. "A Shinn, are ye? There was always somethin' about a Shinn. Joshers, the lot o' ye!"

"If I had the nerve," said Johnny, "I'd ask you to
marry me."

"Ye see?" She chuckled deep in her throat, patting the
chair again. "Who was your mother?"

Johnny was overwhelmed. She was a rawboned old lady
with knotty farmer hands and eyes sharp and twinkly
as snow in Christmas sunshine, set in a face wrinkled
and pungent, like an apple treefall. Ninety-one years had
dragged everything down, a bosom still full, a great
motherly abdomen—everything but the spirit that touched
the wrinkles with grace and kept her ancient hands warm.
Johnny thought he had never seen a wiser, shrewder,
kinder face.

"I never knew her, Mrs. Adams. She died when I was
very small."

"Ah, that's no good," she said, shaking her old head.
"It's the mothers make the men. Who reared ye, your
father?"

"No, Mrs. Adams."

"Too busy makin' a livin'? I saw him last when he was

no bigger than a newborn calf. Never came back to Shinn Corners. How is your father?"

"He's dead, too."

The shrewd eyes examined him. "Ye've got your grandfather Horace Shinn's mouth. Stubborn. And I don't like your smile."

"Sorry," murmured Johnny.

"It's got nothin' behind it. Are ye married?"

"Heavens, no."

"Ought to be," Aunt Fanny Adams decided. "Some woman'd make a man of ye. What d'ye do, Johnny Shinn?"

"Nothing."

"*Nothin'?*" She was appalled. "But there's somethin' wrong with ye, boy! Why, I'm over ninety, and I ain't found time to do half the things I want to! Never heard the like. How old are ye?"

"Thirty-one."

"And ye don't do *nothin'?* Are ye rich?"

"Poor as poor."

"Don't ye *want* to do somethin'?"

"Sure. But I don't know what."

"But weren't ye trained for nothin'?"

Johnny laughed. "Studied law, or started to. The war stopped that. Then afterward I couldn't seem to decide on anything. Sort of drifted, trying one thing and another. Came Korea, and I jumped back in. Since then . . ." He shrugged. "Let's talk about you, Mrs. Adams. You're a far more interesting subject."

But the withered mouth did not relax. "Unhappy, ain't ye?"

"Happy as a lark," said Johnny. "What's there to be unhappy about? Do you know this is a red-letter day in my life, Mrs. Adams?"

She took his limp hand between her warm papery ones. "All right," she said. "But I'm not lettin' ye off the hook, Johnny Shinn. We got to have a real long talk. . . ."

It was eleven o'clock when Judge Shinn had walked him up Shinn Road past the church to turn into the Adams gate and through a garden fragrant with pansies and roses and dogwood trees to the simple stone step and the gracious door overhung by the second story and the steep-pitched roof; and there she had been, this wonderful old woman, receiving her neighbors with dry hos-

pitality, a word for everyone, and a special sharp one
for the Judge.

Her house was like herself—clean, old, and filled with
beauty. Color ran everywhere, the same bright colors
that flamed on her canvases. And the Shinn Corners
folk who crowded her parlor seemed freshened by them,
simplified and renewed. There was a great deal of laughter
and joking; the parlor was filled with nasal good-fellow-
ship. Johnny gathered that Aunt Fanny Adams's "open
house" occasions were highlights in the dull life of the
village.

The old lady had prepared pitchers of milk and great
platters of cookies and heaps of ice cream for the children.
Johnny tasted blueberry muffins and johnnycake, crab-
apple jelly and cranberry conserve and grape butter.
There was coffee and tea and punch. She kept feeding
him as if he were a child.

He had very little time with her. She sat beside him
in her long black dress with its high collar, without orna-
ment except for an oldfashioned cameo locket-watch
which she wore on a thin gold chain about her neck—
talking of the long ago when she had been a girl in Shinn
Corners, how things had been in those days, and how
looking backward was a folly reserved for the very old.

"The young ones can't live in their kinsmen's past,"
she said, smiling. "Life is tryin' to upset applecarts. Death
is pushin' a handplow in a tractor age. There's nothin'
wicked about change. In the end the same good things—
what I s'pose ye'd call 'values'—survive. But I like keepin'
up to date."

"Yet," Johnny smiled back, "your house is full of the
most wonderful antiques." Death, he thought, is standing
still in a hurricane. But he did not say it.

The lively eyes sparkled. "But I've also got me a deep-
freeze, and modern plumbin', and an electric range.
The furniture's for memories. The range is for tellin'
me I'm alive."

"I've read a very similar remark, Mrs. Adams," said
Johnny, "about your painting."

"Do they say that?" The old lady chuckled. "Then
they're a sight sma'ter than I give 'em credit for. Most
times seems like they talk Chinese. . . . You take Grandma
Moses. Now she's a mighty fine painter. Only most of her
paintin's what she remembers of the way things *used* to be.

I like rememberin', too—I can talk your ear off 'bout the way life was when I was a girl in this village. But that's *talkin'*. When I find a paintbrush in my hand, rememberin' and talkin' just don't seem to satisfy me. I like to paint what I *see*. If it all comes out funny-lookin' —what Prue Plummer's friends call 'art'—why, I expect it's 'cause of how I see the colors, the way things *set* to me . . . and mostly what I don't know 'bout paintin'!"

Johnny said earnestly, "Do you really believe that what you see is worth looking at, Mrs. Adams?"

But that was a question she never got to answer. Because at that moment Millie Pangman waddled over to whisper in Aunt Fanny's ear, and the old lady jumped up and exclaimed, "My land! There's lots more in the freezer, Millie," and excused herself to him with a sharp look and went away. And by the time she got back with more ice cream for the children, Johnny had been boarded and seized by Prue Plummer.

Prue Plummer was a thin vibrant lady of valorous middle age with a liverish face coming to a point and lips which she kept preening with a tireless tongue. She was dressed in a smart summer suit of lavender linen which looked as outrageously out of place in that Colonial roomful of plainly dressed farm women as a Mondriaan would have looked on the wall. Two big copper hoops dangled from her ears and a batik scarf, bound round her gray hair, trailed coquettishly over one shoulder.

"*May* I, Mr. Shinn?" said Prue Plummer, digging her bloody talons into his arm. "I've been watching for my chance to monopolize you. I could hug Millie Pangman for luring dear old Aunt Fanny away. Such a darling! Of course, she doesn't know beans about art, and brags about it, which is such a delightful part of her quaintness, because of course she really *doesn't*—"

"I understand," said Johnny rather abruptly, "you sell antiques, Miss Plummer."

"Oh, I dabble at it. I do have some good rock crystal and old Dresden, and rather an amusing collection of miniature lamps, and a few old Colonial and Early American pieces when I can persuade my neighbors to let me market them—"

"I should think," said Johnny, not without malice,

"that this house of Mrs. Adams's would be a gold strike for you."

"Haven't I tried, just," laughed Prue Plummer. "But she's simply making too much money. Isn't it disgusting? You just watch the vultures descend when Aunt Fanny passes on. She has a stenciled 'rockee' in her attic that's worth a fortune. You know there aren't many good old things left undiscovered in New England—oh, dear, such a bother . . . Hello! Our minister and his wife. Mr. and Mrs. Sheare, Mr. Shinn?"

In the exchange, he managed to throw off the grappling iron.

Samuel and Elizabeth Sheare made a sort of clerical Mr. And Mrs. Jack Spratt. The minister was a lean little elderly man with a troubled smile; his wife was stout and anxious. Both had an air of vague alertness. Mr. Sheare, it appeared, had inherited the Shinn Corners parish from his father; Elizabeth Sheare had been a Urie, a family which no longer existed. Between them they had catered to the village's spiritual and educational needs for thirty-five years. They had no children, they said wistfully as they watched Peter Berry's four stuff themselves. Did Mr. Shinn have any? No, said Johnny again, he was not married. Ah, said Mr. Sheare, that's too bad, as if it really were. And he pressed closer to his wife. They were lonely people, Johnny thought, and harried. Mr. Sheare's God must seem very near and dear to them both. He made a mental note to go to church on Sunday.

Johnny met the Hemus family, and the Hacketts, and Merton Isbel, and Drakeley Scott's mother Mathilda (Drakeley was not there), and old Hosey Lemmon, and Emily Berry, and all the children young and grown, and he was a little confused and uneasy. He felt New Yorkish, which he did not often feel. He should be feeling Shinn Cornerish, since it was supposedly in his blood. The truth is, Johnny thought, I've got less kinship with these people than I had with the Koreans and Chinese. What's the matter with them? Is everybody in the world a carrier of nastiness and doubt?

The Hemuses were disturbing. Hubert Hemus was a slight one-syllabled man with dirty hands, stiff in his Sunday clothes. He shed a steady, unpleasant power. Nothing moved in his gaunt face but his sharp jaws; he looked at things with his whole head, as if his eyes had no independent maneuverability. But even with his head turned, he seemed on the watch. He joked and talked to the other men without enjoyment. It was impossible to think of him as capable of changing his mind or seeing another point of view. Johnny was not surprised to learn that Hube Hemus had been First Selectman of Shinn Corners for over twenty years.

His wife, Rebecca, was a great cow of a woman, swinging all over. She giggled with the other women, but always with an eye on her husband.

Their children were formidable. They had twin sons, Tommy and Dave, hulking eighteen-year-olds, powerfully muscled, with heavy blue jaws and expressionless eyes. They were going to make mean and dangerous men, Johnny thought, remembering some of the hard cases he had met in the Army. The daughter, Abbie, had the family eyes—a precocious twelve-year-old with overdeveloped breasts who kept watching the big boys brazenly.

Then there was Merton Isbel and his family. There was something queer about the Isbels. Johnny had seen them coming into the village in a battered farm wagon drawn by a team of plowhorses, the big craggy farmer woodenly at the reins—needing only the beard, Johnny thought, to look like old John Brown—his daughter Sarah and his granddaughter Mary-Ann sitting like mice at his side. Isbel was a widower, Judge Shinn had said, and Sarah and her child lived with him. The Judge had seemed reluctant to talk about them.

Isbel stood about with Hubert Hemus and Orville Pangman and Peter Berry and the Judge talking weather and crops and prices, but his daughter and her child sat by themselves in a corner as if they were looking through a window at an unreachable luxury. No one went near them except Fanny Adams. The old lady brought Mary-Ann a plateful of ice cream and cookies and a glass of milk, and pressed some punch and cake on the woman; but at her evident urging that they join the others, the woman shook her head with a faint smile and the child looked frightened. They remained where they were. The woman Sarah had large, sad eyes. Only when they turned on her little girl did they glow, and then only for a moment.

Johnny was introduced to Merton Isbel by Constable

Burney Hackett. The old farmer barely acknowledged the introduction and turned away.

"Did I say something wrong to Mr. Isbel, Mr. Hackett?" Johnny asked, smiling.

"Shucks, no." Hackett was a lean chinless man with birdlike shoulders and a permanent furrow between his eyes. "It's just Mert's way. You'd have to live here forty-odd years before Mert'd think you had a right to cast a vote. And even then he'd hardly pass the time o' day."

"Nobody in Shinn Corners is what you'd call real modern," said Constable Burney Hackett in his nasal drawl, "but Mert's still back in McKinley's administration. Ain't changed his farmin' methods from the way it was when he was a boy. Won't listen to reason any more'n a deaf Baptist. Does his own horseshoein'! Mighty mulish man, Mert."

Johnny began, "His daughter—"

But Hackett went on as if Johnny had said nothing at all. "Peter Berry tried to sell him a flush toilet once, but Mert said the old three-holer'd been good enough for his pa and by jing it was good enough for him. Things like that. Actu'ly, he ain't got no runnin' water exceptin' what he hand-pumps. No 'lectric lights, no tank gas, no nothin'. Mert Isbel might just as well be livin' back in Asahel Shinn's time. But Mert's a righteous man, God-fearin' as all getout, and ain't nobody bellows a hymn out Sundays louder."

"Why does his daughter—"

"Pa'don, Mr. Shinn. There's my mother havin' a to-do with the youngest," said Burney Hackett quickly; and it was a long time before Johnny got to hear why Merton Isbel's daughter and granddaughter sat in corners.

He was rather taken with Mathilda Scott, the mother of the troubled boy he had met in Berry's store that morning, but he found her shyness too stubborn for a shiftless man. She was a half sister of Rebecca Hemus's; they were both Ackleys, a once numerous family of Shinn Corners. But they were the last. Mrs. Scott's face was a dark hollow mask of old and present pain; drudgery had done the rest. "She was a beautiful girl," Judge Shinn said as she went looking for her thirteen-year-old daughter. "Drakeley got those eyes of his from her. They're about all Mathilda has left." She looked sixty; the Judge said she was forty-four.

And then there was Hosey Lemmon. Old man Lemmon was one of the few Yankees of Johnny's experience to wear a beard. It was a long beard, rain-silver, and it flowed from a head of long silvery hair as from a fountain. The old fellow was broad and spry and heavily sunburned, and he walked softly about Fanny Adams's house, as if it were a church. He wore tattered, filthy overalls and a faded winter farm hat with upturned flaps; on his feet were a pair of manure-caked boots. He avoided the adults, remaining among the younger children, who accepted him as if he were one of them.

Judge Shinn told Johnny about Lemmon. "Hosey was once a prosperous farmer up Four Corners Road, past the Isbel place. One night he had a fight with his wife and went to the barn with a quart of whiskey. He finished it and staggered out into one of his pastures and fell asleep. When he woke up his barn and house were a mass of flames. He'd apparently dropped his pipe in the barn, it had ignited the hay, and a high wind had done the rest. By the time the engine got out there from the village it was impossible to do anything but watch the house burn to the ground and keep the fire from spreading to the woods. His wife and six children were burned to death. Lemmon went up Holy Hill and crept into an abandoned shack, and there he's been ever since. Exactly how he manages we don't know. He won't accept help; Lord knows Aunt Fanny and I have offered it. Traps and hunts some, I expect. When he needs cash, he comes down the hill and hires out to one of the farmers, the way he's doing now at the Scotts'. Probably the only reason he's here today. People don't see him in the village for months on end, and when they do he won't speak to them."

And there was Calvin Waters, edging around the circle of talking men with his empty face, a trace of blueberry muffin on his brown lips—an obscenity, thought Johnny, a perambulating obscenity . . . And Emily Berry, the storekeeper's wife. Em Berry's thin Gothic figure seemed strung on piano wires; dowdy hair was drawn back in a tight brown knot; she wore a dark expensive maternity dress that managed to look cheap. Her voice was sharp and she talked to the other women as if they were dirt. Johnny slipped away from her as soon as he decently could.

And the older boys—the Hemus twins, Joel Hackett, Eddie Pangman—who had drifted out of the house, bored, and were setting off firecrackers under Merton Isbel's team . . .

Johnny was very glad when the Judge looked at his watch, sighed, and announced, "It's time!"

And so Shinn Corners in its near unanimity—the only ones missing, observed the Judge to Johnny, were the three generations of Scott men and Merritt Pangman—set out from the gate of Aunt Fanny Adams's house to straggle down Shinn Road to the intersection and the west corner with its cannon and its flagpole and its monument to Asahel Shinn, the men ahead, the women and children in tow; and they all sat down on campchairs brought over by Burney Hackett and Laughing Waters from the Town Hall, three rows of them in the road, while trestles bearing warning signs guarded them from a traffic that never came; and Judge Shinn mounted the pedestal of the monument and took off his Panama hat in the burning July sun and wiped his scalp with a handkerchief. And everyone grew quiet, even the youngest children.

And the Judge said, "We will begin our annual exercises in the usual way, with a salute to the flag."

And turned and faced the flagpole, and Shinn Corners got up from the campchairs and all the men's hats came off and all right arms came up, and the Judge led his village in pledging allegiance to the flag of the United States, "one nation indivisible, with liberty and justice for all.

And there was a rustle as all took seats again, and then the Judge said, "And now we will render unto God. Our pastor will lead us in prayer."

And Samuel Sheare took his spare body up onto the pedestal, and he no longer wore the troubled smile but a look of solemn responsibility; and he bowed his head, and the Judge bowed his head, and all the people below bowed their heads; and the minister said a prayer in a loud clear voice, as if he had authority to speak without fear at last. And it was a prayer to the Heavenly Father to preserve our liberties as He had bestowed them, to send us rain so that the fruits of our fields might multiply, and to send peace to our aged, and health to our sick, and good will toward all men high or humble. And Mr. Sheare prayed for the security of our country, that it might prevail over its enemies; and for wisdom on the part of the President of the United States and his counselors; and for peace wheresoever on earth. And the people of Shinn Corners murmured, "Amen," and raised their heads obediently as their pastor stepped down to resume his seat and his troubled smile.

And the Judge said with a smile, "Judy Scott, who constitutes in her lone majesty next year's graduating class of our grade school, will now read the Declaration of Independence."

And Mathilda Scott's Judy, her yellow braids shining in the sun, her cheeks pink with excitement, marched stiffly up to stand beside Judge Shinn, and she held up a white scroll printed in rather blurry blue printing with a red border around it, and the scroll shook a little, at which she frowned and began to read in a high tight voice with an occasional squeak in it the Declaration of Independence. . . .

Johnny glanced about him at the Judge's fellow townsmen. It seemed to him that with the exception of Fanny Adams he had never seen a more uniform vacancy. The noble-sounding words flowed over them like a spring tide over stones. Nothing soaked in; and in a little while the stones would be dry again. Well, Johnny thought, why not? What were words but the lawyer's delusion, mockery, and snare? Who but a few old men like Lewis Shinn listened to them any more?

He noticed that when Judy Scott stepped down with relief, to have her shoulder squeezed by Elizabeth Sheare and receive the misty love-glance of her mother, Judge Shinn was silent for a space, as if even he had been impressed by their vacuity.

Then the Judge began his speech.

He began by addressing them as neighbors and saying that he well remembered the village's Independence Day exercises when he was a small boy, and some of them remembered, too. "The river ran through Shinn Corners then. All the houses were white as the Monday wash, and there were lots of fine old shade trees. The dirt roads were rutted and dusty from all the rigs and surreys and farm wagons driving in for the celebration. And the crowds—of purely Shinn Corners folks—spread all over the Four Corners and up and down these roads, there were so many of us. We had a fife-and-drum corps

for stirring us up, and it made good loud music. The
militia company of our district fired off muskets in a
salute, to start things going, and we had our prayer and
the reading and the oration, and in my father's boyhood
this cannon was fired, too; and afterwards there were
bread and cheese and punch for everybody. The orator
of the day made a rousing speech about how our ancestors
had fought and bled and died to win our liberties for us,
and how we were free men and must ever be ready to
lay down our lives in defense of our freedom. And we
yelled and whistled and shot off guns, because the freedom
to be young and strong and prosperous and full of hope
and scared of nothing and nobody seemed to us a mighty
important thing."

The Judge looked down at the vacant faces, and the
vacant faces stared up at him; and he said suddenly,
"And today we're celebrating another Fourth of July. And
the river that ran through our village we now call the
Hollow, and we use part of it to dump our trash and
garbage. The houses that were white are a dirty gray
and falling to pieces. We're worn away to a handful. Nine
children in the grade school, three in the high school at
Comfort. Four farms, all struggling to keep out of the
hands of the Sheriff. And an old man gets up and babbles
about liberty, and you say to yourselves, 'Liberty? Liberty
to what? To get poorer? To lose our land? Liberty to
see our children want? Liberty to get blown up, or to die
in caves like moles, or to see our bones glow like candles
in the dark?' These are hard questions to answer, neighbors,
but I'm going to try to answer them."

They stirred.

They stirred, and the Judge talked of the great conflict
between the free world and Communism, and of what
was happening to Americans' liberties in the name of the
fight against it. How some in power and authority had
seized the opportunity, in the struggle against Communism, to attack and punish all who held opinions contrary
to theirs, so that today a man who held a contrary
opinion, no matter how loyal he might be, was denied
equal justice under law. How today in some cases even
the thoughts of a man's father, or of his sister, were
sometimes held against him. How today men stood con-
victed of high crimes by reason of mere association,

even of the distant past. How today the unsupported word of self-confessed traitors was honored under oath. How today accusation was taking the place of evidence, and the accused were not permitted to cross-examine their accusers, and often were not told who their accusers were—or even, as was happening with increasing frequency, the exact nature of the charges.

"And you ask me," said Judge Shinn, his arms jerking a little, "what all this has to do with you, and I tell you, neighbors, it has everything to do with you! Who wants to be poor? But who'd hesitate if he were given the choice between being a poor freeman and a rich slave? Isn't it better to lose your land than your right to think for yourself? Did the farmers who grabbed their muskets and fought the Redcoats from behind their farm fences take up arms to defend their poverty or their independence of mind and action?

"The attack on free men always begins with an attack on the laws which protect their freedom. And how does the tyrant attack those laws? By saying at first, 'We will set the laws aside for a little while—this is an emergency.' And the emergency is dangled before your eyes while your rights are stolen from you one by one; and soon you have no rights, and you get no justice, and—like Samson—you lose your strength and your manhood and you become a thing, fit only to think and to do what you're told. It happened that way in Nazi Germany. It happened that way in Soviet Russia. Are you going to let it happen here?"

Judge Shinn wiped his face; and he cried, "There is no liberty without justice, and there's no justice unless it's the identical justice for all. For those who disagree with us as for those who hold the same opinions. For the poor man as for the rich. For the man with the furrin-sounding name as for the Cabots and the Lodges. For the Catholic as for the Protestant and the Jew as for the Catholic. For the black as for the white. These aren't mere words, neighbors, pretty sayings to hang on your parlor walls. They're the only armor between you and the loss of your liberties. Let one man be deprived of his liberty, or his property, or his life without due process of law, and the liberty and property and lives of all of us are in danger. Tell your Congressmen and your Senators that. Make yourselves heard . . . while there's still time!"

* * *

When "The Star-Spangled Banner" had been sung, and Peter Berry had hurried ahead to reopen his store, and the children had whooped after him to buy cap pistols and bubble gum, and their elders dispersed in groups talking weather and crops and prices, Johnny took the old man's arm and walked him around the Shinn house and into the woods beyond.

"I thought that was a fine speech, Judge," said Johnny, "as speeches go."

Judge Shinn stopped and looked at him. "What did I say, Johnny, that you don't believe?"

"Oh, I *believe*. I believe it all." Johnny shrugged. "But what can I do about it? Have a cigaret?"

The Judge shook his head irritably. "When a man with paralysis of the vocal chords talks to people who are stone deaf, the net result is a thundering silence. Let's walk."

They walked through the Judge's woods for a long time. Finally the Judge stopped and sat down on a fallen tree. He mopped his face, and swatted at the gnats, and he said, "I don't know what's the matter with me today."

"It's the Yankee conscience," smiled Johnny, "rebelling at a display of honest emotion."

"I don't mean *that*." The Judge paused, as if groping for the right words. "All day I've had the funniest feeling."

"Feeling?"

"Well, it's like waking up on one of those deathly still, high-humidity days. When the air weighs a ton and you can't breathe."

"Seen a doctor lately?" asked Johnny lightly.

"Last week," growled the old man. "He says I'll live to be a hundred."

Johnny was silent. Then he said, "It's tied up with Shinn Corners, of course. You don't get down here much any more, you said. It doesn't surprise me. This place is pretty grim."

"Do you believe in premonitions, Johnny?" asked Judge Shinn suddenly.

Johnny said, "Sure do."

The Judge shook himself a little.

He got up from the log and reached for his handkerchief again. "I promised Mathilda Scott I'd bring you over to meet Earl. Lord, it's hot!"

The next day Aunt Fanny Adams was murdered.

Two

❖━━━━━━━━━━━━━━━❖

He was plastered against the flimsy wall with his eye to the hole in the freezing dark fighting off the stench from the alley and saying don't don't don't he's only a kid from Oklahoma who ought to be kissing his date in a jalopy under a willow by some moonlit river but they went on jamming lighted cigarets against his nipples and other places and telling him to say what he'd dropped from his plane on their people's villages and the hole in the wall got bigger and bigger and bigger until the hole was the whole room and he was the kid flyer twisting and jerking like a trout on a line to get away from the little probing fires the fires the fires . . .

Johnny opened his eyes.

He was in a sweat and the room was black.

"Who is it?" he said.

"Me," said the Judge's voice. The old man's finger was poking holes in him. "For a restless sleeper you're sure hard to wake up. Get up, Johnny!"

"What time is it?"

"Almost five. That's a three-mile walk to the pond, and the big ones bite early."

They hiked up Shinn Road in the dawn with their fishing gear and a camping outfit, the Judge insisting they make a day of it. Or as much of a day as the threatening skies would allow.

"When a man gets to be as old as I am," observed the Judge, "half a day is better than none."

Each carried a gun, taken from a locked commode drawer in the Judge's bedroom, where the weapons lay wrapped in oily rags among boxes of ammunition. The old jurist frowned on hunting for sport; he had his property severely posted to protect the pheasant and deer. But he considered chuck, rabbit, and such pests fair game. "When the fishing runs out we'll go after some. They're thick up around there. Come down into the valley and play hob with the farms. Maybe we'll get a bead on some fox. They've done a lot of damage this year." He had issued to Johnny a 20-gauge double for the rabbits, reserving to himself what he called his "varmint rifle." It was a .22 caliber handloader designed to play a little hob of its own, the Judge said ferociously, with the damn woodchucks. And he sighed, wishing old Pokey were trotting along to heel. Pocahontas had been the Judge's last hunting dog, a red setter bitch whose tenderly framed photograph hung on his study wall. Johnny had seen her grave in the woods behind the garage.

"Pokey and I had some fine times in the woods," Judge Shinn said happily.

"Hunting the butterflies, no doubt," grinned Johnny.

The Judge flushed and mumbled something about all that foolishness being dead and buried.

So the day began peacefully, nothing marring their pleasure but the closing sky. They netted some peepers for live bait and went out in the old flatbottomed boat the Judge had had carted up to the pond the week before, and they fished for largemouthed bass and were successful beyond their dreams. Then they hauled the boat up on shore and did some steelrod casting for pickerel, and they caught not only pickerel in plenty but a couple of husky trout, at which the Judge declared gleefully the coming of the millennium, for Peepers Pond had been considered fished out of trout, he said, for years.

"Did I croak some twaddle yesterday about premonitions?" he chortled. "False prophet!"

Then they made camp on the edge of the pond, broiled their trout and swallowed the delectable flesh along with their pond-cooled beer and Millie Pangman's oatmeal bread, and Johnny brewed he-man's coffee while the Judge cut open the ambrosial currant pie Aunt Fanny Adams had sent over by little Cynthia Hackett the evening before; and they stuffed themselves and were in heaven.

Whereupon the Judge said drowsily, "Don't feel a bit like snuffing out life. Hang the chucks," and he spread his poncho and dropped off like a small boy after a picnic.

So Johnny lay down and did likewise, hoping this time he wouldn't dream the one about the ten thousand men in yellow blanket-uniforms all shooting at him with the Russian guns in their yellow hands.

And that was how the rain caught them, two innocents fast asleep and soaked to the skin before they could scramble to their feet.

"I'm running true to form," gasped Johnny. "Did I ever tell you I'm a jinx?"

It was a few seconds past two o'clock by the Judge's watch, and they huddled under a big beech peering at the sky and trying to determine its long range intentions. The woods about the pond crackled and trembled under lightning bolts; one struck not a hundred feet away.

"Rather be drowned on the road than electrocuted under a tree," shouted the Judge. "Let's get out of here!"

They turned the boat over, hastily gathered their gear, and ran for the road.

They pushed against a curtain of water, squishing along heads down at a steady pace. At two-thirty by the Judge's watch they were half a mile from the crest of Holy Hill.

"We're not doing bad!" roared the old man. "We've come about halfway. How d'ye feel, Johnny?"

"Reminiscent!" said Johnny. He never wanted to see another fish. "Isn't there *any* traffic on this road?"

"Let us pray!"

"Keep your weather eye peeled for anything on wheels. A scooter would look good just now!"

Five minutes later a figure swam into view on the opposite side of the road, heading in the direction from which they had come and leaning into the rain.

"Hi, there!" yelled Johnny. "Enjoying the swim?"

The man leaped like a deer. For a moment he glared in their direction, the width of the road between them. They saw a medium-sized man of spare build with a face dark gray as the skies, a stubble of light beard, and two timid, burning eyes. The rain had fluted the brim of his odd green hat and was coursing down his face in rivers; patched black pants plastered his shanks and the light tweed jacket with its leather elbow patches hung on his body like a wet paper sack. He carried a small black suitcase, the size of an overnight bag, made of some cheap material which was dissolving at the seams —a rope held it together. . . . For a moment only;

then, in a lightning flash, water squirting out of his shape-less shoes, the man ran.

Soaked as they were, Johnny and the Judge stared up the road after the running man.

"Wonder who he is," said the Judge. "Stranger around here."

"Never look a stranger in the mouth," said Johnny.

But the Judge kept staring.

"Foreigner, I'd say," shrugged Johnny. "Or of recent foreign origin. He never got that green velour hat in the U.S.A."

"Probably some itinerant heading for Cudbury and a mill job. Why do you suppose he ran like that, Johnny?"

"Sudden memories of the old country and the People's Police, no doubt. Two armed men."

"Good Lord!" The Judge shifted his rifle self-consciously. "I hope the poor devil gets a lift."

"Hope for yourself, Judge. And while you're at it, put in a good word for me!"

A minute or so later a gray shabby sedan bore down on them from behind, shedding water like a motorboat. They turned and shouted, but it was going over forty miles an hour and before they could half open their mouths it was past them and out of sight over the hill. They stood in the slap of its wake, dejected.

"That was Burney Hackett's car," growled the Judge. "Darn his chinless hide! He never even saw us."

"Courage, your honor. Only a mile or so more to go."

"We could stop in at Hosey Lemmon's shack," said the Judge doubtfully. "It's at the top of the hill there, in the woods off the road."

"No, thanks, I filled my quota of filthy shacks long ago. I'll settle for your house and a clean towel."

As they reached the top of Holy Hill, the Judge ex-claimed, "There's old Lemmon now, footing it for home."

"Another pioneer," grumbled Johnny. "Doesn't he have a car, or a buggy, or a tricycle, either?"

"Hosey? Heavens, no." Judge Shinn frowned. "What's he doing back up here? He's hired out to the Scotts."

"Prefers high ground, of course!"

The Judge bellowed at the white-bearded hermit, but if Lemmon heard the hail he paid no attention to it. He disappeared in his hut, a ramshackle cabin with a torn tarpaper roof and a rusty stovepipe for a chimney.

Nothing human or mechanical passed them again. They fell into the Judge's house at three o'clock like shipwrecked sailors on a providential beach, stripped and showered and got into clean dry clothes as if the devil were after them; and at three-fifteen, just as they were sitting down in the Judge's living room with a glass of brown comfort and rags to clean the guns, the phone rang twice and the Judge sighed and said, "Now I don't consider that neighborly," and he answered the phone and Burney Hackett's nasal voice, more nasal and less lucid than the Judge had ever heard it, announced with total unbelief that he had just walked over to the Adams house and found Aunt Fanny Adams stretched out on the floor of her paintin' room deader than a shucked corn.

"Aunt Fanny?" said Judge Shinn. "Did you say, Burney, Fanny Adams is *dead?*"

Johnny put his glass down.

The Judge hung up and blindly turned in his direction.

"Heart?" said Johnny, wishing he could look elsewhere.

"Brains." The Judge groped. "Where's my gun? Brains, Burney Hackett says. They're spilled all down her smock. *Where's my gun!*"

They splashed up the path of the Adams house to the front door, which resisted. Judge Shinn rattled the brass knocker, pounded.

"Burney! It's me, Lewis Shinn!"

"I locked it, Judge," said Burney Hackett's voice. "Come around the side to the kitchen door."

They raced around to the east side of the house. The kitchen door was open to the rain. In the doorway stood Constable Hackett, very pale, with a yellow undertinge. The cold water was running in the sink near the door, as if he had just been using it. He reached over and turned off the tap and said, "Come on in."

A puddle of muddy water lay inside the doorway. The muddy tracks of Hackett's big feet were all over the satiny inlaid linoleum.

It was a small modern kitchen, with an electric range and a big refrigerator and a garbage disposal unit in the sink. On the kitchen table stood a platter of half-eaten food, boiled ham and potato salad, a dish of berry pie, a pitcher of milk and a clean glass.

There was a swinging door on the wall opposite the outer door, and the Judge went to it slowly.

"Let me," said Johnny. "I'm used to it."

"No."

The old man pushed the door aside. He made no sound at all for a long time. Then he cleared his throat and stepped into the inner room, and Johnny stepped in after him. Behind Johnny the telephone on the kitchen table rattled as Constable Hackett asked fretfully for a number.

The studio was almost square. Its two outside walls faced north and west and were all glass, with a view of Merton Isbel's cornfield to the north and, on the west beyond the stone wall, the church and cemetery. The cornfield stretched to the flat horizon.

She looked small lying on the floor, little more than a bundle of dry bones covered by a smeared smock, the rivulets of blood in the wrinkles already turning to the color of mud, the single exposed hand with its wavery blue veins—like a relief map of its ninety-one years—still grasping the paintbrush as if that, at least, could not be taken from her. The hand lay old and shriveled, at peace. On the easel behind her stood a painting. The palette she had been working with daubed the floorboards gaily under the north window, where it had fallen.

Johnny went back into the kitchen. He yanked a clean huck towel from a rack above the sink and returned to the studio. Burney Hackett put down the phone and followed.

Johnny covered the head and face gently.

"Two-thirteen," said the Judge. "Remember the time. Remember it." He turned to the blackened fireplace on the wall opposite the north picture window and pretended to be studying it.

Johnny squatted. The weapon was on the floor almost within her reach. It was a long heavy poker of black iron, fire-pocked and crusted with the smoke of generations. The blood on it was already dry.

"Does this poker come from the fireplace?" Johnny asked.

"Yes," said the Judge's back. "Yes, it does. It was made by her grandfather, Thomas Adams, in a hand-forge that once stood on this property. The past, she couldn't get away from the past even in death."

Who can? thought Johnny.

"Even this room. It was originally the kitchen and it's as old as the house. When Girshom died and she began to paint she blocked off the east end for a small modern kitchen and turned the balance into a studio. Knocked out the north and west walls for light, had a new floor laid, supply cabinets built . . . But she left the old fireplace. Said she couldn't live without it." Judge Shinn laughed. "Instead, it killed her."

"Two-thirteen," said Burney Hackett.

"I know, Constable," Johnny said softly. "You didn't touch the locket?"

"Nope." Hackett's tone was stiff.

The oldfashioned locket-watch on its gold chain that Johnny had noticed Fanny Adams wearing the previous day was still around her neck. It had died, too. One wild, mad blow had missed her head and scraped down the front of her, smashing the cameo and springing the locket-face, so that the face stood open and the cracked and silenced dial with its delicate roman numerals fixed the moment of eternity. Two-thirteen, it said. Thirteen minutes past the second hour of the afternoon of Saturday, July the fifth. The sooty streak left by the tip of the poker on the battered watch case was as definite as a crossmark on a calendar.

Johnny rose.

"How did you find her, Burney?" Judge Shinn had turned back now, his long Yankee face hardened against the world, or perhaps himself.

Hackett said: "I been after Aunt Fanny for a long time to buy herself adequate p'tection for her pictures. Lyman Hinchley'd wrote her up for fire insurance on the house and furnishin's, but not near enough to cover all them paintin's she's got around. Most a hundred in that slidin' closet, worth a fortune.

"Well, yesterday at the party I fin'ly talked her into lettin' me cover the market value of the pictures. So today I ran over to Cudbury to see Lyman Hinchley 'bout an up-to-date comprehensive policy plan, and I got all the figgers and come back here to put 'em to her. That's when I found her layin' here like you see."

"What time was that, Burney?"

" 'Bout a minute or two before I phoned you, Judge."

"We'd better call the coroner in Cudbury."

"No need to call *him*," said Burney Hackett quickly.

"I already phoned Doc Cushman in Comfort while I was waitin' for you to get here."

"But Cushman's merely the coroner's deputy for Comfort, Burney," said Judge Shinn patiently. "This is a criminal death, directly in the county coroner's jurisdiction. Cushman will merely have to call Barnwell in Cudbury."

"Cushman ain't callin' nobody," said Hackett. "I didn't tell him nothin' but to get over here right away."

"Why not, for heaven's sake?" The Judge was exasperated.

"Just didn't have a mind to." The underdeveloped chin suddenly jutted.

Judge Shinn stared at him. As he stared, a wailing scream began that grew and grew until it filled the house.

It was the village fire siren.

"Who set that off?"

"I just phoned Peter Berry to send Calvin Waters over to the firehouse and start it goin'. That'll bring everybody in."

"It certainly will!" The Judge turned abruptly to the kitchen door. "Excuse me, Burney . . ." The chinless man did not budge. "Burney, get out of my way. I have to phone the state police, the sheriff—"

"Won't be necessary, Judge," said Hackett.

"You've already called?"

"Nope."

"Burn Hackett, don't fuddle me," exclaimed the Judge. "I'm not exactly myself just now. This is a murder case. The proper authorities—"

"I'm the proper authority in Shinn Corners, Judge," said Burney Hackett, "now, ain't I? Duly elected constable. The law states I *may* call the county sheriff to my aid, *when necessary*. Well, it ain't necessary. Soon's my posse forms, we go huntin'."

"But the summoning of a *posse comitatus* is the function of—" Judge Shinn stopped. "Hunting? For whom, Burney? What are you holding back?"

Hackett blinked. "Not holdin' nothin' back, Judge. Ain't had a chance. Prue Plummer phoned me here soon's I hung up after talkin' to you. Says she mistook your two rings for her three. As usual. Anyways, she listened in. Well, Prue had somethin' to tell me before she began

phonin' the news around the Corners. A tramp stopped
at her back door 'bout a quarter of two today, she says.
Dang'rous-lookin' furriner, spoke a broken English. She
couldn't hardly understand him, Prue says, but she figgered
he was after a handout. She sent him packin'. But here's
the thing." Hackett cleared his throat. "Prue says she
watched this tramp walk up Shinn Road and go round
Aunt Fanny's to the back."

"Tramp?" said the Judge.

He glanced at Johnny's back. Johnny was looking out
the north window at Aunt Fanny Adams's barn and lean-
to and the Isbel cornfield beyond.

"Tramp," nodded Constable Hackett. "There's nobody
in Shinn Corners'd beat in the head of Aunt Fanny
Adams. You know that, Judge. It was that tramp murdered her, and it's a cinch he can't have got far on foot
in this pourin'-down rain."

"Tramp," the Judge said again.

The siren shut off in mid-scream, leaving a shimmer of
silence. Then there was confusion in the garden and
the road. The swishy movement of feet in the kitchen, the
creak of the swinging door, a wedge of eyes.

Judge Shinn suddenly pushed the door in and he and
Burney Hackett went into the kitchen. Johnny heard
angry female murmurs and the old man saying something
in a neighborly voice.

The rain was still driving hard in crowded slanting
silver lines, putting up a screen beyond the window
through which the cornfield wavered. Water was pouring
off the Adams barn in the back yard and the pitched
roof of the small lean-to attached to it, a two-sided
affair open at the front and rear. Johnny could see
through to the stone wall of the Isbel field as if the
lean-to were a picture frame.

He turned back to the painting on the easel.

She had caught in her primitive, meticulous style all
the raging contempt of nature. The dripping barn, the
empty lean-to, every stone in the wall, every tall tan
withered stalk in the rainlashed Isbel field, every crooked
weeping headstone in the cemetery corner, cowered under
the ripped and bleeding sky.

And Johnny looked down at the crumpled bones, and
he remembered the dark gray face, the timid, burning
eyes, the green velour hat, the rope-tied satchel, the

spurting shoes as their feet fled in the downpour . . .
and he thought, You were a very great artist, and a
beautiful old woman, and there's no more sense in your
death than in my life.

Then the Judge and Samuel Sheare came in with a
staring man between them, and the Judge said in the
gentlest of voices, I'm sorry, Ferriss, that death had to
come to her this way; and the man shut his eyes and
turned away.

When Mr. Sheare said in his troubled way, "We must
not, we must not prejudge. Our Lord was poorest of the
poor. Are we to lay this crime on the head of a man
merely 'cause he must ask for food and walk in the
rain?"—when the minister said this, Fanny Adams's grandnephew raised his head and said, "Walk in the rain?
Who?"

They had taken him out of the studio into Fanny
Adams's gleaming dining room, and Prue Plummer was
there with Elizabeth Sheare, stroking the pin butterfly
hinge on the door from the death room with patient
avarice. But Ferriss Adams's question brought her mouth
to a point, and Prue Plummer told him avidly about
the man who had begged for food at her back door.

"I saw a tramp," Adams said.

"Where?" asked Constable Hackett.

Mr. Sheare said suddenly, "I ask you to remember
that you're Christians. I'm stayin' with the body," and
he went into the studio. His stout wife sat down in a
corner.

"I saw the tramp!" said Adams, his voice rising. He
was a tall dapper businessman with thinning brown hair
and close-shaven cheeks that had grown pink and blotchy.
"I was on my way over from Cudbury just now to call
on Aunt Fanny and I passed a man on the road . . . Miss
Plummer, what did this tramp look like?"

"Had on dark pants," said Prue Plummer, making a
smacking sound, "and a light sort of old tweed jacket,
and he was carrying a cheap suitcase tied with a rope."

"That's the man! It was just a few minutes ago! What
time is it? He's still up there somewhere!"

"Take it easy, Mr. Adams," said Burney Hackett.
"Where'd you see this feller?"

"I got here just about three-thirty—I passed him only

a few minutes before that," cried Adams. "It was on the other side of Peepers Pond, the Cudbury side, about three-quarters of a mile beyond it, I'd say. He was headed towards Cudbury. Thought he acted queer! Jumped into the bushes when he saw my car coming."

"Less'n four miles from here, it's three thirty-five . . . say you passed him ten-twelve minutes ago . . ." Hackett thought deliberately. "Can't have got much more'n half a mile past where you saw him. Your car's outside here, Mr. Adams, ain't it?"

"Yes."

"I got to stay here get my posse together and make sure everybody keeps his mouth shut. Judge, I'm deputizin' you and Mr. Shinn and Mr. Adams to start out after that tramp. He's likely dang'rous, but you got two guns. Don't use 'em 'less you have to, but take no chances, neither. Got enough gas in your tank, Mr. Adams?"

"Gassed up this morning, thank God."

"Don't figger we'll be more'n five-ten minutes behind you," said Constable Hackett. "Good huntin'."

And then they were in Ferriss Adams's old coupé rattling furiously up the hill in the rain, Johnny and the Judge bouncing around in the jump-seats clutching their guns.

"I hope this windshield wiper holds out," said Adams anxiously. "Do you suppose he's armed?"

"Don't worry, Ferriss," said the Judge. "We have a manhunter with us. Fresh from the wars."

"Mr. Shinn? Oh, Korea. Ever kill anybody, Mr. Shinn?"

"Yes," said Johnny.

They knew it was the same man the moment they saw him. He was slogging along the streaming road at a fast shuffle, the rope satchel bumping off his knees as he shifted its weight from one hand to the other, the absurd velour hat a cloche now clinging to his ears. He kept glancing over his shoulder.

"That's him!" yelled Ferriss Adams. He stuck his head out of the car, squawking his horn. "Stop! In the name of the law, stop right there!"

The man dived off the road to his right and disappeared.

"He's escaping!" screamed the lawyer. "Shoot, Mr. Shinn!"

"Yes, sir," said Johnny, not moving. It was hard to

keep her shattered head in focus; already she was part of his dreamworld. All he could see was a live man, running to stay alive.

"Shoot where, you idiot?" cried Judge Shinn. "Ferriss, stop the car. You can't drive into that muck. It's swamp!"

"He's not getting away from me," grunted Adams, struggling with the wheel. "Say, isn't that a wagon road? Maybe—"

"Don't be a fool, man," roared the Judge. "How far will we get?"

But Ferriss Adams's coupé had already plunged into the marsh, its wheels whining for traction.

They slipped and skidded after the fleeing man. He had been forced onto the path; apparently a few seconds of floundering in swampwater up to his knees had made the road with its mere five inches of mud seem like a running track. He ran stooped over, dodging, weaving, ducking, as if he expected bullets. The satchel was under his arm now.

They were in the marsh area about four and a half miles northeast of Shinn Corners, well beyond Peepers Pond. It was posted with county signs warning against dangerous bogs, and the heavy rain of almost two hours had not added to its charms. Now a rolling mist closed in that made Adams curse.

"We'll lose him altogether in this pea soup! We'll have to chase him on foot—"

"Wait, Ferriss." The Judge was peering ahead, fingering his gun nervously. "Watch it! Stop the car!"

The brakes shrieked. The coupé skidded to a halt. Adams jumped out, looking ahead wildly.

The car had stopped on the brink of a soft black stretch of the marsh. Adams picked up a heavy rock and lobbed it into the stuff. The rock sank out of sight immediately. The surface of the muck quivered as if it were alive.

"Quagmire." Adams cursed again. "We lost him."

The rain bounced off them. Each man stood in a nimbus of spray, peering.

"He can't have got far," said Johnny.

"There he is!" cried Adams. "Stop! Stop, or we shoot!"

The fugitive was wading frantically through the knee-deep morass forty yards away.

"Mr. Shinn—Judge—shoot, or give me a gun—"

Johnny pushed the excited man aside. The Judge was looking at him curiously.

"Stop," called Johnny. "Stop, and you won't be hurt."

The man pressed on in a violent splash of arms and legs.

"Why don't you *shoot?*" Adams shook his fist at Johnny.

Johnny raised the 20-gauge and fired. At the roar of the gun the fugitive leaped convulsively and fell.

"You hit him, you hit him!" shrieked the Cudbury lawyer.

"I fired over his head," said Johnny. "Stay right there!" he called.

"Scared witless," said the Judge. "There he goes!"

The man bounded to his feet, glared about him. He had lost his suitcase, his hat. He crouched and scuttled behind a big swamp oak. By the time they reached the tree he had vanished.

They kept together, calling, occasionally firing a shot into the air. But the tramp was gone as if the bog had caught him.

Eventually they struggled back to the wagon road.

"You should have put a bullet in his leg," Ferriss Adams was saying heatedly. "I'd have done it if I had a gun!"

"Then I'm glad you don't, Ferriss," said the Judge. "He won't get away."

"He's got away, hasn't he?"

"Not for long, I warrant you. If he sticks to the swamp, he's bottled up. If he takes to the main road, he'll be caught in a matter of minutes. Burney Hackett and the others should be along any time now. What is it, Johnny?"

Johnny touched the Judge's elbow. "Look."

They were back at the dead end of the wagon road. Adams's coupé no longer stood on the brink of the bog. It was settling into the quagmire. As they watched, it stopped.

All but a foot of its top had been sucked under.

"My car," said Ferriss Adams dazedly.

Johnny pointed to a series of deep narrow oval holes in the mud midway between the tracks of the car, ending at the edge of the bog.

"His tracks. He released the brake, put his shoulder to the rear end, and pushed the car in. He'd probably doubled back, seen the coupé, and decided he had a better chance of escape if we were forced to foot it, too. Tough luck, Mr. Adams."

The Judge said, "I'm sorry, Ferriss. We'd better get back to the main road and wait for the other cars."

"Give me your gun!" said the lawyer.

"No, Ferriss. We want this man alive, and pushing a car into a bog doesn't call for the death penalty."

"He's a killer, Judge!"

"We don't know that. All we know is that he was seen going around to the kitchen door of your aunt's house some twenty minutes or so before she was murdered."

"That proves it, doesn't it?" snarled Adams.

"You're a lawyer, Ferriss. You know it proves no such thing."

"I know I'm going to get that murdering hobo dead or alive!"

"You're wasting time," said Johnny. "He'll risk the main road again, now that we have no car. We'd better get moving."

They hurried back along the wagon road in the mire, Ferriss Adams laboring ahead in white-faced silence. Johnny and the Judge did not look at each other.

Suddenly they heard a burble of voices, scuffling sounds, a man's laugh. Adams broke into a run.

"They got him!"

They burst out into the blacktop road. Hubert Hemus's sedan and Orville Pangman's farm truck were blocking the road. The fugitive was down on his back at the bottom of a pile of flailing arms and legs—the big Hemus twins, Eddie Pangman, Joel Hackett, and Drakeley Scott. Forming a tight gun circle around the boys were Hubert Hemus, Constable Hackett, Orville Pangman, old Merton Isbel, and fat Peter Berry. As the three men pushed through, the pile-up dissolved and the Hemus boys hauled their quarry to his feet. They slammed him against the side of Orville Pangman's truck.

Eddie Pangman said hoarsely, "Get your lousy hands over your head." He rammed the muzzle of his rifle into the man's belly. The quivering arms went up.

Tommy Hemus grinned and kicked him in the groin. He fell down with a scream, clawing at his middle. Dave Hemus picked him up and pinned him against the truck again. His legs jerked in spasms of effort to raise them.

Johnny Shinn felt something stir deep, deep inside. It was the small cold hard core of an anger he thought he had lost forever. It slowly spread to take in the old woman's head, as if her shattered head and the fugitive's twitching legs were part of the same violated body.

He felt the Judge's hand on his arm and looked down with surprise. His finger was on the trigger of the shotgun and the gun was coming up to Tommy Hemus's belt buckle.

Johnny hastily lowered the gun.

The dripping, muddy, blood-caked gasping man was hardly recognizable as the itinerant Johnny and the Judge had passed on the road in the downpour earlier in the day. Dirty blond hair hung over his eyes; his jacket and pants were torn in a dozen places; thorns had ripped his hands and face; blood oozed from his mouth where a tooth had been kicked out. His eyes kept rolling like the eyes of a frightened dog.

"You flushed the bastard right out to us," said Burney Hackett.

"Saw your tracks where ye turned into the ma'sh," said burly Orville Pangman, "then heard your guns."

"We spread out along the road and ambushed him," panted Peter Berry. "Real excitin'."

Old Merton Isbel said: "Scum. Dirty whore scum."

Eddie Pangman, great red boy-hands opening and closing on his rifle: "Put the cuffs on him, Mr. Hackett!"

"Aw, Pop don't have no cuffs," said stocky Joel Hackett disgustedly. "Didn't I always say you ought to get cuffs, Pop? Cop's got to have at least one pair, anybody knows that."

"You mind your tongue," said Constable Hackett.

"Cops without cuffs . . ."

Tommy Hemus drawled: "He ain't goin' no place."

Dave Hemus, sucking on a torn knuckle: "Not any more he ain't."

Hubert Hemus, to his sons: "Shut up."

Drakeley Scott said nothing. The thin-shouldered boy was staring at the jerking fugitive with heat, almost with hunger.

"Was he armed?" asked Judge Shinn.

"No," said Constable Hackett. "I kind of wish he was."

Ferriss Adams walked up to the man and looked him over. "Has he talked?" he asked harshly.

"Jabbered some," said Peter Berry. "Try him, Mr. Adams."

"You killed her, didn't you?" said Ferriss Adams.

The man said nothing.

"Didn't you?" shouted the lawyer. "Can't you talk, damn you? All it needs is a yes or no!"

The eyes merely kept rolling.

"Ferriss," said Judge Shinn.

Adams sucked in some air and stepped back. "Also," he said coldly, "you went and pushed my car into the bog. How am I going to get it out? Won't you talk about that, either?"

"Car in the bog?" said Peter Berry alertly. "Now that's a darn shame, Mr. Adams. S'pose I take a look—"

"Not now," said Hube Hemus. The slight man had not moved. "Burney, put the halter on him."

"Wait!" said the Judge. "What are you going to do?"

"Got to secure the prisoner, Judge, don't we?" said the constable. "Brought along a calf halter. It ought to just fit." Hackett slipped a muddy halter over the fugitive's head. The man dropped to his knees. His eyes rolled back so far only the whites showed.

"He thinks he's going to be hanged or shot," exclaimed Judge Shinn. "Can't you see this man is in the last stages of fright? Not to mention pain! Take this nasty thing off him, Burney."

"Ain't nobody goin' to hurt him, Judge." The constable tightened the neck-strap and buckled it. "Nobody's goin' to shoot you, killer. Not for a while, anyway." He snapped a lead-rope to the ring of the halter. "There we are. Try gettin' out of that."

The nose-piece of the halter gave the man a ridiculous animal appearance. It seemed to annoy him. His torn hands tugged at it violently.

"Better tie his hands, too," said Hube Hemus. "Dave, Tommy, hang on to him. Anybody got another rope?"

"There's some rope under the seat of the truck, Eddie," Orville Pangman said to his son.

The Hemus twins took hold of the man's arms, one pulling one way, one another. The man stopped struggling. Eddie Pangman scrambled off the truck with a length of tarred rope. His father took it from him. The twins slammed the prisoner's wrists together behind his back and the big farmer trussed them.

Judge Shinn stepped forward.

"Now he's all right, Judge," said the elder Hemus politely. "Orville, I'll take him in my car with Tommy and Dave. He might get a notion to jump out of an open truck. Burney, get him on his feet."

"Come on, get up." Hackett pulled on the rope. The kneeling figure resisted. "Nobody's goin' to do nothin' to you. Up on your pins!"

"Would you mind waiting a minute, Hackett?" Johnny heard his voice say.

They stared at him.

Johnny went over to the cowering man, wondering at his own energy. He was beginning to get a headache. "Miss Plummer said this man talked in a foreign accent. Maybe he doesn't understand English too well." He stooped over the prisoner. "Do you know what I'm saying?"

Bruised lips moving; the eyes were closed.

The lips kept moving.

Johnny straightened. "Sounds like Russian, or Polish."

"Told you he jabbered!" said Peter Berry triumphantly.

"Commie spy, I bet," grinned Tommy Hemus.

"What's he saying?" demanded Joel Hackett. "Huh, Mr. Shinn?"

"My guess is," said Johnny, "he's praying."

"Then he can't be a Commie," said Eddie Pangman. "They don't pray."

"That's right," said Dave Hemus. "Them bastards don't believe in God."

"Some of 'em do," said Drakeley Scott unexpectedly. "They got churches in Russia."

"Don't you believe it," sneered Joel Hackett. "That's a lot of Red propaganda."

"What's the matter, Drake," said Tommy Hemus, "you a Commie-lover?"

"You shut your damn mouth!" The Scott boy doubled his thin fists.

"All o' ye shut your mouths," said Merton Isbel. He walked up to the kneeling man and deliberately measured the distance between the toe of his heavy farm shoe and a point midway between the prisoner's thighs. "Git up, ye godless furrin whoreson. Git up!"

He let fly.

The man fell forward on his face and lay still.

Judge Shinn's blue eyes flashed at Johnny with a sort of contempt. Then he went up to Merton Isbel and struck him a heavy blow on the shoulder with the heel of his hand. The old farmer staggered, his mouth wide open with astonishment.

"Now you men listen to me," said the Judge in a throbbing whisper. "This man is a prisoner. He's suspected of murder. Suspicion isn't proof. But even if we knew he was guilty, he'd still have his rights under the law. I will personally swear out a warrant for the arrest of anyone who manhandles him or harms him in any way. Is that clearly understood?" He looked at Constable Hackett. "And since you make so much of your constabulary office, Burney Hackett, I'm holding you responsible for the safety of the prisoner."

The chinless man said soothingly, "Sure, Judge. I'll go right along with him in the Hemuses' car."

The old jurist stared around at his neighbors. They returned his stare without expression. His lips flattened and he stepped aside, shifting his rifle slightly.

"Boys." The First Selectman of Shinn Corners nodded toward the fallen man.

The Hemus twins bent over the prisoner, hooked his armpits, and lifted.

He was only half-conscious. The dark gray of his skin had a greenish tinge. His face was a twist of pain.

His legs refused to straighten. They kept making weak attempts to come up tight against his belly.

Tommy Hemus winked. "Now this ain't manhandlin', Judge Shinn, is it? You see he won't walk." And the brothers dragged the prisoner to their father's car, his shoetips scraping on the road. Constable Hackett cradled his gun and followed. Hube Hemus was already behind the wheel, looking impatient.

Hackett pulled open one of the rear doors.

"Upsadaisy," said Tommy Hemus pleasantly. He and his brother heaved, and the fugitive tumbled into the car head first.

The car immediately began to back up. Hemus's sons jumped in with the prisoner, grinning; Hackett yelped and scrambled in beside their father.

The car was fifty feet down the road before the doors slammed.

"I'm sorry, Judge," said Johnny in a low voice. "But I've either got to go berserk or mind my business." Judge Shinn said nothing. "I wish I hadn't met her!" said Johnny.

Orville Pangman was climbing into the cab of his open truck. The other men were pulling themselves up over the tailboard.

"Better ride up here with me, Judge," called Pangman as he kicked his starter. "Ye'll get jounced around back there."

"I'll ride with the others, Orville," said the Judge quietly.

Eddie Pangman vaulted in beside his father.

Johnny helped the old man onto the truck in silence. He was about to follow when the truck shot backward; he was almost hurled under the wheels. He clung to the tailboard chain, dragging; if not for the helping hands of the Judge and Ferriss Adams he would have been torn loose. The others looked on curiously, not stirring.

His head ached abominably.

All the way back to Shinn Corners the Cudbury lawyer complained about his sunken car, trying to get a salvage price out of Peter Berry. The rain dripped off his nose bitterly. The storekeeper kept shaking his head and saying in his boomy-smily voice that he couldn't set a price beforehand, didn't know how long the job would take, it was a question if his old wrecker had the power to pull a car out that was almost completely buried in bog, though of course he'd be glad to give it a try. Likely need a dredger, too. Might be a mite expensive. If Mr. Adams wanted him to tackle it on a contingency basis . . . "'Course, you could always get 'Lias Wurley from over Cudbury to come way out here, Mr. Adams, but Wurley's a high-priced garage . . ."

In the end Adams threw up his hands. "Couldn't possibly be worth it," he said disgustedly. "Anyway, I got a new car on order from Marty Zilliber and all the robber'd allow me on a trade-in was a hundred twenty-five. Hundred twenty-five! I said sure it's gone a hundred and thirty-two thousand miles, Marty, but I only had a ring job and complete overhaul done at the hundred thousand mark, the rubber's in good condition, seems to me it's worth more than a hundred twenty-five, book or no book. But that's all he'd give me on the trade. So I guess the hell with it. Let the insurance company worry about it. If they want to spend a couple hundred dollars for a dredge and wrecker . . ."

He had apparently forgotten all about his aunt.

Johnny lay down flat on his stomach with his head over the tailboard and was sick all over the road. The Judge held onto his legs, looking away.

The rain stopped and the late afternoon sun came out just as they passed old man Lemmon's hovel on Holy Hill.

Hubert Hemus's car was parked just beyond the Adams house, before the church. The prisoner, Burney Hackett, the three Hemus men were nowhere to be seen.

"Where is he?" demanded Judge Shinn, pushing through the crowd of women and children at the church gate. "What did they do with him?"

"Don't you worry, Judge, he's safe," said Millie Pangman. The sun flashed off her gold eyeglasses. "They're fixin' up the coalbin in the church cellar as a jail. He won't get away!"

"Too good for him, I say," bellowed Rebecca Hemus. "Too good for him!"

"And that Elizabeth Sheare runnin' to make him a cup of tea," said Emily Berry venomously. "Tea! Poison's what I'd give him. And gettin' him dry clothes, like the church was a hotel. Peter Berry, you get on home and take those wet things off!"

"Wouldn't it be better if you all went home?" asked the Judge evenly. "This is no place for women and children."

"What did he say?" shouted old Selina Hackett. "Who went home? At a time like this!"

"We have as much right here as you men, Judge," said Prue Plummer sharply. "Nobody's going to budge till that murdering foreigner gets what's coming to him. Do you realize it was only by the grace of God and the fellowship of the Holy Ghost that I wasn't the one he murdered? How many times I told Aunt Fanny, 'Don't take in every dirty stranger who comes scraping at your kitchen door,' I told her. 'Some day,' I said, 'some day, Aunt

Fanny, you'll let in the wrong one.' The poor dear wouldn't ever listen. And now look at her!"

Mathilda Scott said in a low voice, "I'd like to get my hands on him. Once, just once."

Judge Shinn looked at her as if he had never seen her before.

Hackett and the Hemuses appeared on the church steps. As the Judge led the way through the group of women and children to meet them, Johnny noticed Mert Isbel's daughter Sarah and her child hanging about the edge of the crowd. The woman's face was lively. But the liveliness died as her father pushed by her. She drew away, gripping her little girl's hand.

"Burney, what's the meaning of this?" cried Judge Shinn. "Locking him in a coalbin!"

"Got no jail to lock him in, Judge," said the constable.

"He shouldn't be here at all! Have you notified Coroner Barnwell yet?"

"I got to talk that over with Doc Cushman. Doc's waitin' for us over at Aunt Fanny's."

"All Dr. Cushman can legally do is bring in a finding that death was caused by a criminal act, and report that finding at once to Coroner Barnwell in Cudbury. From that point on, the case is in Barnwell's hands. He will either summon a coroner's jury of six electors—"

"Judge." Hubert Hemus's gaunt face was granite, only the jaws moving, like millstones grinding away at the words to come. "For ninety-one years Fanny Adams belonged to the town. This is town business. Ain't nobody goin' to tell us how to run town business. Now you're an important judge and you know the law and how things ought to be done, and we'll be obliged for your advice as a judge and a neighbor. We'll let Coroner Barnwell come down here and make his findin's. If he wants a coroner's jury, why, we got six qualified electors right here. We'll do everythin' legal. Ain't nobody goin' to deprive this murderin' furrin trash of his legal rights. He'll have his lawyer and he'll have his chance to defend himself. *But he ain't leavin' Shinn Corners, no matter what.*"

A murmur formed behind them like an oncoming wave. The sound tickled Johnny's scalp. He fought down another attack of nausea.

Hube Hemus's cheerless glance went out over his neighbors. "We got to get this organized, neighbors," the First

Selectman said. "Got to set a day and night guard over the prisoner. Got to set guards against outside meddlin'. Got to see that the milkin's done—we're a full hour late now!—got lots to do. Right now I b'lieve the big boys better get on home and attend to the cows. Mert, you can send Calvin Waters back in your wagon with Sarah and the child to do your milkin'; we need you here. We men stay and figger out what we got to do. The women with small children can take 'em home, give 'em somethin' to eat, and put 'em to bed. Bigger children can watch over 'em. The women can get together and fix a community supper . . ."

Somehow, the Judge and Johnny found themselves shut off. They stood about on the periphery, watching and listening, but groups fell silent and drifted apart at their approach.

"It must be me," Johnny said to the Judge. "Shinn or no Shinn, I'm an outsider. Wouldn't it make it easier all around, Judge, if I packed and got out?"

"You'd like that, wouldn't you?" said the Judge scornfully.

"What do you mean?" said Johnny.

The Judge looked suddenly quite old. "Nothing. Nothing, Johnny. It has nothing to do with you. It's me. I've sat on the bench in Cudbury for too many years to be *en rapport* with Shinn Corners. Hube Hemus has passed the word around."

It was from Ferris Adams that they learned what had happened in the cellar of the church when the prisoner was brought down to the coalbin. Adams had the story from Samuel Sheare, whom he had sought out to discuss arrangements for Fanny Adams's funeral. Mr. Sheare had been present in the cellar; he had insisted on providing the prisoner with dry clothing—the man's teeth were clacking from immersion and chill. When he brought the clothing, the minister had asked Constable Hackett and the Hemuses to leave him alone with the prisoner; they had refused and ordered the man to strip. Either he misunderstood or he understood too well—doubled over in agony still, the man had resisted furiously. The Hemus twins had torn the clothes from his body.

In his jacket Burney Hackett found a paper identifying him as one Josef Kowalczyk—"Mr. Sheare spelled it for me," Ferris Adams said, "it ends in c-z-y-k, which

Mr. Sheare says the fellow pronounces 'chick' "—aged forty-two, a Polish immigrant admitted to the United States under a special refugee quota in 1947. They had also found, in a dirty knotted handkerchief tied to a rope slung around Kowalczyk's naked waist, a hundred and twenty-four dollars.

"And that's the clincher," snapped the Cudbury lawyer. "Because Mr. Sheare says that yesterday, at Aunt Fanny's open house, she took him into her kitchen for a private talk. She told him she'd noticed Elizabeth Sheare's summer dresses were pretty shabby, and she wanted him to buy his wife a new one. She reached up to the top shelf of her old pine cabinet, where she's always kept her row of spice jars, and she took down the cinnamon jar. There was some change in it and a roll of bills. When Mr. Sheare protested, Aunt Fanny said to him, 'Don't ye worry none about my runnin' short, Mr. Sheare. You know I keep some cash here for emergencies. There's a hundred and forty-nine dollars and change in this jar, and if I can't give Elizabeth Sheare a new dress out of it without her knowin', what in the land's sake can I do with it?' And she peeled off two tens and a five and pressed them into Mr. Sheare's hand. A hundred and forty-nine dollars in Aunt Fanny's cinnamon bank only the day before," said Ferriss Adams, "she gave twenty-five of it to Samuel Sheare, there's *nothing* left in Aunt Fanny's cinnamon jar —they've already checked that—and here's a hundred and twenty-four dollars hidden under Kowalczyk's undershirt . . . smelling of cinnamon. It's what the Judge and I as lawyers, Mr. Shinn," said Adams dryly, "call circumstantial evidence, but I'd say those are pretty damning circumstances. Wouldn't you, Judge?"

"As presumptive of theft, Ferriss, yes," said the Judge.

"Judge, he's guilty as hell and you know it!"

"Not legally, I don't. Ferriss, are you staying around the village this evening?"

"I'll have to. I've got to see about the undertaking arrangements. As soon as the coroner gets here and gives us a release—it'll have to be tonight!—I'm having Cy Moody of Comfort pick up the body. Why, Judge?"

"Because, Ferriss," said Judge Shinn slowly, "I don't like one little bit what's going on. I've got to appeal to you as a practicing lawyer sworn to uphold the laws of the state to disregard your personal feelings, Ferriss, and help me stop . . . whatever's brewing. As Fanny Adams's kin you ought to be able to exercise some sobering influence on these upset people. Tonight may be crucial, Ferriss. I'll stay out of the way. Will you try to talk them into handing Kowalczyk over to the sheriff or the state police?"

"Hube Hemus is the man," muttered the Cudbury lawyer. "The tail that wags your wacky community. Why is Hube acting so God-Almighty, Judge? What's Hube's beef?"

"It's compounded of many things, Ferriss. But principally, I think, the murder of his brother Laban before the war."

"The Gonzoli case! I'd clean forgot about that. Cudbury jury acquitted him, didn't it? Then I'm afraid, Judge," said Adams, shaking his head, "you're asking for the impossible."

"Do your best, Ferriss." The Judge squeezed Adams's arm and turned away. He was shivering.

"I think, your honor," said Johnny, "I'd better get you into your house before you go off on a pneumonia kick. Did you ever get a Japanese rubdown? March!"

But the Judge did not smile.

They sat on the Shinn porch that night and watched the arrival of Coroner Barnwell. They watched the coroner's excited gestures, the eddy of villagers, the arrival of the Comfort undertaker's truck, the departure of Fanny Adams's remains. With the crickets shrilling, the peepers roaring, the mosquitoes humming, the millers and beetles cracking against Shinn Corners's sole street light, outside Peter Berry's store, the weird performance on the village streets that night was played to fitting music. Through it all the Hemus twins flitted about the church grounds like spirits of darkness, each armed with a shotgun. One patrolled the front yard of the church, the other guarded the rear.

When, at ten o'clock, the Cudbury County coroner strode from the Town Hall to the intersection and began to cross Shinn Road to his parked car, Judge Shinn called softly.

"Barnwell, come up here a moment."

The heavy figure looked startled. Barnwell hurried over the green and across the Judge's lawn. "I thought they'd strung you up or something, Judge Shinn! What the devil's come over this one-horse agglomeration of two-footed he- and she-asses?"

"That's what I want to talk to you about. Sit down, Barnwell. By the way, meet a young cousin of mine, John Shinn."

"Heard the Judge had a long-lost relative floating around town." Coroner Barnwell groped for Johnny's hand and wrung it. "Fine mess you've stepped into. Judge, what's going on in Shinn Corners? Do you know they won't give up this fellow Kowalczyk? Won't give him up!" The coroner sounded baffled. "Why?"

"I'm afraid there are a great many reasons, all pretty complicated," sighed Judge Shinn, "but the only fact that need concern us at the moment, Barnwell, is the fact of their refusal. What happened over at Town Hall? Did you have a coroner's jury?"

"Yes, and they brought in a perfectly proper finding from the testimony and evidence. Kowalczyk obviously must be held for arraignment. But then they handed me my hat and politely asked me to get the hell out of Shinn Corners. I'm still flabbergasted. Of course, I'll run these local yokels of yours clean back to their primitive privies as soon as I can get some cops down here—"

"That's exactly what I wish you wouldn't do, Barnwell. Not right away, anyway."

"Why not?" The coroner was astonished.

"Because there'll be a heap of trouble."

"Who cares!" said Barnwell violently.

"I care," said the Judge. "And so, I think, Barnwell, will you. I'm not exaggerating the danger. There's real trouble ahead. Ask an outsider's opinion. Johnny's an ex-Intelligence officer, a trouble-shooter of experience! Johnny, what do you think?"

"I think," said Johnny, "that to bring armed men into this village in its present frame of mind—any armed men, Coroner Barnwell—is to invite a nastier mess than anything New England's seen since Daniel Shays's rebellion."

"Well, I swan to Marthy," said Barnwell sardonically, "I do believe you two picklepusses are serious. I'll tell you, Judge. I've got my duty, too, though it's hardly my place to remind you of it, since in our beloved state county coroners are appointed by the judges of the Superior Court, on whose altitudinous bench you've parked your fanny with such distinction for so long. In other words, Judge, you share the awful responsibility of my appointment. Consequently, you have a vested ethical interest in seeing that I carry out my duties faithfully and to the last jot and tittle of the law. My duty is to secure custody of the accused, Josef Kowalczyk, and see him lodged in the sacred precincts of our county jail, where the sonofabitch belongs. I'm not going to do it personally; I'm far too sinister for that. Me, I'm going to toss this squishy little old punkin into the mitts of those whose duty in turn it is to assist me in performing mine—to wit, the police power. Rebellion!" Barnwell tramped off the porch, snickering. "Go to bed and sleep it off," he called back; and he drove off up Shinn Road towards Cudbury with a flirt of his exhaust.

After Barnwell's departure, the Judge and Johnny went back to their silent watch. They saw the villagers emerge from the Town Hall, straggle up Four Corners Road, stand about the intersection, disperse, regroup. They heard arrangements discussed for the milking and other farm activities that had to go on. Chores were to be taken care of on a communal basis, by women as well as men; cars and weapons were to be pooled. So-and-So was to tend the stock at the Pangman barn, this boy was to relieve Calvin Waters at the Isbel farm, that one was to run over to the Scotts' while Drakeley was on duty in the village. They saw Ferriss Adams let into the Adams house by Burney Hackett, and old Merton Isbel being given a gun to patrol the Adams property. They saw Hube Hemus and Orville Pangman relieve Tommy and Dave Hemus on the church grounds, and the twins roar down Shinn Road past the Shinn porch in their father's car, presumably to go home for a few hours' sleep. Plans were made for regular four-hour watches, with each man and able-bodied boy of Shinn Corners assigned his place and time. Older children of the immediate vicinity, like Dickie Berry and Cynthia Hackett, ran here and there on mysterious errands. Kitchens were lit up until past midnight, as Millie Pangman and Prue Plummer and Emily Berry busied themselves making sandwiches and pots of coffee.

But at last the lights blinked out, the Corners emptied, the children disappeared, the town settled down. Except for the street lamp on Berry's corner and the floodlight illuminating the church grounds, Shinn Corners was in darkness. The only sounds were the sounds of the insects, an occasional faint bark from the Scotts' dog far down Four Corners Road, and the tread of the farmer sentries.

"Incredible," said Johnny.

"What?" The Judge started.

"I said all this strikes me as unbelievable," Johnny said. "For the first time I begin to grasp Lexington and Concord and the Boston Tea Party. How can people get so worked up over anything?"

"They believe in something," said the Judge.

"To this extent?" Johnny laughed.

"It shows they're alive, at any rate."

"I'm alive," argued Johnny. "But I've got more sense than to stick my neck out. For what? The old lady, God rest her soul, is dead; nothing's going to bring her back. Why get into a hassle?"

Judge Shinn's rocker creaked. "Are you referring to me, or to them, Johnny?"

"To both of you."

"Let me tell you something about people like us," said the Judge. "You have to go back a lot further than 1776. You have to go back more than three centuries to when the Puritan nature was molding itself to the rough shape of the new England. To Miles Standish, for instance, under orders by the Pilgrim Fathers to destroy the Mount Wollaston settlement and kick out Thomas Morton because of his uninhibited life and his success at Indian trading—moral issues and economics, you see, the Holy Book and the Pocketbook, in defense of either or both of which the good Puritan more or less cheerfully risked his life. Or to the John Endecott expedition against the Pequot Indians in reprisal for the murder of John Oldham, a simple exercise in revenge against the benighted heathen furriners—well, their skin color was different and they spoke English with an accent when they spoke it at all, which amounted to the same thing. As I recall it, they followed that up by wiping out the main Pequot settlement and massacring every big and little Pequot they could find. The Puritan is a mighty stubborn citizen when aroused."

"In other words," Johnny grinned in the darkness, "they were swine."

"They were people. People with beliefs, some right and

some wrong. More important—they did something, rightly or wrongly, about their beliefs." The rocker stopped creaking. "Johnny, what do you believe in?"

In the darkness Johnny felt the old man's eyes groping for him.

"Nothing, I guess."

"A man has to believe in something, Johnny."

"I'm not a man, I'm a vegetable," laughed Johnny.

"So you're vegetating."

"It follows, doesn't it?" Johnny suddenly felt too tired to talk. "I used to believe in a great deal."

"Of course you did—"

"It was painful."

"Yes," said the Judge dryly.

"I even did something about my beliefs. I lapped up all the noble sludge, shipped out to be a hero. I knew what I was fighting for. You betcha. Democracy. Freedom. Down with the tyrants. One world. Man, those were the days. Remember?"

"I remember," said the Judge.

"So do I," said Johnny. "I wish I didn't. Remembering is the worst pain of all. The trouble is, I'm not a *successful* vegetable. I'm not a successful anything. That bothers me a little. It would be nice just rooting in the sun, performing my little photosynthesis for the day, watching the animal life go by. But I'm like the rose in a story I read by Roald Dahl. When it was cut, it shrieked."

"Go on," said the Judge.

"You like to listen to this stuff?" Johnny lit a cigaret; the flame trembled, and he snuffed it out quickly. "All right, I will. I think the first hint I got that I was going to be the missing link between the fauna and the flora came to me when I saw Hiroshima. Know anything about real fear, Judge? It's the only hell there is. Hiroshima was hell on earth. Hell is a man's shadow printed on the side of a building. It's a radioactive bloodstream. It's a kid with his bones lit up like a Christmas tree. There's nothing in Dante that comes within a million miles of it."

Johnny smiled his queer smile in the warmth of the night. "So I came home. I felt out of sorts . . . out of touch with business-as-usual, but I put that down to the labor pains of readjustment. I really tried. I tried sitting in a law class again. I tried watching movies and TV commercials. I tried to understand prices going up and industry blaming it on labor and labor blaming it on industry. I tried to understand the UN. The one thing I didn't try was Communism. I never fell for that crap. Some of the men did—I knew a fighter pilot who'd flown fifty-nine missions and came back and after a while joined the party, said there had to be hope somehwere. I was denied even that. I began to realize that there was no hope anywhere, at all. Then Korea. Am I boring you?"

"No," said Judge Shinn. "No."

"Korea, God help us," said Johnny. "I was no hero that time. I just wanted to get back into something I knew. And all the time I was keeping my eye on what was going on outside that pustulated pimple on the hide of Asia. I saw nothing that stirred me in the direction of the fauna. Quite the contrary. And when it was all 'over'—as if it's over!—the hopelessness simply shifted from one phase into another. But it was the same damned thing. More TV commercials. More gripes about taxes. More politicians promising better protection for less dough. And more speeches at the UN. And—always— bigger and better bombs.

"I'm not being emotional about this," said Johnny. "I dream some, but I manage to sleep. . . . You take this Commie business. Suppose there were no Commies. There'd still be Africa, India, China—there'd still be Spain and Germany, and the Arabs, and the Peronistas—there'd still be a world full of poverty, hate, ambition, greed. There'd still be atom bombs, hydrogen bombs, nerve gas. And there'd still be the book burners and the witch hunt- ers and the doubletalkers. About the only note of reas- surance the brass keep sounding is that we've got all of three years left before the bombs start falling. . . . So what do you want me to do, Judge—find a job, get married, have kids, buy a house, water a lawn, save up for Junior's college and my old age? What for?"

The Judge was silent.

Johnny said apologetically, "Well, you asked me. Mind if I hit the sack?"

He went into the house and climbed the polished stair- way to his musty bedroom to try out Coroner Barnwell's parting advice.

After a long time, Judge Shinn followed.

Johnny was awakened from his dream by the church bell. His first drowsy thought was, What a nice way to be reminded that I promised myself to attend Mr. Sheare's service Sunday morning. But as his senses sharpened it seemed to him the reminder was too insistent. The old bell, with its flat and cracked clang, was pealing away like a 1900 fire alarm.

He rolled out of bed and went to a window.

The people were running toward their church from all directions. He saw Burney Hackett burst out of his house on the south corner, struggling to get into his Sunday jacket and hold on to his gun at the same time. Peter Berry came lumbering up Four Corners Road from his house behind the store as if a bull were after him. Children were darting everywhere, surrounded by wildly barking dogs. The Pangmans and Prue Plummer were trotting down the middle of Shinn Road, urging one another on. Two cars shot up to the north corner, one from the south and the other from the west, almost colliding at the intersection. One deposited Dave Hemus, Merton Isbel, and Calvin Waters, the other Drakeley Scott and his mother. A group was already waiting before the church; Johnny saw Samuel Sheare and his stout wife hurrying across the lawn from the parsonage, their faces unnaturally white.

Then Judge Shinn pounded on his door.

"Johnny, get up!"

"What's happening?"

"Someone was posted out beyond Comfort, near the Petunxit police barracks. Just phoned a warning in. The state police are on their way over. Damn Barnwell!"

Johnny threw on his clothes and scuttled downstairs.

They were all congregated now—every man, woman, and child of the village except the Scott invalids and the hermit of Holy Hill. The women and children huddled on the steps of the church. The men and older boys were deployed in a loose arc formation before them, covering the approach to the church and the drive on its east side where the cellar windows were. Judge Shinn and Mr. Sheare were talking earnestly to Hubert Hemus and Burney Hackett. Ferriss Adams paced nearby, nibbling his fingernails.

Johnny got across to the north corner just as two state police cars and a private car came up Shinn Road from

the direction of Comfort at a leisurely gait. They slowed
down at the intersection and fanned out a little; then
they stopped. Both police cars were full; the passenger
car held one man.

The driver of the passenger car, a big stout man in a
blue-striped seersucker suit and a new straw hat, got slowly out and stood in the road. He took off his hat and
wiped his half-bald head with a big blue polka-dot handkerchief. Large halfmoons of sweat darkened his jacket
below the armpits. He kept glancing from the silent crowd
before the church to one of the police cars.

Finally a uniformed man joined him. He was sandy-
haired, with a red hard face. He wore the insignia of a
captain of state police. A gun was holstered at his hip;
the flap of the holster was buttoned.

The other police remained in the cars.

The police captain and the stout civilian walked slowly toward the church in the bright sunshine.

Johnny remained where he was. He leaned against the
horse trough. But only for a moment. Curiosity made
him move again. He crossed over the curve of path that
separated the north corner from the church lawn. He
stopped near the Sheares.

The troopers had their heads out the car windows,
watching in silence.

The police officer and the civilian went up the church
walk side by side, very slowly now. They stopped altogether about ten feet from the line of armed men.

"Mornin', Judge Shinn. Mornin', folks," said the stout
man. "Heard the terrible news, thought I'd stop by with
Captain Frisbee to see what we could do."

"This is Sheriff Mothless of Cudbury County," said the
Judge. "Constable Burney Hackett, Hubert Hemus, Merton
Isbel, Peter Berry, Orville Pangman . . . Glad to see you,
Captain Frisbee. Shake hands with my neighbors."

The policeman and the sheriff hesitated. Then they
came forward and shook hands all around.

"And this is Mr. Ferriss Adams, Fanny Adams's grandnephew," said the Judge. "I think you know the sheriff,
Ferriss . . ."

The Cudbury lawyer shook the fat hand silently.

"Can't tell you what a shock it's been, Mr. Adams," said
Sheriff Mothless, wiping his head again. "Never had the
pleasure of meetin' that grand old lady, but we've always

been mighty proud of her in this county, mighty proud. Great credit to her town, state, and country. Famous artist, they say. Captain Frisbee and me just stopped down Comfort way at Cy Moody's parlors and took a real good look at her. Ter'ble. Brutal. I tell you, it like to made my blood boil. Man who'd commit a murder like that don't deserve any more mercy than a mad yellow dog. And by goshamighty, I'm goin' to see he gets what's comin' to him! And damn quick! Right, Captain Frisbee?"

"No need for you folks to fret any more about him," said the state policeman. "We'll take him right off your hands."

He stopped expectantly.

Nobody moved.

Sheriff Mothless wiped his forehead once more. "Hear you got him locked up in the church cellar," he said. "Fine work, neighbors! Leaves us nothin' to do but go on down there, yank him out, and shoot him straight over to the county jail. Easiest manhunt I ever heard of. Hey, Captain?"

"I sure appreciate the help," said Captain Frisbee. "Well." He glanced over his shoulder at the police cars, but Sheriff Mothless nudged him, and the policeman turned back.

"Well, it's gettin' on," the sheriff said, glancing at his wristwatch. "I expect you folks'll be wantin' to get into church. So if you'll all kindly step to one side while Captain Frisbee's men haul that skunk up out o' there . . ."

The sheriff's heavy voice dribbled off. Not a man or woman had stirred.

Captain Frisbee glanced over his shoulder again, a little impatiently.

"Just a moment, please!" Judge Shinn nudged Ferriss Adams forward.

The Cudbury lawyer faced the villagers with respectful friendliness, as if they were a jury. "Neighbors," he said, "you all know me. I've been coming into Shinn Corners on and off for forty years, since the days when my Aunt Fanny jiggled me on her knee. So I don't have to tell you there's nobody in this town wants to see this Kowalczyk, or whatever his name is, pay the penalty for his crime quicker than I do. I'm asking you good folks to hand him over to these officers of the law so they can throw him into one of those escape-proof cells we've got in that fine modern county jail in Cudbury. Step aside and let this officer do his duty."

From the crowd of women in the church doorway came the voice of Rebecca Hemus, a shrill challenge. "So a Cudbury jury can let him go, the way they let that Joe Gonzoli go when he murdered my brother-in-law Laban?"

"But that was a case of self-defense," protested Adams.

Hubert Hemus said, "He ain't gettin' out of our jurisdiction, Mr. Adams, and that's that."

Judge Shinn touched Adams's arm. The lawyer stepped back, shrugging.

"That's fine talk from the First Selectman," said the Judge. "For twenty years and more, Hube Hemus, Shinn Corners has looked to you for counsel and leadership. How do you expect your children—all these children— to grow up respecting law and order when you set such a poor example?"

Hemus shifted his rifle suddenly and spat. "Seems to me you got it wrong, Judge," he said in a mild voice. "It's law and order we're upholdin'. Aunt Fanny Adams was one of us—born here, growed up here, married here, buried her husband Girshom and her children here, did all that paintin' that made her famous here, and she died here. We're a community. We take care of our own. Our law enforcement officer arrested Aunt Fanny's murderer, a coroner's jury of our electors brought in a findin', and we aim to follow right through as our just due. We don't need no outside help, didn't ask for none, don't want none. That's all there is to it, Judge. Now I'm goin' to ask you, Sheriff, and you, Captain Frisbee, to kindly get on out of Shinn Corners and take your men with you. We got to go to church service."

"Do you talk about church, Hube Hemus?" cried Samuel Sheare. "Where's your humility? Have you no shame, carryin' a gun on the Lord's day, incitin' your neighbors to do the same—yes, even to the steps of the house of the Lord's congregation? And defyin' the mandate of the law, in the persons of these men who are only doin' their sworn duty? You're the instigator and ringleader, Hubert Hemus. Come back to your senses. Talk your neighbors into comin' back to theirs!"

Hube Hemus said gently, "We had a town meetin' last night, Mr. Sheare. You were there. You know this matter was voted on in the manner prescribed by town regulations, and minutes were duly taken of the proceedin's. You know nobody had to talk nobody into nothin'. You know there wasn't a single nay vote on the motion exceptin' yours and Mrs. Sheare's."

The minister looked over his congregation, at those whose dead he had buried, whose sick he had comforted, whose troubled he had given faith—at the brides and the grooms, the mothers and the fathers, at the children he had received into his church. And everywhere he looked, the familiar faces were rock, implacable.

Mr. Sheare made a small gesture of despair and turned away.

"I'm saying it again," said Hube. Hemus to the sheriff and the policeman. "Go away and leave us to our own."

Sheriff Mothless jammed his straw hat over his ears. "What is this, a dime-store revolution? Shinn Corners secedin' from the forty-eight states? You folks stop this time-wastin' tomfoolery and stand aside! Captain Frisbee, do your duty!"

The captain nodded at the two police cars. Ten troopers climbed down into the road. They shuffled to form a line. Then they came slowly up from the north corner and turned into the church walk, feeling their holsters.

The thin arc of village men and boys began to finger their guns.

Johnny watched, fascinated.

"Stop right there, please!" Judge Shinn's voice cracked out like a rifle shot. The advancing troopers glanced at their captain; he nodded, and they halted. The Judge turned to his fellow townsmen. "May I say something more? This is the United States of America, neighbors, one of the few places left on earth where men live by just laws, or try to, and where the law is the same for all. I told you only Friday on the green there what some men are trying to do in our country, how they are undermining the legal structure that protects the principle of equal justice for all, what a catastrophe this could be if it isn't put a stop to. Yet what do I find less than forty-eight hours later? My own neighbors proposing to commit the same criminal folly!

"One of the keystones of our system of law is the protection of the rights of accused persons. We proudly guarantee that every person charged with a crime—no matter who he is, no matter how sickening his offense —that every such person get a fair trial, in a court of competent jurisdiction, before a jury of responsible citizens, with open minds, so that they may weigh the facts of the case without prejudice and arrive at a just decision.

"Now," said the Judge, "we have a murder case on our hands. Hube, Orville, Burney, Peter, Mert, all of you—can you provide a court of competent jurisdiction? No. The laws of our state specifically designate the Superior Court as the court of jurisdiction in serious criminal cases, with certain exceptions such as the counties having Courts of Common Pleas, of which Cudbury County is not one. True, we have a trial justice, in common with all small communities in our state that lack a town court; and you, Orville Pangman, are the justice of the peace by town election. But if you've read the laws regulating your office, Orville, you know that a case as serious as a murder is not within your jurisdiction, that the accused must be bound over to the next term of the Superior Court or, where such courts are provided for, the Court of Common Pleas.

"And do you think—Hube, Orville, Burn, Peter, Merton, all of you," cried the Judge, "that this accused, Josef Kowalczyk, can get a fair trial in Shinn Corners? Is there one man or woman within range of my voice who is without prejudice in this case? Is there one of you who hasn't already made up his mind that this man Kowalczyk is guilty of the murder of Fanny Adams?"

Johnny thought, You may as well try arguing with the stones in the cemetery there.

"Well?" demanded Judge Shinn. "Answer me!"

And again Hube Hemus spoke out of his gaunt inflexibility. "Fairness works two ways, Judge. He'll get as fair a trial in Shinn Corners as Joe Gonzoli got in Cudbury. We want justice, too." He was silent; then, with his first show of defiance, he added, "Maybe we can't trust nobody but ourselves no more. Maybe that's it, Judge. Anyway, we voted it that way, and that's the way it's goin' to be."

Captain Frisbee said instantly, "All right, men."

Sheriff Mothless hopped aside.

The troopers moved forward in a sort of drift, as if they felt everything was in delicate balance and must not be weighted down on their side by so much as a heavy footfall. The men and boys watched them coming, the boys a little pale but with half-grins, the men's mouths flattening.

Hube Hemus brought his gun up.

The sun flashed along the whole steel barrier.

The troopers halted.

Captain Frisbee looked astounded. Then his red face went redder. "I ask you people to get out of our way. If you don't, we've got to come through anyway. There's nothing we can do about it. The choice is yours."

"Don't force the issue, Captain." Hube Hemus's jaws ground. "We'd have to shoot."

The guns steadied.

The police officer hesitated. The hands of his troopers hovered over their holsters. They were watching him uneasily.

"Judge, please step out of the way," said Captain Frisbee in a low voice. "I ask the minister there to do the same."

Neither Judge Shinn nor Samuel Sheare obeyed. The little minister's hands fluttered; that was all.

"I not only ask you to step aside," snapped the officer, "but if there's anything you can say to get those women and children away from the doorway you'd better say it now. A lot of people are going to get hurt. I call you to witness that I'm not responsible if—"

"Wait," said the Judge in a gritty voice. "Will you wait? Give me ten minutes, Captain, just ten minutes."

"For what?" said Captain Frisbee. "These people, Judge, are plain loony. Or they're bluffing, which is more likely. Either way—"

A nervous trooper jerked out his revolver and lunged.

There was a shot.

Johnny thought, This is one of those dreams.

The revolver flew out of the trooper's hand and thudded to the grass beside the walk. The trooper cried out and stared at his hand. Blood was welling from a long crease across the web of flesh between his thumb and forefinger.

Smoke snaked out of Hube Hemus's gun.

"I warned ye. Next time it's through the heart."

Judge Shinn jumped up and down like a marionette, waving his arms. "For God's sake, Captain, ten minutes!" he shouted. "Don't you realize yet what you've stepped into? Do you want a blood bath on your conscience? Women and children victims as well as yourselves and these mules? I want a chance to phone the Governor!"

Captain Frisbee said in a murderous voice, "Grady, take Ames over to the car and fix up that flesh wound. The rest of you stay where you are. Hollister, take over till I get back." He nodded bitterly to Judge Shinn. "Lead the way."

Johnny trailed them across the road to the Shinn house. The Judge sat down in the foyer beside the telephone, wiped his face and hands with a handkerchief carefully. Then he picked up the phone.

"Operator, this is an emergency call. I want to speak to Governor Bradley Ford in the state capital. Governor Ford is either at the Executive Mansion or somewhere in the Capitol Building. I must speak to him in person. This is Superior Court Judge Lewis Shinn calling."

As he waited, the Judge wiped his ear and the earpiece of the receiver. The foyer was cool, quiet. The sun, still in the eastern sky, streamed in through the screen door. A horsefly crawled and buzzed on the screen, black against the light. The red of Captain Frisbee's face was so deep it was alarming.

Johnny found his pulse throbbing. He made the discovery with some surprise.

"Governor Ford?" said Judge Shinn. Then he said through his teeth, "No, damn it, I want the Governor himself! Put him on!" He wiped his mouth this time.

There was no sound from outdoors at all. Through the screen door Johnny could see the whole tableau before the church. It had not changed. He had the absurd feeling that it would remain fixed that way in time and space, like a photograph.

"Governor? Judge Lewis Shinn," said the Judge rapidly. "No, I'm calling from my home in Shinn Corners. Governor, Fanny Adams was murdered here yesterday afternoon—yes, Aunt Fanny Adams. I know—I know you haven't heard about it, Governor. Governor, listen—Governor, a man has been caught by our constable and a posse of the townspeople. He's an itinerant of Polish origin and speaks very little English. There is circumstantial evidence that he may have been the murderer. No, wait! Our people have locked him in the cellar of the church and refuse to give him up. That's right, Governor, they insist on retaining custody of the suspect and trying him themselves—I know they *can't*, Governor Ford, but they say they're going to just the same! At this moment a detail of state police under command of Captain Frisbee of the Petunxit barracks is facing almost the entire male population of Shinn Corners before the church. And they're all armed. No, I mean the villagers are armed, Governor. In fact, one shot has already been fired . . . No, no, Governor, how would militia help the situation? It would only aggravate matters. That's not why I'm calling . . . *Talk* to them! Governor, you don't understand. I tell you if these troopers try to take the prisoner out of that church, blood will run in the streets. I might add that every woman and child in the village is in the direct line of the troopers' fire and refuses to move. I know—I know, Governor, it is fantastic. But it's also a fact— That's exactly the point. There is something you can do, and that's why I'm calling. First, I suggest you give Captain Frisbee the direct order—he's standing by—to retire with his men. Sheriff Mothless of Cudbury County is here; he's to get out, too. Secondly, and this is of vital importance, Governor, I want you to appoint me special judge in this case, authorized to hold a trial in Shinn Corners—Governor . . . Governor . . . No, wait. You don't understand my purpose. Obviously any trial conducted here will be a travesty of justice. Legally speaking, it won't be a trial at all. But it will pacify these people and get us past the critical period, which is my sole concern at the moment . . . If they find him guilty and insist—? Of course not, Governor! If it should come to such an extremity, I'll notify you at once and you can send the state police in force, if necessary call out the National Guard . . . No, the status of the accused in my opinion wouldn't change an iota, regardless of what they find. There will be so many errors of legal process—I'll compound them!—so many statutory safeguards, trampled on . . . That's it, Governor. For the record you should make it clear that my request and your authorization constitute a ruse of convenience only, to avert bloodshed, and that they're designed solely to allow tempers to cool down so the prisoner can be got safely away. Then he can be tried in the regular way in a court of proper jurisdiction— No, no, Governor, I don't *want* the

State's Attorney of Cudbury County involved! For exactly the reason that he should be! . . . That's right, Governor. That's it—thank you. Oh, one thing more. Will you keep this quiet? The fewer know what's happened the better. If word gets out and reporters start pouring in here . . . Yes, yes. Please instruct Captain Frisbee to that effect for himself, his men, and Sheriff Mothless. I'll take care of the county coroner and the one or two others here who know— Yes, I'll keep you informed . . . God bless you, Governor. Captain Frisbee's right here."

With the departure of the troopers and the sheriff everything softened into natural shapes and colors. The air lightened as if a gas had blown away and the people changed from stiff figures in a photograph to men and women and children.

Samuel Sheare turned away, his lips moving. His wife went up to him, putting her stout body between him and the danger that had passed.

The women chattered and scolded the children; the big boys elbowed one another, horsing around; the men grounded their weapons and looked sheepish. Only Hube Hemus did not change expression; if he felt a personal triumph, no sign of it appeared on his gaunt features.

Judge Shinn held up his hand, and after a moment, good-naturedly, they listened.

"With the consent and cooperation of the Governor of our state, neighbors, you are going to have your chance to demonstrate that Shinn Corners is as strong for protecting the rights of an accused murderer as you are for asserting your own. Governor Ford has just empowered me to conduct the trial of Josef Kowalczyk in Shinn Corners."

They murmured their approval.

"I assume," the Judge continued dryly, "you consider me qualified. But so that there will be no misunderstanding, will you signify that you consent to my sitting in this case, and that you will abide by my rulings without argument except as they are properly argued by prosecutor and defense counsel?"

"Let's call a town meetin'," said Burney Hackett.

"No need for that," said Hube Hemus indulgently. "Trial's got to have a judge, and a judge's got his prescribed powers. All those in favor say aye!" There was a roar of ayes. "All those opposed motion carried. Go ahead, Judge."

"Then I set the trial of Josef Kowalczyk as beginning Monday morning, the seventh day of July, at ten o'clock A.M. That's tomorrow morning, late enough so the chores can be got out of the way. The place of the trial will be Aunt Fanny Adams's house. We'll all be more comfortable there, and we'll have the additional advantage of being on the scene of the crime, so that exhibits need not be toted from one place to another. Is that agreeable to everyone?"

They were pleased. Johnny thought, Crafty old conniver. You've set it in the one place calculated to reassure them.

"The first thing we will do tomorrow morning," the Judge went on, "is empanel a jury. The law states that the accused must be tried by a jury of his peers, consisting of twelve legal voters of good character, sound judgment, and fair education, aged at least twenty-five, plus an alternate in case one of the twelve takes sick or otherwise cannot continue as a juryman during the trial. There will have to be a bailiff to take charge of the prisoner and keep order in the courtroom, a clerk of the court to keep the record of the trial, a prosecutor, and a defense attorney. The accused will be given the opportunity to select his own counsel and, if he does so, you must abide by his choice. If he has no preference, the court will appoint counsel to defend him; and in that case, I shall have to call in a lawyer from outside at town expense. Is that understood?"

They looked at Hubert Hemus.

Hemus reflected. "Aya. He's got to have his lawyer. But who's goin' to prosecute?"

"Good question, Hube," said the Judge, still more dryly. "I'll have a suggestion on that point at the proper time, one that I'm sure will meet with everyone's approval."

He looked around. "All qualified voters will be present in the living room of Aunt Fanny Adams's house by a quarter of ten tomorrow morning. Court will convene at ten sharp. And now, neighbors, I think we've held up church long enough, don't you? Mr. Sheare?"

The women and children trooped into the church. The men conferred in low tones; then Tommy and Dave Hemus were given instructions and came down off the steps to take posts before and behind the little white building, trailing their guns negligently. Eddie Pangman and Drakeley Scott hurried up the walk and out into Shinn Road. They halted in the middle of the intersection. Eddie Pangman faced east, in the direction of Cudbury; Drakeley Scott faced west, in the direction of Comfort. Both boys were in high spirits. They joked to each other over their shoulders.

The men of Shinn Corners stacked their guns carefully outside the church and went in to their Sunday worship.

Three

❖━━━━━━━━━━━━━❖

Judge Shinn was preoccupied during the service. Almost as preoccupied, Johnny observed, as Mr. Sheare. The minister mumbled throughout, and during the singing of the hymns he stood with eyes closed as if communing with the only Authority that had never failed him. To the Judge's frank relief, Mr. Sheare dispensed with his sermon.

Johnny found his thoughts wandering to the man in the cellar. Kowalczyk was probably a Roman Catholic, and if he was devout this imprisonment in the coalbin of a Low Protestant church during a sacred service must seem to him a cruel and unusual punishment. No Latin, strange-sounding hymns, a priest who dressed like other men . . .

He dismissed Kowalczyk with an effort.

After the service the Judge conferred with Ferriss Adams. Then he took Hube Hemus aside. He was talking earnestly to Elizabeth Sheare when Millie Pangman waddled over and hovered.

"Yes, Millie, what is it?"

"Your Sunday dinner's goin' to be awful late, Judge," the farmer's wife said timidly. "I've got my own family's dinner to get, and what with everythin' that's happened and all—"

"It's all right, Millie," the Judge barked. "We'll manage," and he turned back to Mrs. Sheare.

Millie Pangman drew little Deborah away, crushed. Johnny went up to her. "Now don't you worry about our dinner, Mrs. Pangman. I'll fix it."

"But I don't like you havin' to do that, Mr. Shinn."

"Why not? I'll enjoy it," Johnny lied gallantly. "Is there anything in the house to make dinner with?"

"There's a roast of beef in the refrig'rator I was goin' to fix—"

"Say no more. I cut my eyeteeth on roasts of beef. We'll make out fine."

So Sunday afternoon found Johnny in the big Shinn kitchen up to his armpits in one of Millie Pangman's aprons, pondering the mysteries of a boned rolled roast while Judge Shinn busied himself with equally mysterious telephone calls on the extension in his study. Johnny solved the culinary mystery when he dug a cookbook out of a cupboard drawer, and the discovery of a roast-thermometer he crowed over. But the mystery of the Judge's phone calls remained one. Johnny found himself rather resenting the old man's reticence. He wondered why. He prepared some dough for biscuits thoughtfully.

While he set the table in the dining room, the Judge passed through the hall without a glance. Johnny saw him cross the road and disappear in the church.

The Judge came back an hour later, frowning. Again he shut himself in his study; and Johnny had to knock five times before he answered.

They ate Johnny's dinner in silence—rare roast beef, hot biscuits with country butter, gooseberry jam (found on the top shelf of a cupboard), and bread-and-butter pickles that came in a jar with a homemade pictorial label bearing the signature "Fanny Adams." The Judge might have been eating fried woodchuck. He ate with a scowl, his gray brows bunched over his shrewd blue eyes.

But after dinner the old man suddenly chuckled and took Johnny's arm. "Don't know when I've savored a meal more, Johnny. Beats Millie's cooking all hollow! Never mind the dishes, Millie'll do 'em. . . . I wanted to do some thinking and checking. Come on into my study."

*   *   *

"First," said the Judge, sinking into his leather swivel chair, "understand that I'm not trying to drag you into this, Johnny. But as long as you're here, do you mind if I use you as a sounding board?"

"Well, I'm here," said Johnny. "Sound off."

"I don't want you to think—"

"Cut the psychology, your honor," said Johnny. "The maiden is willing. To listen, anyway."

"Thank you," said the Judge solemnly. "Let's understand our position—excuse me, my position . . ."

"See here," said Johnny, "apparently you have some notion that all breathing has ceased and somebody forgot to inter the remains. This thing interests me, Judge. If only as a confirmation of my thesis that God's in His heaven, all's wrong with the world. Where do we stand?"

"Well," said the Judge, settling back carefully, "we have a thin edge to walk. My purpose is to make this proceding as legally preposterous and indefensible as I can get away with."

"Then why that speech about court personnel, defense counsel, and the rest of it? Seems to me all that makes it too real."

"You didn't let me finish. At the same time, let's not underestimate my neighbors. They're provincial and ignorant of a great many things, but they're not fools. To the extent of their minimal knowledge we'll have to conform to normal courtroom procedure. They certainly know that in every trial there must be someone to administer the oath, keep order, and so on. As a New England community steeped in the tradition of town meetings, caucuses, selectmen meetings and the like, they're also minutes-conscious and will expect someone to keep a record of what goes on. And so on down the line."

"That's a complication," frowned Johnny. "Seems to me there aren't enough people available."

"There's a rather curious result mathematically," said the Judge. He glanced at a pad of lined yellow paper on the desk. "Let's take the problems in order. Bailiff. The natural choice is Burney Hackett. As town constable Burney can take charge of the prisoner's comings and goings—they'll consider that fitting and proper; as bailiff of the court he can keep order, serve as messenger, jury usher, and administer the oaths.

"Next: Court stenographer. We can't avoid this, obviously, and we don't want to avoid it. We want the most accurate transcript of what happens in the 'courtroom' for the permanent record."

"Means you'll have to call in some one from outside."

"As it happens, no. Elizabeth Sheare trained herself in shorthand years ago to help her in her teaching work."

"But don't you need Mrs. Sheare as a jurywoman?"

"Love to have her as both," remarked the Judge. "That would make a fine black smear on the trial record! But unfortunately Hube Hemus knows it, too. I can't chance arousing Hube's suspicions. He's our key man. If we keep him satisfied, we'll have no trouble with the others.

"Next: The prosecutor. I have the perfect choice—"

"Ferriss Adams," said Johnny.

"Right. He couldn't possibly be improved upon for our purposes. You heard Hube this morning; he was worried about it. In my capacity as a judge of the Superior Court, my appointment of Adams to be 'special assistant state's attorney' is bound to please Hube and everyone else. As Aunt Fanny's kin, Ferriss has strong feelings about the case and they'll expect him to prosecute with a vengeance; they'll have confidence in him. I've talked to Ferriss and explained confidentially what I'm after. He's agreed to do it.

"Now for the defense: I've been over to see Kowalczyk—"

"Don't think I don't know it," said Johnny. "All on your lone."

"Now, now, I had my reason. Kowalczyk knows no lawyer, doesn't know anyone around here, he says, and I'm going to appoint counsel, someone I can trust to play his part in this farce convincingly. In fact, I've already talked to him. He's coming down from Cudbury this evening."

"Who is he?"

"I introduced you to him last week. Andy Webster."

"Judge Webster? But I thought you said he was retired and raising prize chrysanthemums."

"He's itching to get into this." The Judge glanced at his pad. "That brings us to the jury.

"The jury, of course," said the Judge, leaning back again, "is our real secret weapon. Almost without exception it will be packed with avowedly prejudiced jurymen whose opinions as to the defendant's guilt have been fully formed in advance. Which is, for our purposes, just dandy!

"Let's go through the voting population of Shinn Corners and see what we get.

"The Berrys, Peter and Emily, make two.

"Hubert and Rebecca Hemus, four. The Hemus twins are only eighteen.

"Hacketts. Burney's our bailiff-etcetera, so he can't serve, and Joel's under age. Selina's so deaf the others wouldn't let her sit even if we wanted her. Their aim is a quick trial, and Selina's insistence on having every-thing repeated to her till she hears it would prolong this thing into the next century. Therefore no Hacketts.

"Pangman." The Judge referred again to his notes. "Orville and Millie, Eddie being under age and Merritt off in the Navy somewhere."

"Two more, making six."

"Prue Plummer."

"Seven."

"Scott. Earl's helpless—hasn't been out of the house for five years except on his porch. Old Seth's not only in a wheelchair, he's senile. And Drakeley's only seven-teen. Leaving Mathilda. She'll have to serve while Judy takes care of the invalids."

"Mathilda Scott, eight."

"The Sheares." The Judge fingered his chin. "Eliza-beth is our stenographer. Samuel Sheare, let us pray, will be in. Or on."

"But you can't do that," protested Johnny. "A minister of the gospel serving on a jury in a first-degree murder case? For one thing, Mr. Sheare probably doesn't be-lieve in capital punishment—"

"And in this state," nodded the Judge, smiling, "con-viction in a first-degree murder case carries with it the death penalty. Exactly. And, by the way, Samuel Sheare does have conscientious scruples against capital punish-ment. My problem's going to be to get him to refrain from expressing them in the courtroom. If he'll keep quiet we may have a fighting chance to slip him into the panel."

"Nine," said Johnny, shaking his head. "It's hard to keep

in mind that as far as this trial is concerned we're on the side of lawlessness and disorder. Keep going!"

"You'll see a lot worse before it's over," said the Judge. "Calvin Waters. Now Calvin's another problem. A juryman who hasn't been right in the head since the age of three is, of course, just in line with what we're looking for on this jury. Trouble is, they know Calvin, too. Well, they haven't much choice. It's Calvin Waters, alias Laughing, or we won't reach the sacred number twelve.

"Let's see now . . . beginning to scrape bottom . . ."

"Wait a minute. Calvin Waters, number ten. How about that old man on the hill? Hosey Lemmon?"

"Won't serve. Hube's already sent Burney Hackett up to sound old Lemmon out. Hosey grabbed his shotgun, said he wouldn't have anything to do with killings and trials, that he knew nothing about Fanny's murder, didn't want to know, and refused to take any part. Burn almost got his leg blown off."

"Then who's left? The Isbels! That's two right there. There's your twelve."

"It might appear so to you," said Judge Shinn, "which shows how tricky appearances can be. Yes, there's Mert, and there's Sarah, who's twenty-nine, and that's two, and ten plus two make twelve. Only in this case they don't. Those two add up to one."

"Coventry," murmured Johnny. "I noticed Friday that Aunt Fanny's guests steered clear of Sarah and her little girl. The others wouldn't accept her, eh?"

"Oh, they'd accept her, especially in a thing like this," said the Judge. "It's Mert who wouldn't."

"Her own father?"

"I didn't tell you about Sarah. Can't think of a better illustration of what we're up against." The Judge sighed. "It happened—yes, Sarah was nineteen—about ten years ago. Mert's wife Hillie was alive then; Sarah was their only child. She was a bouncy, pretty girl, not the washedout dishrag you see today.

"Well, it happened around Christmas time. A traveling man from New York, drygoods or notions or something, had his car break down during a blizzard, and between waiting for the county plows to come through and clear the road and his car to be fixed by Peter Berry, he was snowed in here till after New Year's. Stayed with the Berrys, as I recall, in their spare room. At a fee, of course. With the holiday goings-on and all, Sarah was in the village a good deal that week. And when the traveling man left, she left with him."

"Elopement?"

"That's what we thought. Mert and Hillie were fit to be tied. Not only was the man a New Yorker, he had a furrin-sounding name—at least it wasn't Anglo-Saxon—and, what was worse, he was an atheist, or pretended to be. Good deal of a smart aleck; I don't doubt he was pulling the yokels' legs. His gibes at religion made Mert Isbel froth at the mouth. And this was the man who'd run off with his only daughter.

"As if that wasn't bad enough, about a year later Sarah came home. She hadn't written once during that year, and when she got home we realized why. She showed up with a baby, Mary-Ann, and no husband. In fact, she hadn't seen the man she'd run away with for months. He'd got her pregnant and abandoned her, and of course he'd never married her."

"Dirty dog," said Johnny pleasantly.

"Well, there are dirty dogs and dirty dogs," said the Judge. "I give you Mert Isbel as a relative example."

"What do you mean?"

"Hillie died. Between her daughter's disgrace and her husband's Biblical tantrums—and a heart that was never very strong—Hillie just gave up the ghost. And from the day Mert buried his wife, he hasn't uttered one syllable of recognizable human speech to Sarah or the child."

"You're kidding!"

"Well, you've seen them together. Have you noticed Merton Isbel so much as glance Sarah's way, or at Mary-Ann? They live in the same farmhouse, Sarah keeps house for him, prepares his meals, makes his bed, darns his socks, separates his cream, churns his butter, helps him with the milking and in the fields, and he pretends she has no existence whatsoever. The invisible woman, with an invisible child."

"And Shinn Corners?" said Johnny in a clipped way.

"No, no, you've got the wrong picture, Johnny. The people here feel very sorry for her. Mert's an exceptional case.

"Adultery to the Puritan," said the Judge, "has always been a serious crime, because like murder it endangers the family and the town. But fornication was, and is, different. It's a private misdemeanor, hurting the offender chiefly."

"And it's always been so common," remarked Johnny.

"Yes, indeed. Remember, the Puritan is a practical man. He keeps the statute making fornication a crime on the books as a matter of principle, but he winks at it more often than not because he knows if he didn't there wouldn't be enough jail room to hold all the criminals.

"No, the stone in this furrow is Mert Isbel. We feel sorry for Sarah and Mary-Ann, but we can't show it except when Mert isn't around. And that's practically never. He compounds his cruelty by making sure Sarah doesn't get out of his sight. At church, or whenever they make a public appearance, we ignore Sarah and the little girl because if we didn't he'd make their lives even more hellish than they are. And he's quite capable of going on a rampage if he's balked. Then, too, of course, they're his daughter and granddaughter. In old Yankeeland, my boy, you don't interfere in a family affair. . . . Only one in town who ever gave Mert his comeuppance was Aunt Fanny. She didn't care if Mert was around or not. She invariably singled out Sarah and the child for special attention. For some reason, Mert was afraid of old Aunt Fanny. At least, he ignored her kindness to the outcasts."

"Well, that's the story," said Judge Shinn, "and now you know why Sarah Isbel can't serve on this jury. Mert simply wouldn't have it. It would have to be either Mert or Sarah, and of the two the town obviously will pick Mert. He's the head of a family, the taxpayer, the property owner, the deacon of the church."

"And that," said the Judge, "makes eleven."

"But there's no one left," said Johnny. "Or have I forgotten somebody?"

"No, that's all there are."

"Oh, I see. You're going to put an eleven-man jury over on them."

"I doubt if I could get away with it."

"But . . . then what are you going to do, Judge?"

"Well," said the Judge, doodling on his pad, "there's you."

"Me!" Johnny was flabbergasted. "You mean you're counting on *me* as the twelfth juror?"

"Well, I suppose you wouldn't want to bother."

"But—"

"It would be kind of convenient, though," said Judge Shinn vaguely.

"In what way, in God's name?"

"You sitting among these people, Johnny? Why, I'd have someone I could trust sitting in on the trial, hearing and seeing everything that goes on."

"Might be a kick at that," said Johnny.

"Then you'll do it?" The Judge dropped the pencil. "That's fine, Johnny! Even if a slipup occurs and by some miracle Sarah Isbel gets on the jury to make a twelfth —or Hosey Lemmon changes his mind or Earl Scott insists on being wheeled over—I'd still have you as the alternate; you heard me lay the groundwork for a thirteenth juror."

"But how can I serve on a jury here?" asked Johnny. "I'm not a voter. I'm not even a resident of this state. They'd never accept a stranger."

"Well, not exactly a stranger, Johnny. You do carry the Shinn name. Anyway," said the Judge, "they're going to have to accept you. Did I ever tell you I know a dozen ways to skin a balky calf? Here's one of them." He opened the top drawer of his desk and took out two sheets of legal-size paper clipped together. It was a printed form, its blank spaces filled in by typewriter.

"You finagler," said Johnny. "You have that all made out. What is it?"

"Where defending constitutional democracy and due process is concerned," said Judge Shinn, "I'm an unmitigated scoundrel. Why, Johnny, this is a warranty deed relating to a piece of property I own at the western boundary of my holdings, a house and ten acres. The house is usually rented under a lease, but the last lessee moved two years ago and it's stood untenanted ever since. This," and the Judge took another paper from the drawer, "is a bill of sale. Under its terms I, Lewis Shinn, am selling you, John Jacob Shinn, the house and ten acres covered by the deed for the sum of—what do you offer?"

"At the moment," said Johnny with a grin, "my checking account shows a balance of four hundred and five dollars and thirty-eight cents."

"For the sum of ten thousand dollars in imaginary currency, and you will kindly sign a paper—this is my Yankee heritage apeaking—promising to 'sell' the property back to me at the same terms when this is over. I don't know how many laws I'm breaking," said the Judge, "and I find myself singularly unable to worry about it just now. The point is, when Andy Webster gets here he can witness my signature and yours, and first thing tomorrow morning we'll take the deed over to the Town Hall and have Burney Hackett in his capacity as town clerk record same, for which you will pay him out of the hand the sum of four dollars, thereby becoming a Shinn Corners property owner entitled to all the responsibilities thereof, which under the ruling I'm going to make when the jury is empaneled will include your responsibility to serve on a Shinn Corners jury. There's nothing impresses a Yankee more than the recording of a deed to a piece of land. Little side issues like length of residence, non-voting, and so forth, we shall conveniently ignore."

Johnny was staring at the Judge in a puzzled way.

"What's the matter?" said the Judge.

"I'm trying to squeeze a feeling of reality out of this," said Johnny. "I don't get it. I really don't. All these shenanigans . . . Aren't you whipping up an awfully big tempest for such a little teapot, Judge?"

"You think it's little?"

"It's subatomic. One man, who's probably guilty to begin with! And you stand a whole town on its head, befuddle a bunch of perfectly capable cops and county officials, drag the governor of your state into it . . ."

Judge Shinn got out of his chair and began to pace up and down before his law books, his brows coming together as if meeting a challenge.

"One man," he said slowly. "Yes, put that way it sounds ridiculous. But that's only because you're thinking of Josef Kowalczyk as if he existed in a vacuum. What's one man? Well, Johnny, one man is not merely Josef Kowalczyk. He's you, he's me, he's Hube Hemus—he's everybody. It always starts with one man. A man named John Peter Zenger, a German immigrant, was tried for seditious libel in 1735 in New York for having published some polemical articles in his weekly. One man. Another man, named Andrew Hamilton, defended Zenger's right to print the truth. Hamilton's success in securing Zenger's acquittal established freedom of the press in America.

"Someone has to keep on the alert, Johnny. We've been lucky. Luckier, maybe, than we deserve. We've always had someone to watch over us.

"You take the debates during the founding of the Constitution," said Judge Shinn. "The debaters who demanded guarantees of procedural due process weren't arguing from mere theory. The adoption of the Bill of Rights, in particular the Fifth and Sixth Amendments, had behind it real fears, fears that had grown out of actual happenings in colonial history. For instance, the witchcraft trials in Massachusetts in 1692.

"In those trials," said the Judge, "the judges were laymen, the Attorney General was a merchant. Not a single person trained in the law was involved with the court or the trial proceedings in any way whatsoever. The witch court, under the highsounding name of Special Court of Oyer and Terminer, allowed its prosecutor to present what they called 'spectral evidence' and to put on the stand a parade of confessed or reformed 'witches' to testify against the accused. Anybody from the crowd who clamored to be heard, irrespective of the relevance or legal propriety of his testimony, was allowed to do so. Result: twenty persons smeared by hearsay, superstition and hysteria, found guilty, most of them hanged—one, an octogenarian, was actually pressed to death. The same kind of thing is going on today before the so-called Supreme People's Courts in Communist China. And for that matter in Washington, where men's reputations are destroyed and their capacity to earn a living is paralyzed without a single safeguard of due process.

"And let's not shunt the blame onto the Congressional committees," said the Judge. "The blame is ours, not theirs. The demagogue in Congress couldn't operate for one day in an atmosphere of common horse sense. It's public hysteria that keeps him going strong.

"Proving, Johnny," said Judge Shinn, "that people *can't* always be trusted. Human beings, even in a democracy, are too prone to degenerate into mobs. That's why the Shinn Corners versus Josef Kowalczyk teapot, Johnny, contains a tempest big enough to destroy all of America. Who's going to protect the people from their worst enemy—themselves—except the individual here and there seizing on an individual case and refusing to let go?"

"Hear, hear," said Johnny.

Judge Shinn stopped pacing. He bent over his desk to finger the yellow pad, throwing a sidelong look at Johnny.

"Sorry," said Johnny. "But I'm so damned fed up with words."

The Judge nodded. "Don't blame you," he said briskly. "Let's get down to cases. Suppose I tell you, Johnny, my real reason for wanting you on that jury."

Johnny stared.

The Judge studied him speculatively, pinching his lip.

"Yes?" said Johnny.

"No," the Judge said. "I'll let you tell me. Let's go across the road and pay a visit to Josef Kowalczyk."

Eddie Pangman was on late afternoon guard duty before the church. He no longer looked unhappy. He whistled as he marched, and he executed his sentry turns with a military gusto, in an excited solemnity that enlivened his long face and made it curiously little-boyish.

He passed the Judge and Johnny along gravely.

Drakeley Scott, patrolling the rear, was another story. Drakeley Scott was not a boy exuberantly playing games. He was like a man who, under servere strain to escape the pressures of manhood, has gone back to the child. His pimpled face was pinchy, with a ghastly overcast; he held his narrow shoulders in tense readiness; there was something furtively eager in his excitement.

When he saw the two men he looked uncomfortable, and something of the hurt Johnny had seen in his eyes in Peter Berry's store Friday morning came back into them; but only for a moment.

He said defiantly, "I don't know if I'm s'posed to let you through, Judge. Hube Hemus said—"

"I'll tell you what, Drakeley," said Judge Shinn with tremendous earnestness. "At the first move Johnny Shinn or I make to let the prisoner escape, you shoot to kill. Fair enough?"

The Scott boy flushed scarlet.

"Who has the key to the bin?"

"There's a guard down there," mumbled the boy.

They went past him down the crumbling stone steps to the church cellar. Johnny blinked after the sunshine. As he accommodated to the gloom he made out rough rafters overhead bearing irregular axmarks. They had been hewn out of whole oak trees; some of the original bark clung, looking petrified. There was a storage bin, an oldfashioned coal furnace, and the coalbin.

The coalbin was large and entirely enclosed. The door was slightly ajar, a lock hanging open from a new-looking hasp. Light came through chinks in the walls.

On a chair facing the bin door, a shotgun across his knees, sat Merton Isbel. The chair was part of an old broken pew, which seemed to Johnny fitting. The craggy features bunched at sight of him.

"Someone in there with him, Mert?" asked the Judge.

"Mr. Sheare." Isbel's bass voice had an unused sound.

Judge Shinn touched Johnny's arm. "Before we go in," he said in a low voice.

"Yes?"

"I want you to pretend you're interested in him."

"In Kowalczyk? But I am."

"Question him, Johnny."

Johnny nodded.

The minister's voice answered the Judge's knock, and they entered the bin.

The only coal Johnny saw was a small heap in a corner, apparently the leftovers of the previous winter's supply. But coal dust was everywhere. An attempt had been made—by the Sheares, he felt sure—to sweep it up, but the prisoner's movements had scattered it again; and nothing could be done about the soot on the walls, which looked as if they had been sprayed with lampblack.

The one window high in the rough foundation wall, the chute window, had been newly boarded up. Light came from a 25-watt bulb in a naked ceiling socket protected by a wire cage.

Josef Kowalczyk sat on the edge of a cot drinking hot tea out of a water glass. A folding table was strewn with the remains of a meal. Mr. Sheare was stacking the dishes on a tray when they came in.

"He's had a hearty dinner," said the minister cheerfully. "Wanted his tea in a glass with lemon and jelly, European style. Judge, don't you think he's lookin' a good deal better?"

"I do, Mr. Sheare." The Judge glanced at the dishes. "Some of Elizabeth's famous boiled dinner, I see."

The minister said in a firm voice, "Someone must take care of his bodily needs. I wish we could do somethin' about this coal dust."

"You've done wonders, Mr. Sheare."

A white chamberpot stood in one corner.

The minister's troubled smile returned. He picked up the tray and went out. The door remained open.

Merton Isbel sat watching them.

The prisoner set down his empty glass with a start, as if he had just noticed them. He started to rise.

"Sit down, sit down, Kowalczyk," said the Judge testily.

Kowalczyk sank back, staring at Johnny.

He was wearing his own clothes again; Elizabeth Sheare had evidently tried to clean as well as mend them, with indifferent results. The gray flannel shirt she had washed and ironed. Either his shoes were beyond repair or the village fathers had decreed their confiscation: he wore old carpet slippers, presumably Mr. Sheare's. His colorless hair was combed; aside from a badly swollen lower lip, where he had lost the tooth, his face was unmarked.

The stubble of blondish beard was salted with gray and white now; Johnny suspected that Mr. Sheare had been forbidden to provide a razor. Beneath the stubble and the dark gray skin the face was skeletal, with flaring jaws and high cheekbones, the ears wide and prominent, the forehead low with heavily furred bulges of bone above the eyes. The eyes themselves, still timid, still burning, were deep in his head. His neck was loose and stringy over a large Adam's apple; it looked like the neck of a gobbler. His hands were work hands, joints swollen, nails cracked, fingertips splayed. He kept them clasped between his thighs and his torso bent forward, as if his groin still ached.

He looked sixty-five. It was hard to remember that he was in his early forties.

"This gentleman," said Judge Shinn to the staring man, "is interested in your story, Kowalczyk. He's had a lot of experience talking to men in trouble. His name is Mr. Shinn."

"Sheen," said the prisoner. "Mister Sheen, what they do to me?" He spoke awkwardly, with a thick accent.

Johnny glanced at the Judge. The Judge nodded.

"Kowalczyk," said Johnny. "Do you know why you are here in this cellar, a prisoner?"

The man raised his thin shoulders, dropped them. It was an Old World gesture, saying: I know, I do not know, what does it matter?

"Tell me everything that happened yesterday," said

Johnny. "But first I wish to know more about you, Kowalczyk, your life, where you came from, where you were
going. Will you tell me?"

"Tell Judge before," said the prisoner. "What they do
to me?"

"Tell me," Johnny smiled.

The prisoner unclasped his hands and rubbed the palms
slowly together, addressing the floor of the coal-bin. "Me
Polish. Had got wife, two child, old mother, old father
in Poland. Nazis come, kill them. Me, put labor camp.
After war, Communists. No good. Escape, come America,
have cousin New York, live by cousin three year. Try
get job—"

"Did you have a trade in the old country?"

"Work l'ather."

"Lather?" said Johnny. "You mean you were a barber?"

"No, no. L'ather, like for shoe."

"Oh, leather! Leather worker? Tanning, that sort of
thing?"

"Yes," said Josef Kowalczyk with a trace of animation. "Good worker, me. Old father, he learn me trade."
Then the shoulders went up and down again, and the
animation died. "In America no can get job l'ather worker. No got union card. I like belong union, but got no
money pay dues. Got no ref—no ref—"

"Work references?"

"Yes. So no can work l'ather job. Then cousin die,
heart. Go live Polish family Brooklyn, friend my cousin.
Work odd job, one day here, two day there. Friend got
'nother baby, no more room Kowalczyk. Say why not
go country, Josef, get work farm. I go, I walk country.
Get job one farm, two farm, walk more, work again—"

The prisoner stopped, glancing at Judge Shinn helplessly.

"Apparently," explained the Judge, "he's been an itinerant farm worker for the past several years, wandering all
over New England. From what I gather he doesn't like
farm work, feels it's beneath him, and has never given up
the hope that he'd find a job at his old trade. Where
were you coming from, Kowalczyk, when you passed
through this village yesterday?"

"Come long. From far. Walk eight-nine day." Kowalczyk frowned, concentrating; then he slapped his forehead impatiently. "No 'member name place last work.

Sleep barn, do chore for eat, walk more. Lose money—"

"Oh, you had some money?" said Johnny.

"Seven dollar. Lose. Fall out hole pocket." Kowalczyk frowned again. "No like lose money. People say you tramp, I show money. No tramp, see? But people say you tramp, no can show money—lose—so tramp!" Kowalczyk jumped up, his broad jaws rippling. "No like for be call tramp!" he cried.

"Not many of us do," said Johnny. "Where were you going?"

"Polish farmer Petunxit say can get job Cudbury l'ather factory," muttered Kowalczyk. "He say no union that factory. So walk quick for to get job . . ." He sank to the cot again. He lay down and turned his face to the sooty wall.

Johnny glanced at Judge Shinn. The Judge's face was impassive.

"Kowalczyk." He touched the prisoner's shoulder. "Why did you kill the old lady?"

The man sat up with such violence that Johnny stepped back. "Not kill!" he shouted. "Not kill!" He rolled off the cot and seized Johnny's lapels with both hands. "Not kill!"

Over Kowalczyk's head Johnny saw Merton Isbel beyond the bin door with the shotgun across his knees and his eyes glittering.

"Sit down." John took the man's bony wrists and gently forced him back on the cot. "Before you go on, I'm going to try to tell you why the people in this village believe you murdered the old lady."

"Not kill," whispered the prisoner.

"Listen, Kowalczyk. Try to understand what I say. You were seen going up to the old lady's house twenty minutes or so before she died—"

"Not kill," repeated Kowalczyk.

"You actually spent some time in the old lady's house. How do I know this? Because the Judge and I met you walking on the road in the rain, no more than a mile and a quarter from the village, at twenty-five minutes to three yesterday afternoon. It certainly didn't take you three-quarters of an hour to walk a trifle over a mile. A man walks about three miles an hour, and we saw with our own eyes how fast you were walking. So you couldn't have been on the road more than twenty or twenty-five minutes when we passed you. That means you left the village at ten or fifteen minutes past two o'clock. But it was no later than ten minutes to two when a woman of the village saw you walk up to the old lady's house. So, we say, between ten minutes to two and about a quarter past two you must have been in the old lady's house. If you were, you were there about the time she was killed, which was two-thirteen. You see?"

The prisoner rocked, his hands clasped tightly again. "Not kill," he groaned.

"If you were in the house, you had the opportunity to kill her. If you were in the house, you also had the means—the poker from her fireplace. If you were in the house, you also had motive—the hundred and twenty-four dollars hidden in the handkerchief about your waist.

"That's the case against you, Kowalczyk. In fact, we don't have to suppose you were in the house. We know it. The money proves you were there. The stolen money." Johnny paused, wondering how much of this the man understood. "Do you understand what I am saying?"

"Not kill," said the prisoner, rocking. "Steal, yes. Kill, not!"

"Oh, you admit stealing the hundred and twenty-four dollars?"

"Never I steal before!" cried Josef Kowalczyk. "But lose seven dollar—I see lots money in jar . . . Is not good. Is wrong. Is terrible do that. But lose seven dollar . . . Steal, yes. But not kill, not kill . . ."

Kowalczyk began to cry. It was dry and soundless, the kind of weeping a man might have learned in the nightmare reaches of the European darkness—a slave laborer's weeping, kept silent because silence was a locked door insuring the dignity of grief.

Johnny turned away. He took out a pack of cigarets and, without quite knowing why, set it down on the folding table with a packet of matches.

"No matches!" The rumble came from Merton Isbel.

Johnny lit a cigaret and placed it between the prisoner's lips. At the contact Kowalczyk recoiled. Then he sucked hungrily on the cigaret, and after a moment he began to talk.

He had reached the old lady's kitchen door a few minutes after being refused by "the other lady." He had knocked, and the old lady had come to the door. He had asked for something to eat. The old lady had said she did not feed beggars, but that if he was willing to work for his food she would feed him well. He had said yes, he would do anything, he was not a beggar, he would work for his meal, what work did she have for him to do? She had said to him, you will find some logs behind the barn and an ax in the barn. Take the ax and split the logs in quarters for firewood, they are too heavy for an old woman as they are, and they will burn better in quarters. He had gone to the barn, found the ax, walked through the lean-to and around behind the barn, where the logs were lying, and he had set to work splitting them with the ax. He had split many logs in the past three years during his wanderings from farm to farm, and he was expert. It took him only a few minutes—

"How many logs did you split?" interrupted Johnny.

"Six log," said the prisoner.

"You split each log into four pieces?"

"Four. Yes."

"And this took you only a few minutes, you say?"

"Go quick when know how."

"How many minutes, Kowalczyk?"

The prisoner shrugged. He was no man to count the minutes, he said. But very few. He remembered that just as he had finished splitting the last log, the rain began.

"Two o'clock," murmured Judge Shinn.

He had hurriedly but neatly stacked the firewood in the empty lean-to, replaced the ax in the barn, and run back to the house. The old lady had made him wipe his feet on a mat before he could enter.

He had thought her a very queer old lady. First, she had refused him food unless he worked. Then, the work she had given him to do was to split firewood—in July! Then, when he had split the firewood, she had not only had ready for him on the kitchen table a plate piled high with boiled ham and potato salad and a big piece of berry pie and a pitcher of milk, but while he was eating she had taken down from the top shelf of a kitchen cabinet a jar stuffed with money and she had given him from it a fifty-cent piece. Then she had put the jar back and gone through the swinging door into another room, and he was left alone with the money.

He choked on the food, temptation had been so strong. It was no excuse, he said, but his pockets were empty, and this old woman seemed to have so much. If he was to get a job in the Cudbury leather factory at his old trade, he would need money to make himself look clean and prosperous, to rent decent lodgings as a working man of self-respect should, instead of bedding down on hay in a barn like a beast. It was no excuse, but temptation was too strong. He had bolted down only half the food on the plate, he had not touched the berry pie or the milk. He had got noiselessly out of the chair and tiptoed to her door and swung it open a little. The old lady was standing in the other room, her back to him, painting a picture. He had swung the door shut without sound, reached up to the jar, taken out all the paper money, and run out of the old lady's house. And he had walked very fast up the road leading to Cudbury, clutching the money in his pocket. Only once had he stopped in the rain, to go behind some bushes, wrap the stolen money in his handkerchief, tie it to a length of rope he had in his satchel, and tie the rope around his waist beneath his clothing.

And that was all he knew about the old lady, said the prisoner. He had done wrong, he had stolen her money, for this he should be punished. But kill? No! He had left her alive, painting a picture in the room beyond her kitchen. He could not kill. He would not kill. He had seen too much killing in his life. Blood made him sick. He swore by the Holy Mother of God, crossing himself, that he had not touched so much as a hair of the old lady's head. Only her money . . .

Judge Shinn was regarding Johnny quizzically, as if to ask, Now you've heard his story, how sure are you he killed Aunt Fanny?

The prisoner lay back on the cot again. He seemed indifferent. Evidently he had not expected to be believed, he had told his story only because it was required of him.

Kowalczyk close his eyes.

Johnny stood over him, puzzled. In the course of his Intelligence and Criminal Investigation work in the Army, he had questioned many men, and long ago he had learned to detect the subtle aroma of falsehood. About this man he was not sure. By every physical and psychological sign, Josef Kowalczyk was telling the truth. But there were serious discrepancies.

Judge Shinn said nothing.

Johnny said, "Kowalczyk."

The man opened his eyes.

"You say that the wood you split you stacked in the lean-to next to the barn. How long were the logs you split?" How many feet?"

The prisoner held his hands apart.

"About three feet. They were all the same length?"

Kowalczyk nodded.

"Why do you lie, Kowalczyk?"

"I not lie!"

"But you do. There is no firewood in the lean-to, the lean-to is empty. There is no firewood in the barn, in the house, or anywhere about the house. There are no fresh chips of wood around the wood block behind the barn, such as there would have been had you split logs there as you claim. I know, Kowalczyk, because I myself have searched. Why do you lie about this?"

"I not lie! Split wood with ax, put in shed!"

"And why did you run away when we passed you on the road in the rain? Was this the act of a man who is innocent?"

"Money. Steal money . . ."

He had stolen money and so he had carried around his thin waist the dragging weight of guilt. But it had been guilt for having stolen, not for having killed. . . .

They left him in the coalbin, his gray face turned once more to the sooty wall. As they stepped out of the bin Merton Isbel slammed the door and snapped the lock in the hasp. Then the farmer resumed his seat facing the door, the shotgun balanced on his knees.

"Well?" demanded the Judge as they strolled back to the Shinn house.

Johnny said: "I don't know."

"I'd hoped you'd form a more positive opinion than I. However, even this doubt is important. We've both had plenty of experience weighing the reliability of testimony. If neither of us can say this man is definitely lying or telling the truth, there may be something wrong. Something that has to be followed up."

"The firewood story alone," muttered Johnny, "will be enough to hang him. I mean as far as these people are concerned. Because there's not the slightest evidence to corroborate his story. And yet—if he didn't split any wood for Aunt Fanny, why does he insist he did?"

"It might be simply this," said the Judge as they mounted to his porch, "that in his twisted mind a story of having worked for a meal gives him an aura of honesty not usually associated with murderers."

"Then why does he admit to having stolen her money?"

"He could hardly deny it, since the money was found on him."

They were both silent.

But back in his study, the Judge said, "Now you know why I want you on that absurdity of a jury, Johnny. Kowalczyk's story brings up an interesting alternative . . ."

"Which is that if he's innocent," nodded Johnny, "somebody else is guilty."

"Exactly."

They stared at each other across the desk.

The Judge said slowly, "Unless we can come up with another stranger in Shinn Corners yesterday, for which there's no evidence whatever—I've already sounded out everyone within reach—Fanny Adams was beaten to death by someone in this village who'd known her all his life. I use the masculine pronoun," growled the Judge, "in its inclusive sense. It doesn't take much strength to smash the skull of a ninety-one-year-old woman with a heavy poker."

"In other words, you want me on that jury as a detective? My job being to detect who among your neighbors clobbered Aunt Fanny if Josef Kowalczyk didn't?"

"Yes."

Johnny thought of what he had had to cover with the kitchen towel in the Adams studio. . . . He had the queerest sense of personal loss. Ten minutes of conversation in a noisy room, one touch of the dry warm hand—how could he feel that he had known this old woman from the cradle? Yet her death touched a vital, secret center in him. It left him uncomfortable. Almost emotional.

"All right, Judge," said Johnny.

An altercation outdoors about nine o'clock that night brought them on the run. They found Burney Hackett and Orville Pangman at the intersection being tough with the ancient driver of an ancient Cadillac.

It was ex-Judge Andrew Webster of Cudbury, com-

plete with sleepy eyes, gaunt little fine-boned face, and
the trembling movements of a centenarian. Johnny had to
help him out of his car.

"It's the bones," he said to Johnny as Judge Shinn explained his identity and status to the constable and the
farmer. "Get drier and stiffer by the year. Bones and skin.
I'm beginning to look like something dug out of an Egyp-
tian tomb. Seems to me medical science could find a cure
for old age. It's the curse of mankind. . . . Well, well,
Lewis, what have you got yourself into? Armed men!
Insurrection! I can hardly wait to hear the silly details."

Johnny drove Judge Webster's car around to the Shinn
garage. When he went into the house carrying Andy Webster's bag, the two jurists had their heads together in the
study. Johnny took the suitcase upstairs to one of the
guest rooms, opened the windows, rummaged until he
located the linen closet, made the bed, laid out towels.
He reflected that Millie Pangman could hardly have done
better.

He went back downstairs to find Ferriss Adams with
Judge Shinn and Webster, looking harassed.

"Just got back from Cudbury," Adams complained.
"Had to hire Peter Berry's car, darn him. There's a man
who would try to make a profit selling tickets to his wife's
labor pains. Had to get some fresh clothes and leave a
sign on my office door—my girl's on her vacation, of
course, just when I need her most!" He had been busy
all afternoon between his personal affairs in Cudbury and
the more immediate matters relating to his grandaunt. He
had had to ask Orville Pangman to take charge of her
cow; the Jersey was now with the Pangman herd. He
had also locked up the old lady's paintings for safekeeping,
pending the appointment of an executor by the county
judge of probate. She had left no will despite his fre-
quent urgings, Adams explained in answer to Judge
Shinn's question, and the settling of her estate was bound
to be a long-drawn-out process. As a further safeguard,
he had assumed the responsibility of authorizing Burney
Hackett to write the comprehensive policy on the paintings which had led Hackett to Fanny Adams's kitchen and
the discovery of her body. He himself was going to stay
at the Adams house until the emergency was over, a pre-
caution the older lawyers approved.

They sat around for an hour discussing the conspiracy.

The object, they agreed, was to go through the motions of a murder trial, giving it a sufficient appearance of legality to satisfy the Shinn Corners insurgents and wean them step by step away from their rebellious mood.

"Consequently you must prosecute with vigor, Ferriss," said Judge Shinn, "and Andy, you must defend in kind. We're in the position of a referee and two prizefighters getting together to cook up a fixed fight. We've got to make it look good while nobody gets hurt. There must be objections, arguments between counsel, rulings and overrulings by the bench, recesses out of hearing of the jury, and all the rest of it. At the same time, I want as many rules in the book broken as possible, for the record. We are in the remarkable position of deliberately invading as many of the accused's legal rights as we possibly can for the ultimate purpose of protecting them. In many ways, the protection of Kowalczyk's rights is more important at this time than the establishment of his guilt or innocence."

"I suppose," said Adams, "there's no chance that Kowalczyk may slip through on a double jeopardy plea later?"

"No, Ferriss," said Judge Shinn. "If this jury finds him guilty, as of course it will, he himself will want the proceeding declared no trial, so that he'll have a legitimate chance to draw a not-guilty verdict in a future trial. And if by some mircale Shinn Corners lets him go, we've got the whole farce on the record, with all the breaches and errors, to prove non-trial. In either event, the law's rights will be protected equally with Kowalczyk's."

"I hope so." Fanny Adams's grandnephew sounded grim. "Because for my money the s.o.b. is as guilty as the Polish hell he's booked for!"

Old Andy Webster was shaking his head. "Unbelievable. Incredible. Wouldn't miss it for the world."

He and Adams solemnly witnessed the signatures of Judge Shinn and Johnny on the documents relating to the "sale" of the house and ten acres, and then the three men left—Adams to circulate among the villagers breathing prosecutional fire, Judge Shinn to escort Andy Webster to the cellar of the church to interview his "client."

Johnny went to bed, on the theory that there was something indecent about a man's dreaming in an up-right position.

* * *

The dream illusion persisted all day Monday. The day was excessively humid, with the shimmering quality of such days, but it was crisp and sharp compared with the wavery nature of events. From the early morning march up Four Corners Road with Town Clerk Burney Hackett to the Town Hall for the recording of the deed, Johnny kept fighting fuzziness.

Hube Hemus drove up to the little building as Hackett wrote laboriously in the huge town ledger; Judge Shinn had phoned him during breakfast. The Judge gravely explained to the First Selectman the purpose of the property sale.

"If we're to try the defendant in a special Shinn Corners court as authorized by Governor Ford, Hube," said the Judge, "we've got to be very careful to do things right. Have you gone over the panel?"

"Aya," said Hemus. "Been worryin' me, Judge. Don't figger to come out to the twelve jurors the law requires."

"My point exactly."

"But bein' a property owner don't make a man eligible for jury duty right off," said Hemus. "Got to come from the votin' list."

Johnny felt a chill. Not once had Hemus glanced his way. He might have been one of the campchairs.

"That's true, of course," said Judge Shinn. "You certainly know the law, Hube. So this is going to have to be irregular. I'll make a special ruling in my cousin's case. After all, this is a special sort of trial."

"Might get Earl Scott over," muttered the First Selectman.

"Might," agreed Judge Shinn. "Might at that, Hube. Only thing is, a man who's paralyzed, chronic invalid, hasn't been out of his house for five years . . . might not look very good in the record."

Hube Hemus thought this over. "Guess you're right, Judge. But Mr. Shinn ain't a voter. Ain't even took up town residence. Maybe Sarah Isbel . . ."

"Why, Hube, that's right!" said the Judge, looking relieved. "Never thought of Sarah at all. Just naturally figured if we got Sarah we'd lose Mert. But if you think Mert wouldn't kick up a fuss . . ."

Burney Hackett spat into the spittoon at his feet. "That's ridic'lous. He'd kick it up faster'n Orville's herd bull."

"And we've got to have twelve, Hube. At least twelve." The Judge frowned. "Rather be irregular on a special ruling about one juror than go into court with fewer jurors than the law insists on and have the whole case ruled a mistrial afterwards by the Supreme Court of Errors."

Hube Hemus wriggled. "Durn that Hosey Lemmon!"

"Of course, if we could get old Lemmon to change his mind, our problems are solved."

"Can't. Went lookin' for Hosey myself late last night and couldn't even find him. He's lit out for somewheres. . . . Mr. Shinn," said Hemus suddenly, "hear you went over yesterday afternoon and talked to the tramp."

"Oh?" said Johnny, startled. "Why, yes. Yes, Mr. Hemus, I did."

"My suggestion, Hube," the Judge put in, to Johnny's relief. "Mr. Shinn's had a heap of experience with criminals in the Army. Wanted to see if he could make Kowalczyk confess."

"He ain't confessin' nothin'." Hackett hit the spittoon again. "Knows better."

Hemus's whole head swiveled toward Johnny again. "Mert Isbel says he told you his cock-and-bull story."

Johnny managed a sneer. "I did catch the prisoner in what appears to be a mighty big lie, Mr. Hemus."

" 'Bout the firewood?"

"That's right."

Hemus grunted. His jaws ground exasperatingly for a long time. Then he said to Judge Shinn, "Well, I guess we got no choice," and he stumped out and got into his car and drove away.

Burney Hackett went into the back room to lock up the ledger.

"You're in," said the Judge softly.

Johnny found himself yawning.

The day's next dream followed hard on the Hemus fragment. A few minutes past nine, County Coroner Barnwell showed up from Cudbury in a car driven by a redhaired man with golden freckles and a roving eye.

"My God, it's Usher Peague of the *Times-Press*," said Judge Shinn tragically. "Now we're in the soup for fair. That Barnwell! Come on before Peague gets hurt!"

The car had been surrounded at the intersection by

armed men. They pushed their way through, the Judge waving frantically.

"Hello, Ush! Barnwell, I want to see you."

The editor of the Cudbury *Times-Press* grinned as he stood at bay beside his car. "It's okay, men," he was saying. "I haven't got a thing on me but a pad and a pencil." He waved at Johnny, whom he had interviewed with great skill the week before.

Judge Shinn said wrathfully to the coroner, "Barnwell, have you lost what little mind you have? I thought I'd made myself clear over the phone. Why did you tell Usher Peague, of all people!"

"I didn't tell Peague," retorted Coroner Barnwell, "Peague told me. He heard about it somewhere—from Doc Cushman, for all I know, or Cy Moody. A country newspaper gets automatic coverage on deaths, Judge; they're one of its most important items. Peague queried me on it, and I thought I'd better bring him over myself rather than let him run around loose. You didn't think you could keep this a secret from the newspapers forever?"

"I could hope. Well, we'll have to face it. But what do we say to him?"

"If you want my advice," said Johnny, "take Peague into your confidence. He'll get the story anyway. For another thing, he edits a weekly paper that comes out on Thursdays. This is only Monday morning. By Thursday we ought to be well out of this thing. The only problem is to get Peague to agree not to tip off the wire services, and that's no problem if he wants a scoop on the story."

Judge Shinn convinced Hubert Hemus that the presence of the press was a necessary evil, and then he hustled Peague away from the villagers, who seemed to fascinate the Cudbury editor.

"Who's declared war on whom, and who gets shot?" the newspaperman was saying. "What goes on here, Judge?"

"All in good time, Usher," said the Judge soothingly. "How's Remember?"

"She blooms. Listen, don't con me! There's something rotten in Shinn Corners, and I'm not leaving till I find out what."

When Peague saw old Andy Webster in the Shinn house, his reddish eyes widened. "They got you away from your 'mums! This must be big. Come on, men. What's the story?"

"Tell him, Johnny," said Judge Shinn.

Johnny told him. Peague listened in suspicious silence. He was a former big-city newspaperman who had settled in Cudbury, married Remember Bagley, publisher of the Cudbury weekly, and taken over the editorship. During Johnny's recital Peague glanced at the two old men as if he suspected a practical joke; but at the end his eyes were glistening.

"Peague the Lucky," he said softly. "What a story! You mean if I tried to leave Shinn Corners now Remember'd maybe be picking buckshot out of my rear? They're not kidding? Man, oh, man. I'm going to try it."

Johnny grabbed him. "What would you do with the story now, anyway? Donate it to the Associated Press?" They closed in on him. "Look, Peague. We're at your mercy. You can't use the story till Thursday. Why not stick it out with us here? Report the trial!"

"They'll let you sit in as a spectator, Ush," said Judge Shinn. "I've got the First Selectman's promise. I'll go further. If you're worried about other reporters, I give you my word that if any other newspaperman shows up he'll have to stay out of town to wait for your story. You can be our sole representative of the press. Does anyone else on your paper suspect anything?"

"No."

"What about Remember?" demanded Judge Webster. "That wife of yours has the pickup of a vacuum cleaner."

"I'll handle Remember," said Peague absently. "Okay, it's a deal. If I can also interview this Whatsisname, that is. By the way, is he guilty?"

Fanny Adams's living room looked distorted, too. Most of the furniture had been hauled into other rooms. Midway between the front windows an old chestnut drop-leaf table had been set up for Judge Shinn, before a tall wing chair. A hickory Windsor stood beside the table as the witness chair. Elizabeth Sheare had been installed at a small kneehole desk before the corner cupboard containing Aunt Fanny's collection of Sheffield.

Two rows of six campchairs each, from the Town Hall, were arranged along the fireplace side of the room at right angles to the "bench," as the jury "box." A long

pine trestle table from Aunt Fanny's dining room, blackened and rubbed by time, faced the Judge; this was for
defendant and opposing counsel. Other campchairs and
chairs from the house stood in rows behind the counsel
table for the panel; in a front seat sat Usher Peague, an
endtable before him to write on. (Coroner Barnwell had
been ordered back to Cudbury. He went in Peague's car,
his chin over his shoulder longingly.)

At ten minutes of ten everyone was there.

Josef Kowalczyk was brought in by the Hemus twins.
His arrival precipitated an argument. Constable-Bailiff
Hackett remarked in tones of nasal displeasure that the
conveyance of the prisoner to and from the coalbin cell
was part of his, Hackett's, official duties; the twins might
go along as extra guards, but the defendant was to be in
his personal charge and might not be moved or removed
except under his direction. The twins replied in expressionless drawls that they were the bastard's guards this
morning and don't let your tin badge go to your thick
head. Judge Shinn ruled in Constable-Bailiff Hackett's
favor.

"Moreover," said the Judge, "there will be no profanity
in this court. Any use of bad language, any outburst
against the defendant or other interruption to the orderly
conduct of these proceedings, will expose the violator to
a citation for contempt of court. I will not entertain as
• an excuse the youth of the violator. Take off those
chains!"

The twins had lashed Kowalczyk's wrists with a length
of chain, which they had then passed around his waist
and secured at his back. Another length of chain was
hooked to the waist chain, and the prisoner had come
in on this lead like a dog on a leash, Dave Hemus gripping
the end of it while Tommy Hemus prodded the chained
man along with the muzzle of his gun.

Hubert Hemus said something from his seat; his sons
immediately removed the chains.

"The defendant is not to be secured in this fashion
again, Constable," said the Judge sharply. "You may take
proper precautions against a possible attempt at escape,
of course, but this is an American court, not a Communist one."

"Yes, your honor." Burney Hackett glared at the Hemus
boys. "Won't happen again!"

"All persons not eligible for jury duty, or not required as witnesses or for other purposes, will leave the courtroom. There are to be no children here. Has any provision been made for the care of the youngsters?"

Hubert Hemus spoke up from his chair: "Judge, we decided that durin' sessions of the court the young children would be kept on the school grounds in charge of Selina Hackett, seein' that Selina can't serve on account of bein' so deef, with the older girls like my Abbie and Cynthy Hackett helpin' out, and Sarah Isbel."

"All persons addressing the court will please rise when doing so," said Judge Shinn curtly.

Hube Hemus's jaw dropped. "Yes, Judge," he said. He rose uncertainly. Then he sat down again.

Someone—Johnny thought it was Prue Plummer—tittered. Hemus flushed.

Johnny wondered why the Judge had gone out of his way to humiliate the all-powerful First Selectman. It seemed an unnecessary discipline. To antagonize Hemus when the object was to conduct the proceedings so smoothly as to cover up the deliberate infractions they planned . . .

"Counsel, are we ready to select a jury?"

Andrew Webster and Ferriss Adams rose and said they were.

Johnny swallowed a grin. His honor was back in the groove and off to the races. Court had not been formally convened, no charge had been read into the record, no "People Against Kowalczyk" . . . the defendant had not even entered his plea. For all the record would show, they might have been preparing to try Andy Webster.

But then Johnny lost all appetite for humor. He saw Josef Kowalczyk's face.

The prisoner sat by Andrew Webster's side at the pine table with the quivering rigidity of a man who expects a bullet in the back. The two jurists had felt it wiser not to reveal their plan to Kowalczyk; clearly, he thought he was on trial for his life.

He had made an effort to present a decent appearance. His hair was carefully brushed; he had tried to scrub the coal dust from his skin; he wore a dark tie, whose sobriety suggested Pastor Sheare's wardrobe. But his skin was even grayer and darker this morning, the timid eyes wilder and more sunken. Even the bruise on his lower lip was white. He sat gripping the edge of the table with both hands.

"The town clerk will read the selectmen's roll of eligible jurors," said Judge Shinn. "One at a time, please."

Burney Hackett read from a paper in a loud voice: "Hubert Hemus!"

The First Selectman rose from his campchair and went to the witness chair.

"Mr. Adams?"

Ferris Adams came away from the pine table.

"Your name."

"Hubert Hemus." Hemus was still smarting under Judge Shinn's reprimand.

"Mr. Hemus, have you formed an opinion as to the guilt or innocence of the defendant, Josef Kowalczyk?"

"Do I have to answer that?" He glared at the lawyer.

"The state's attorney must ask that question, Mr. Hemus," the Judge said sternly. "And you must answer it truthfully if you wish to serve on this jury."

"Sure I've formed an opinion!" exploded the First Selectman. "So's everybody else. That murderin' tramp was caught practic'ly redhanded!"

Johnny apologized mentally to Judge Shinn, who was putting a handkerchief to his mouth. Get Hemus mad enough . . .

"But if the evidence should cast a reasonable doubt on the defendant's guilt," Adams asked quickly, "you would not vote to convict him, Mr. Hemus, even though as of this moment you're convinced he's guilty?"

And that nailed it to the record.

Hemus looked grateful. "Mr. Adams, I'm a fair man. If they convince me he's not guilty, why, I'll vote that way. But they got to convince me."

Some of the women giggled.

"Let the record show that there was laughter from the panel at that last remark," said the Judge to Elizabeth Sheare complacently. "There must be no demonstrations in the court! Proceed, Mr. Adams."

Adams turned to old Andy Webster. "Does counsel wish to challenge?"

Ex-Judge Webster rose solemnly. "In view of the limited panel, your honor, I submit that the utilization of challenges during the selection of this jury would effectually prevent a jury from being selected. Consequently, if we

are to have a trial—and I assume that to try Josef Kowalczyk for murder is what we are all here for—I cannot
challenge and I do not challenge."

Neatly done, thought Johnny as Andrew Webster sat
down.

...ubert Hemus will be entered as Juror Number One.
Clerk will proceed with the panel."

"Orville Pangman," read Burney Hackett.

The comedy went on. By one device or another, between them Ferriss Adams and Andy Webster, with occasional help from Judge Shinn, maneuvered each panelist
into admitting his bias for the record. None was chal-
lenged.

It went quickly. Orville Pangman was Juror Number
Two. Merton Isbel was Juror Number Three. Burney
Hackett read his own name and was disqualified. Mathilda
Scott was Juror Number Four; neither her husband's nor
her father-in-law's name was brought up. Peter Berry was
Juror Number Five. The name of Hosey Lemmon was
called; no one responded, and Lemmon was stricken from
the rolls at the Judge's direction.

Johnny awaited with curiosity the examination of Samuel Sheare. They had to ask the minister the same questions they were throwing at the others; and Adams did
so.

"Have you formed an opinion as to the guilt or innocence of the defendant?"

"I have not," said the minister in a firm voice.

Johnny looked around. But none of Mr. Sheare's flock
seemed resentful of their pastor's affirmation of open-
mindedness. They expected him to carry the burden of
Christian charity as befitting his spiritual calling. Apparently they did not consider it possible that he might vote
for an acquittal when the evidence should have been presented. There were sometimes advantages, Johnny grinned
to himself, in dealing with single-track minds.

Mr. Sheare became Juror Number Six. He was not
asked if he believed in capital punishment, and he did
not volunteer a statement of his belief. Mr. Sheare had
been got to, and Johnny, watching Judge Shinn's bland
benignity, thought he knew by whom.

Elizabeth Sheare was excused as not qualifying, since
she was acting as court stenographer.

Rebecca Hemus, Millie Pangman, Emily Berry, and

Prue Plummer were selected in rapid succession as Jurors Number Seven, Eight, Nine, and Ten, and they took their seats behind the six men in the jury "box."

There was some difficulty in getting Calvin Waters to understand what he was being called upon to do. In the course of his examination the conspirators managed to get into the record the town handyman's having fallen on his head as a baby, his lifelong reputation for dull-wittedness, and the fact that he was barely able to write and could read only a few simple words. Hube Hemus looked uncomfortable, but he voiced no objection.

Calvin Waters was recorded as Juror Number Eleven and duly shuffled to the fifth chair in the second row of jurors, his empty face momentarily filled with bewilderment.

"Continue, Mr. Clerk."

"Sarah Isbel."

She was the only one left in the spectators' section except Johnny and Usher Peague.

At the reading of her name, Sarah Isbel went white. Merton Isbel was gathering himself, his craggy features stormy. The woman jumped up and said faintly, "I can't serve on any jury. I have my child to . . ." The rest went away with her. When the front door banged, Merton Isbel sat down again.

"A member of a panel may not arbitrarily refuse to serve on a jury," said Judge Shinn. "The bailiff will return Sarah Isbel to the courtroom."

"Your honor." The old farmer got up, rumbling. "I serve on no jury with *her*. Ye let the daughter of Sodom sit, I leave."

The room was very quiet. Judge Shinn rubbed his chin as if here loomed a formidable problem. Then he said, "Very well, Mr. Isbel. I yield to necessity. There is no profit in gaining one juror while losing another. In view of your threat, Sarah Isbel is excused."

And all this, Johnny thought with wonder, is going down in Elizabeth Sheare's notebook. Yielding to necessity! Threats! It would undoubtedly make the most remarkable transcript in the history of American jury trials.

"Proceed, Mr. Clerk," snapped Judge Shinn.

"I can't, your honor," said Burney Hackett feebly. "That's all we got. Except for Mr. John Jacob Shinn, who got to be a property owner only this mornin'—"

"Oh, yes," said the Judge, as if he had quite forgotten.
"I said I'd make a special ruling on that, didn't I? Because
it appears, ladies and gentlemen, that unless we avail ourselves of the services of Mr. Shinn, we can't satisfy the
legal requirements of a twelve-person jury and therefore
we can't try the defendant in Shinn Corners."

The jurors were staring at Johnny with distaste, whispering among themselves. Cruel, cruel the dilemma. Either a trial with a rank outsider sitting among them in a
vital village affair, or no trial.

Judge Shinn waited.

And at last their heads inclined toward Hubert Hemus,
and the First Selectman said something in an impatient
undertone, and they all sank back, troubled but nodding.

The Judge promptly said: "So, although Mr. John Shinn
is so newly in residence among us that he is not yet on the
voting list from which the jury panel must be drawn,
I rule that he may sit as a juror in this case if he otherwise qualifies."

And there, thought Johnny as he went up to the witness chair assisted by a sly prod from Ush Peague's pencil,
is as grandly garbled a ruling as ever was delivered from
a bench. How could a man otherwise qualify when the
"otherwise" was what disqualified him?

Yes, he was familiar with the facts of the case. No, he
had formed no opinion as to the defendant's guilt or
innocence . . . At this, in contrast to their genial suffer-
ance when Samuel Sheare had made the same answer,
the people of Shinn Corners glowered. . . . And Andy
Webster waved him cheerily away, and Johnny took the
last vacant chair in the second row and immediately discovered that certain powerful emanations from the person and clothing of Laughing Waters were going to
create a major problem of the case—for Juror Number
Twelve, at any rate.

The last dreamlike development of the morning was
Judge Shinn's recessing of the trial in order to allow
court, jurors, prosecutor, defense counsel, stenographer,
and bailiff to attend the funeral of the victim whose
alleged murderer they were in process of trying.

"Court will reconvene," said the Judge, "at one P.M."

Even the funeral had the quality of something seen in
a dream. Or a play, Johnny thought. This might be *Our*

Town, minus the rain. The burying ground was uneven,
little swells of ground running into one another, with the
bleached and blurry edges of the headstones sticking out
of them in all directions, old, old, older-seeming than
the soil that held them drearily. Johnny felt an unreason-
able reluctance to setting foot among them.

The Comfort undertaker's hearse had started from the
Adams' house and all of Shinn Corners—men and women
and children—trudged along behind it up Shinn Road
toward the Corners, women fanning themselves with their
hands, men wiping their foreheads in the sticky forenoon
haze; and they had slowly turned right at the intersection into Four Corners Road and passed the horse trough
and the parsonage and come to the sagging iron gate of
the cemetery. And Cy Moody and his helper eased the
expensive-looking casket out of the hearse, and Ferriss
Adams and Judge Shinn and Hubert Hemus and Orville
Pangman and Merton Isbel and Peter Berry took hold of
the handles and began the death march among the ancient
stones to the raw hole dug by Calvin Waters in the very
early morning; and Johnny shivered.

He hardly heard the nasal monotone of Samuel Sheare
reading the service for the dead, for it was not good
to listen closely to such things read in the dedicated mum-
ble of a man addressing God directly, without regard for
neighbor or murderer or even his own troubled soul.
Johnny looked instead among the graves and beyond, to
Isbel's cornfield, and farther to the south the barn and
lean-to of the departed old woman, so near to the place of
her birth and yet so far from its living beauty. How often had Fanny Adams stood here listening to Samuel
Sheare mutter the final farewell to others? How often
had she painted this very scene—the field, the cemetery,
perhaps these same mourners? He remembered the liveliness of her eyes and the warmth of her old hands, the
deep wise voice with its touch of Yankee asperity; and
Johnny was saddened and depressed.

He searched the headstones and saw Shinns scattered
among them like sterile seed, Shinns whose blood ran
in his veins and who were stranger strangers to him than
the Chinese and Koreans. He saw dates so old they had
worn away, names so forgotten they seemed visitants from
another planet. *Thankful Adams, She was an empty tale,
a morning flower, cut down and withered in its hour . . .*

Widow Zilpha, relict of Reverend Nathaneal Urie . . . Je-
buon Waters, O Mortality . . . Here Lieth Elhanon Shinn
Died of Scalding but God will Heal him . . .

And you, Fanny Adams, he thought. You and me both.

Four

❖━━━━━━━━━━━━━━━━━━━━━❖

"Ladies and gentlemen of the jury," said Ferriss Adams,
standing before the twelve campchairs, "I'm not going
to make a long speech. On trial for his life before you is
one Josef Kowalczyk, who came tramping through your
fine little town on the afternoon of Saturday last, the fifth
of July, was here less than one hour, and left behind him
a tragedy that none of you will ever forget—the murdered body of Aunt Fanny Adams, good neighbor, bene-
factor of Shinn Corners, from one of your oldest families,
and a world-famous person.

"The question before you is: Did Josef Kowalczyk
willfully, and with malice aforethought, and during the
commission of a felony, pick up a poker belonging to
deceased and with it beat her so savagely on the head as
to cause her death?

"The People believe that Josef Kowalczyk did so murder Fanny Adams and that his guilt can be proved. . . ."

As Adams went on to sketch in general terms the nature of the "People's" proofs, Johnny watched the faces
of his fellow jurymen. They were listening with grim in-
tensity, nodding at every third word. Even Calvin Waters's
blank features were lightly stamped with intelligence.

Josef Kowalczyk was mercifully so occupied in trying
to follow Ferris Adams's English that he might have been
a mere spectator. The furred brows were painfully one;
the bruised lips curled back over his poor teeth in the
effort. When Adams sat down and Andy Webster rose, a
look of pleasure passed over Kowalczyk's face.

Old Judge Webster said: "When a man is on trial, the
law says that he doesn't have to prove he did *not* commit

the crime, the People have to prove that he *did.* In
other words, as you all know, a man is held to be innocent unless and until he is proved guilty beyond the shadow of a reasonable doubt. The burden of proof is on the
People. And proof isn't a matter of belief, like faith in
God Almighty or an opinion about politics. Proof is a
matter of fact. . . . We won't attempt to make ourselves
out lily-white angels, ladies and gentlemen; there are very
few angels walking the earth. The defendant in this case
is a man who, handicapped by being in a strange land
and having trouble understanding and speaking our language, nevertheless has tried to make an honest living
by the sweat of his hands. The fact that he's failed, that
he's poor—poorer than any of you here—should not be
held against him, any more than you should hold
against him his foreign origin or his other outward differences from yourselves. . . . Josef Kowalczyk doesn't deny
that he stole money from Aunt Fanny Adams. In his
poverty he was tempted, and he knows now that in yielding to temptation he committed a sin. But even if you
can't find it in your hearts to forgive his stealing, the fact
that he stole money from Fanny Adams does not legally
prove that he murdered her.

"That is the crux of this case, neighbors of Shinn Corners. Unless the People can lay the *murder* at his door,
you will have to find Josef Kowalczyk not guilty."

But their doors were shut, locked, and bolted.

So it began.

Ferriss Adams put into the record the statement by
Kowalczyk on his capture, relating his arrival at the
Adams' house before the rain Saturday, Fanny Adams's
offer to feed him if he would split some firewood, and
all the rest of his story as he had told it to the Judge
and Johnny, including his admission of theft. The statement had been taken down by Elizabeth Sheare in the
cellar of the church on Saturday night, and it had been
signed by Kowalczyk in a stiff European hand.

Andrew Webster did not contest.

Judge Shinn directed Adams to call his first witness,
and Adams said: "Dr. Cushman."

"Doc Cushman to the stand," cried Burney Hackett.

A white-haired old man with a steamy red face and
eyes like coddled eggs rose from one of the spectator

seats and came forward. Bailiff Hackett offered him a Bible, the old man placed one shaky hand upon it and raised
the other, and in guitar-string quavers swore to tell the
whole truth and nothing but the truth so help him God.

He sat down in the witness chair.

"Your full name and title?" said Ferriss Adams.

"George Leeson Cushman, M.D."

"You reside and practice medicine where, Dr. Cushman?"

"Town of Comfort, Cudbury County."

"You are the Cudbury County coroner's medical exam-
iner for Comfort and Shinn Corners and certain other
nearby towns, Doctor?"

"I am."

"Did you examine the body of Mrs. Fanny Adams,
ninety-one years of age, of Shinn Corners, on the afternoon of Saturday, July the fifth—this past Saturday, Dr.
Cushman?"

"I did."

"Tell us the circumstances."

Dr. Cushman jerkily brushed his neck. "Received a
phone call 'bout three-twenty P.M. Saturday from Constable Burney Hackett of Shinn Corners, askin' me to come
right off to the Adams house in this village. Told Hackett
I couldn't get away just then, I'd had an office full of
patients since one o'clock and was still goin' strong, was
somebody sick? He didn't say, just said to come soon as
I could. I didn't get away till after five. When I got to
the Adams house Constable Hackett took me to a room
at the back, off the kitchen, where I saw the body of
Fanny Adams layin' on the floor, her head covered by a
towel. I removed the towel. I'd known Fanny Adams
all my life, and it was a shock." Dr. Cushman dabbed
at his head nervously. "I determined at once she was
dead—"

"At the time you first examined her body, Dr. Cushman, how long would you say she had been dead?"

" 'Bout three hours."

"And your examination took place at what time?"

" 'Tween five and five-thirty, thereabouts."

"Go on."

"Saw right off it was a case of homicide. Fierce mul-
tiple blows on top of the head, compound and complicated fractures of the skull—it was cracked in several

places like a dropped squash and the gray matter'd been smashed right into. Worst head injuries I've ever seen outside some bad auto accidents."

"Could these frightful wounds, in your opinion, have been self-inflicted?"

"Absolutely not."

"Could Mrs. Adams have lingered after being struck?"

"Instantaneous death."

"What did you do then, Doctor?"

"Phoned the county coroner in Cudbury, then waited beside the body till Coroner Barnwell got there. We agreed an autopsy wasn't necessary, as the cause of death was so plain to see. I signed the death certificate, then I went back to Comfort leavin' Coroner Barnwell there."

"When you first examined the body, Doctor, did you see anything that might have been the weapon lying near the body?"

"I did. A heavy iron poker. It was spattered with blood and bits of brain tissue and it was bent out of shape a bit."

"Is this the poker you saw?" Ferriss Adams held it up, and the room was deathly still.

"Aya."

"You mean yes, Dr. Cushman?"

"Yes."

"Is there the slightest doubt in your mind that this poker was the instrument of Fanny Adams's death?"

"No."

"Have you any additional reason for that opinion, Dr. Cushman, besides the bloody appearance of the poker?"

"Fracture lines in the cranium, and the shape and depth of the wounds in the brain, were just such as would have been produced by an instrument of this kind."

"Exhibit A, your honor . . . Your witness, Judge Webster."

Andy Webster tottered forward. Two or three of the women murmured resentfully. Judge Shinn had to rap on his table with the darning egg he had filched from Aunt Fanny Adams's sewing basket.

"You have testified, Dr. Cushman," said Cudbury's oldest legal light, "that when you examined the deceased she was dead about three hours, and you have also testified that the time of your examination was 'between five and five-thirty.' Can you be a little more exact about the time?"

"Time I examined?"

"Yes."

"Don't know's I can. Got there, I said, a bit after five, finished with the body around five-thirty."

"Was she dead three hours figuring from 'a bit after five,' or three hours from 'around five-thirty'?"

"Now I can't answer that," said Dr. Cushman indignantly. "Mighty hard to put your finger on an exact time of death. Lots of considerations—temperature of body, rigor mortis, post mortem lividity, temperature of room, whether the body's been moved—don't know how many questions come up. You couldn't get it to the minute, anyway. Most times you're lucky if you can get it to the hour."

"Then it's your opinion that if other evidence indicated the time of death as having been, say, thirteen minutes after two on the afternoon you saw the body, that would square with your guess as to the time of death?"

"Yes!"

"Dr. Cushman, did you form any opinion as a result of your examination regarding the relative positions of the deceased and her attacker during the commission of the crime?"

The boiled eyes blinked. "Pa'don?"

"Would you say," said Judge Webster, "that the blows were struck as Mrs. Adams faced her murderer, or as she was partly turned away from her murderer, or as she had her back turned to her murderer?"

"Oh! Facin' him. Dead on."

"That's a fact? The blows were all frontal?"

"That's right."

"She was *facing* her murderer. He could not have crept up on her from behind?"

Ferriss Adams leaped to his feet with a display of fury. The question, he shouted, was not within the witness's competence, it was improper cross-examination, and so forth. Andy Webster shouted back with surprising vigor. Judge Shinn allowed them to shout for some time. Then he calmly overruled the objection and directed the witness to answer.

"Crept up on her from behind?" Dr. Cushman shrugged. "Might, might not have. If he did, she must have heard him and turned round in time to get whacked from in front."

Ferris Adams grinned ferociously at Andy Webster, and Andy Webster made a fine show of chagrin. He was about to sit down when Johnny got out of his campchair and said, "Your honor, may I say something to defense counsel?"

"Certainly, Mr. Shinn," said Judge Shinn cheerfully.

Johnny came around and whispered to Andy Webster for a moment. The jury whispered, too, angrily. Rebecca Hemus made an audible remark about "interferin' furriners."

The old man nodded, and Johnny went back to his seat.

"Dr. Cushman," said Judge Webster, "what was the height of deceased, do you know?"

"Five foot five. Good height for an old woman—"

"Would you say that the wounds on Fanny Adams's head, five feet five inches from the floor, are such as could have been inflicted by a man only five feet seven inches in height?"

"Objection!" roared Ferriss Adams; and again they went at it. And again Judge Shinn directed the witness to answer.

"I couldn't form such an opinion," said Dr. Cushman, "without knowin' in exactly what position she was when she was hit. If her head was bent forward, it'd make all the difference."

"Nevertheless, assuming deceased was standing erect with her head in the normal position, isn't it true—"

"Objection!"

In the end, the Judge had the question struck. He was gauging his rulings, Johnny thought, more or less by the measure of the expressions on the face of the jury. Peague was writing away furiously, looking awed.

Andy Webster waved and sat down and Ferriss Adams jumped up again.

"Just to get this one point clear, Dr. Cushman. It is your opinion that a man five feet seven inches in height *could* have inflicted the wounds in question?"

"Object!" yelped Andy Webster.

"Overruled." It seemed to Johnny that Judge Shinn's reason for this ruling had little or nothing to do either with proper examination or his overall plan to foul up the record. He simply wanted to hear the answer.

"Could, *if* her head was in a certain position. Couldn't, if it wasn't." Dr. Cushman was eying old Andy with great hostility. "Just can't say. Expect nobody could."

The Comfort physician was excused.

The next witness called by Ferriss Adams was the bailiff himself. In all gravity the presiding justice rose, came around his "bench," picked up the Bible, and administered the oath. Then he went back to presiding.

"You found the body of Fanny Adams, Constable Hackett?"

"Yep."

"Tell us what happened on the afternoon of July fifth —how you happened to find the body and what happened afterwards."

Burney Hackett told his story. How at ten minutes after three on Saturday afternoon he had left his house to walk over to the Adams house to see Aunt Fanny about an insurance plan for her valuable paintings, how he had arrived a few minutes later to find the kitchen door open and the rain beating in, and how he had discovered Aunt Fanny's dead body on the floor of her "paintin' room" next to the kitchen. He identified Exhibit A as the poker he had found beside the body.

He had telephoned to Judge Shinn, Hackett said; as soon as he hung up the phone rang and it was Prue Plummer, who had listened in on his conversation with the Judge (Miss Plummer glared from the jury "box"), to inform him that a tramp had stopped at her back door about a quarter of two, Prue Plummer had refused him food, and she had watched him slouch up Shinn Road and turn into Aunt Fanny Adams's place and go around to the kitchen door. Hackett had then phoned Dr. Cushman in Comfort, at which point Judge Shinn and Mr. Shinn ran in . . .

"When you first saw the body, before the arrival of Judge Shinn and Mr. Shinn, Constable," said Ferriss Adams, "did you notice a locket-watch hanging from a gold chain about the neck of the deceased?"

"I did."

"In what condition was the watch?"

"The cameo on the front was smashed and the case'd

sprung. Way it looked to me, one of the blows had kind of missed and scraped down the front of her, hittin' the watch on her chest and breakin' it."

"Is this the watch?" Adams handed it to Hackett.

"Yep."

"Exhibit B, your honor . . . What was the time shown on the face of the watch when you first saw it?"

"What it shows right now. Thirteen minutes past two."

"It was not only broken, it was also not running?"

"Not runnin', no. It'd stopped."

The constable told of Ferriss Adams's arrival and his story of having passed a tramp on the road a short time before; and of how he, Hackett, had then deputized Adams, Judge Shinn, and John Shinn to go after the tramp; and of how, a few minutes later, he followed them with a posse and they captured the tramp as he ran out of the swamp beyond Peepers Pond.

"Was that the man you captured?" asked Adams, pointing to Josef Kowalczyk. Kowalczyk's mouth was open.

"Yep."

"Did he surrender peaceably, Constable Hackett?"

"He put up a fight. We had our hands full."

Hackett then told of bringing Kowalczyk back to the village, fixing up the coalbin in the church cellar as a jail, searching the prisoner and finding money hidden under his clothing. . . .

"Constable, I show you some U.S. paper money in bills of varying denominations, totaling one hundred twenty-four dollars. Is this the money you and Hubert Hemus took from the person of the defendant when you stripped him?"

Burney Hackett took the bills, shuffled through them, put them to his nose.

"This is the same money."

"How do you know?"

"For one thing I put it in an envelope and marked it—"

"This envelope, with the notation: *Money taken from prisoner Sat'y aftn. July 5* written on it in your handwriting?"

"That's it. There were thirteen bills—four twenties, three tens, two fives, and four ones."

"Have you an additional reason for believing these thirteen bills are the same thirteen bills you took from the defendant?"

"Sure do. They smelled strong of cinnamon. You can still smell it on these."

"Your honor, I enter this envelope and contents as Exhibit C, and I think we all ought to have a whiff of the bills."

The bills were duly passed to the counsel table and from there to the jury box. Everyone sniffed. The scent of cinnamon was faint, but unmistakable.

"Now, Constable Hackett," said Ferriss Adams, "you have testified that on finding Aunt Fanny's body, you telephoned to Judge Shinn. Did you do anything between finding the body and making the phone call?"

"I run out through the kitchen door and took a quick look around, thinkin' I'd maybe spot somebody. At that time I didn't know how long she'd been dead. I hadn't yet noticed the stopped watch."

"When you say you 'took a quick look around,' Constable, do you mean you stood at the kitchen door and looked, or did you actually go somewhere?"

"I run across the back yard, looked in the barn, behind the barn, in the lean-to—"

"You went *into* the lean-to, Constable?"

"Right through it."

"Did you see or find anything in the lean-to?"

"Not a thing."

"You saw no firewood of any kind?"

"Lean-to was empty," said Burney Hackett.

"Did you see any evidence whatever behind the barn that logs had been recently split?"

"Nary a splinter."

"Did you see any sign whatsoever, either in the lean-to or anywhere else about the premises, either during that first quick search on finding the body or at any time subsequently, of freshly split firewood?"

"No, sir."

"Your witness, Judge Webster."

Andrew Webster (and this time, Johnny noted, the tip of his thorny old nose was white with determination): "Constable Hackett, did you examine defendant's clothing on the afternoon of Saturday last, July fifth?"

"Me and Hube Hemus. It was when Mr. Sheare come down with some dry duds for the prisoner and we removed his wet ones."

"Did you find any bloodstains on defendant's clothing?"

"Well, no, though that's what I was lookin' for. But they were soakin' wet and plastered with mud and sludge from the swamp. Any blood'd got on his clothes or hands had been washed out."

"Ignoring the totally unwarranted inference, Constable," snapped Andy Webster, "didn't it occur to you as an officer of the law that there is such a thing as chemical analysis of clothing, which might definitely have established the presence—or absence—of bloodstains even on wet, muddy clothing?"

"Object!"

"Overruled," said Judge Shinn gently.

"Never occurred to me," Burney Hackett said in a sulky tone. "Anyway, we got no facil'ties for such things—"

"There is a modern scientific laboratory in Odham regularly used by nearby Cudbury County police departments for just such purposes, is there not, Constable Hackett?"

"This isn't proper cross—" began Ferriss Adams automatically. Then he shook his head and shut up.

"Constable, what happened to the clothing you tore from the defendant's body?"

"Elizabeth Sheare cleaned 'em—"

"In other words, it is now impossible to establish the presence or absence of bloodstains. Constable Hackett, did you attempt to bring out any fingerprints on the murder weapon?"

Burney Hackett's underdeveloped jaw waggled. "Fingerprints . . . Heck no, Judge Webster. I don't know nothin' 'bout fingerprints. Anyway, the poker was too messed up—"

"You did not send the poker to a qualified police or other laboratory for fingerprint examination?"

"No . . ."

"Have you handled the poker since Saturday, Constable?"

"Well, I did, yes. So did Hube Hemus, Mr. Adams, Orville Pangman . . . I guess most everybody's handled it since Saturday." Hackett's large ears were now a bright, pulsing red.

Ferriss Adams's glance appealed to Judge Shinn. But the Judge merely sat judgelike.

"One thing more, Constable. For the record, where were you at two-thirteen o'clock Saturday afternoon?"

Johnny relaxed. He had asked Andrew Webster to establish the whereabouts of every witness at the time of the murder, on any pretext, and he had begun to think the old man had forgotten.

Hackett was startled. "Me? I'd drove over to Cudbury Saturday morning for a talk with Lyman Hinchley 'bout figgerin' out the insurance plan for Aunt Fanny Adams's paintin's. I got the figgers from Lyman and started on back from Cudbury——"

"What time did you leave Hinchley's insurance office?"

"About two o'clock. The rain was just startin' to come down. Got back home at twenty minutes of three. Parked my car—I remember I was madder'n hops at my Jimmy, he'd left his trike in the middle of my garage and I had to get out, it's only a one-car garage, and got soakin' wet——"

"Never mind that, Constable. It took you forty minutes, then, to drive from Cudbury to Shinn Corners, leaving Cudbury at about two o'clock. At two-thirteen, then, you were somewhere between Cudbury and this village?"

"Well, sure. I'd say . . . coverin' twenty-eight miles in forty minutes, goin' a bit over forty miles an hour all the way . . . I'd say at two-thirteen I was 'bout nine miles out of Cudbury. Say nineteen miles from Shinn Corners."

"That's all."

The next witness Adams called was Samuel Sheare.

The little pastor rose slowly from the last seat in the first row of jurors—Johnny, directly behind him, could see his bony shoulders contract and his skinny neck telescope into itself. He made his way to the Windsor chair, where Burney Hackett was waiting with the Bible. The touch of its limp cover seemed to reassure him. He took the oath in a clear voice.

At the trestle table old Andy Webster put his hand up to his eyes, as if to shut out the horrid spectacle of a juror preparing to testify in a murder case. Usher Peague was watching incredulously.

"Mr. Sheare," said Adams, after the minister had given his name and occupation, "you were present in Fanny Adams's house on the morning of July fourth—the day before the murder—and you had a conversation with her at that time?"

"Yes."

"Will you please tell the jury what Aunt Fanny Adams said to you on that occasion, and what you said to her."

Mr. Sheare looked distressed. His hands clasped and unclasped. He addressed the hooked rug at his feet, telling how Mrs. Adams had taken him into her kitchen for a talk, how she had offered him twenty-five dollars to buy his wife a new summer dress—

"Just a moment, Mr. Sheare. Where did Aunt Fanny get the money she offered you?"

"Out of one of her spice jars on the top shelf of the kitchen cabinet." Mr. Sheare's voice faltered.

"What kind of spice jar was it? Was it marked in any way?"

"Yes. The word *Cinnamon* was printed on it in kind of Old English gilt letters."

"Is this the jar, Mr. Sheare?" Adams held it up.

"Yes." Johnny had to strain to hear the response.

"Exhibit D, your honor, entered in evidence."

Josef Kowalczyk had his hands flat on the table, staring at the jar, his gray skin a muddy grave color. And the jury looked at him without expression.

"Mr. Sheare, do you know how much money was *left* in this jar after Aunt Fanny gave you the twenty-five dollars?"

"Yes . . ."

"How much?" Adams had to repeat the question. "How much, Mr. Sheare?"

"A hundred and twenty-four dollars."

A sound, very slight, rippled through the room. It raised the short hairs on Johnny's neck.

"How do you know she had a hundred and twenty-four dollars left in this jar after she gave you the twenty-five dollars?"

" 'Cause she told me the jar contained a hundred and forty-nine dollars in bills, besides some loose change."

"And twenty-five from a hundred and forty-nine, by simple subtraction, left a hundred and twenty-four, is that correct, Mr. Sheare? That's how you know?"

"Yes . . ."

"What did she do with the cinnamon jar after she gave you the money?"

"She put it back on the cabinet shelf."

"In the kitchen?"

"Yes."

"And this happened on Friday, the day before the murder?"

"Yes."

"Thank you, Mr. Sheare. Your witness."

Andy Webster waved.

"I call as my next witness," said Ferriss Adams bashfully, "er . . . Judge Lewis Shinn."

But while the presiding judge left his bench to come around and take the oath as a witness in the case he was trying, Johnny edged out of his seat and stole away.

He went into Aunt Fanny's kitchen, looked up a number in the telephone book on the cabinet, and gave it to the operator. It was a Cudbury number.

A girl's voice answered. "Lyman Hinchley's office."

"Mr. Hinchley, please. Tell him it's John Shinn, Judge Shinn's cousin. I met him at a Rotary lunch in Cudbury about ten days ago."

The brassy tones of Cudbury's ace insurance broker belled into Johnny's ear almost at once. " 'Lo there, Shinn! Enjoying your stay with the Judge?"

Then Hinchley hadn't heard. "Real vacation, Mr. Hinchley," Johnny said with genuine heartiness. "Fishing, lazing around . . . Oh, I'll tell you why I'm calling. It's going to sound silly, but I've been having an argument with Burney Hackett here—you know Burney, don't you?"

"Sure do," chuckled the insurance broker. "Real hick constable. Harmless, though. Fancies himself as an insurance man."

"Yes. Well, Burney tells me he was over to see you Saturday about some insurance advice and says he drove the twenty-eight miles back from your office to Shinn Corners in forty minutes by the clock. I said he couldn't do it in that jalopy of his, but he swears he left your office at two o'clock Saturday. Did he, or is he pulling my leg?"

"I guess he's got you, Shinn. At least he did leave here around two. I remember he hadn't been out of my office two minutes when the rain started. And that was two o'clock on the nose."

"Well, I'll have to apologize to his heap! Thanks, Mr. Hinchley . . ."

* * *

And returned to his campchair in time to hear Judge Shinn finish the recital of their movements Saturday and to be called to the stand himself.

Johnny's story corroborated the Judge's in detail, including the meeting with Josef Kowalczyk in the rain about a mile and a quarter from the village.

"You say, Mr. Shinn," said Ferriss Adams, "that you passed the defendant on the road at twenty-five minutes to three. How sure are you of the time?"

"Pretty sure. Judge Shinn had looked at his watch at two-thirty. My estimate is that about five minutes passed, and then we spotted Kowalczyk across the road going toward Cudbury."

"What time did you and Judge Shinn arrive at the Judge's house?"

"Just about three o'clock."

"In other words, it took you and Judge Shinn twenty-five minutes to get from the spot where you met Kowalczyk to the Judge's house?"

"Yes."

"Did you walk steadily?"

"You mean without pausing?"

"Yes."

"We paused three times," said Johnny. "First, we stopped to stare after Kowalczyk when he passed us and before we resumed our hike. Second, Burney Hackett's car passed us without seeing us and gave us a splashing, and that held us up for a short time. Third, we halted at the top of Holy Hill near Hosey Lemmon's shack."

"How long would you say, Mr. Shinn, those three pauses took altogether?"

"Maybe a minute."

"Now the twenty-five minutes you gave us as the allover time between first sighting Kowalczyk and arriving at the Judge's house comes out longer, does it not, than if you figured it between first sighting Kowalczyk and passing the Adams house on your way to the Judge's?"

"If you mean how much time it took us to walk the last leg of the trip between the Adams house and the Shinn house, I should think no longer than two minutes."

"Then with the one minute of delays en route and the two minutes after passing the Adams house, you'd say, Mr. Shinn, that the actual walking time between the place where you met Kowalczyk and the Adams house was twenty-five minus three, or twenty-two minutes?"

"Roughly," agreed Johnny. "You'd need a stopwatch to be accurate."

"You and the Judge walked fast?"

"Yes."

"Was the defendant walking fast when you sighted him?"

"Yes."

"As fast as you two, or faster, or not as fast?"

"I really couldn't say," Johnny shrugged. "Fast."

"Is it a fair inference that he was walking at about the same pace as you and the Judge?"

"Object!" growled Andy Webster.

"Sustained," said Judge Shinn.

"Do you agree, Mr. Shinn," said Ferriss Adams, "that if it took you and the Judge twenty-two minutes' walking time between the meeting place on the road and the Adams house, then it took Kowalczyk about the same time to get from the Adams house to the meeting place—"

"Object!"

"—and consequently that Kowalczyk must have left the Adams house at two-thirteen, or in other words *just about the time of the murder?*"

"*Objection!* Your honor, I move that this entire line of testimony, both questions and answers, be stricken!"

"Oh, I think we'll let it stand, Judge Webster," murmured Judge Shinn.

Usher Peague rubbed his ears. Then he went back to his headlong scribbling.

Ferriss Adams brought out Kowalczyk's "suspicious actions" on sighting the two men in the rain—"Yes, sir, he started to run"—and Andy Webster came back on cross-examination to establish that Johnny and the Judge had been toting guns, implying that any ignorant stranger encountering two armed men on a lonely road might have started to run, too . . . but in the main it was a cut-and-dried exchange, and Webster did not embroider the point.

Then Johnny resumed his place among the jury and Peague had more wonders to jot down in his notes . . . the prosecutor taking the stand as a witness while the judge took over the role of prosecutor!

Ferriss Adams told of his arrival at the Adams house at three-thirty Saturday afternoon, how a remark about a tramp had recalled to his mind the man he had seen walking along the road towards Cudbury in the rain a few minutes before, how Burney Hackett had deputized him and the two Shinns to go after the tramp; and of the events that followed, including defendant's "malicious act" in pushing his, Adams's, car into the bog in the swamp to delay pursuit—an episode which, to judge from Adams's bitter tone, still rankled.

On cross-examination Andrew Webster said: "Mr. Adams, you have testified that your visit to Fanny Adams Saturday afternoon was occasioned by an urgent request from her that you come to see her. Will you tell us the circumstances?"

"What's the relevance of the question?" asked the acting prosecutor, stepping out of his role momentarily to become the judge again.

"Anything the victim did or said just prior to her murder, your honor, especially cast in terms of urgency," said Andy Webster, "may throw light on the crime. If, for example, Mrs. Adams was in some sort of trouble with a neighbor and wished to discuss it with her grandnephew, who is a lawyer, surely that fact would be relevant and possibly important."

"Answer the question, Mr. Adams."

"I can't," said Ferriss Adams. "I don't know what she wanted. She didn't say, and by the time I got to the house she was dead." He related that he had locked his Cudbury office in the Professional Building on Washington Street Saturday about five minutes to one, his secretary being on vacation, and had gone out to lunch and to see some people. On his return about two-thirty he had found a note under his door. The note was from Emily Berry—Mrs. Peter Berry, Juror Number Nine—saying that she was at Dr. Everett Kaplan's dental office with the children and that he was to phone her there, she had a message for him from his Aunt Fanny. He had called Emily Berry immediately from his office phone and found her still at Dr. Kaplan's office.

"Mrs. Berry told me my aunt had been trying to reach me all morning but my phone was busy—that was true. I was on the phone all Saturday morning on a real estate matter involving a lawsuit. So Aunt Fanny'd asked her to stop by my office and give me a message. She'd got to my office about one o'clock, a few minutes after I left for lunch, and not finding me in she slipped a note under my door. Mrs. Berry said the message was that I was to go see Aunt Fanny in Shinn Corners right away."

Adams had started out from Cudbury at once, he said. The time couldn't have been later than twenty-five minutes to three. The rain had been heavy, and he had lost some time when his windshield wiper went blooey and he had to stop to fix it. When he did arrive at his aunt's house, it was to find Burney Hackett and the others there over the murdered body of his aunt.

"You have no idea, Mr. Adams, what your aunt had in mind?"

"No. She didn't usually call me unless it had something to do with one of her contracts, and I thought that's what it was. It didn't occur to me till you just brought it up that it might have had something to do with her murder. I still think it was about a contract or some other business matter. I don't see any reason to believe otherwise."

Emily Berry—with Ferriss Adams and Judge Shinn restored to their proper stations—corroborated Adams's testimony. The storekeeper's wife had dressed stylishly for her dual role of juror-witness, in a flowered silk dress, a straw picture hat, and white elbow-length gloves; but the severity of her Gothic features, the tight plainness of her bun, the piano-wire tension of her pregnant figure, gave her the look of a department store dummy on display in a street window.

She spoke sharply, never taking her eyes off Josef Kowalczyk. Johnny thought, Put some knitting in her hands and a guillotine where Kowalczyk sits, and you've got Citizeness Defarge.

"Aunt Fanny asked me to deliver the message to Ferriss Adams because she knew his office is in the same buildin' as Dr. Kaplan's. Not that I care much for Everett Kaplan's kind, after all he is the brother of that Morrie Kaplan who runs the moving picture show in Cudbury, you know what *they* are, but everybody says he's the best dentist around. Of course, if it wasn't for my children . . . Got the children in the sedan a bit after twelve— Dickie, Zippie, Suky, and Willie—and why Peter couldn't relieve me of that job once in a blue moon I don't know, but no, he had to stay home and tinker with the new delivery truck, that cost three thousand dollars and is always needin' fixin', leaving me to drive four hoodlums twenty-eight miles and back!"

"Mrs. Berry," said Ferriss Adams, "if you'd please—"

"I'm testifyin', ain't I? Seems to me a body's got a story to tell, they ought to let her tell it!"

"The witness," began Judge Shinn, "will please—"

"I'll get to it," said Emily Berry grimly, "if you'll all stop interruptin'. Well, I got to the Professional Building in Cudbury about one o'clock, and I had to climb the four flights with the elevator right there—I mean to your office, Mr. Adams, they insisted on racin' up the stairs— if they'd behaved like normal children I could have saved myself all that climbin'—"

"You found my door locked," said Adams desperately, "you thereupon scribbled a note to me—"

"*Yes.* And slipped it under your door. Then we walked down to that Dr. Kaplan's office, had a one o'clock appointment, we were late and his nurse was darn snotty about it and I told *her* a thing or two! Anyway, they all needed attention to their teeth, not that I wonder, with the junk children keep stuffin' themselves with these days, though of course havin' a store makes it kind of hard to give their poor little stomachs a rest, they're always runnin' in for somethin', and we didn't get away till after three o'clock—"

"My phone call," said Adams with a sigh.

"Did I leave that out? You phoned me at the dentist's office around two-thirty, said you'd just found my note under your door, and I told you what Aunt Fanny'd said, and anyway when we left after three we walked over to that new parking lot behind the Billings Block where they charge thirty-five cents an hour and if that isn't an outrage I don't know what is, you can't *ever* find a place to park on the streets in that town any more, and they hold you up somethin' terrible—"

"You got the children into your car," urged Adams, "and you began to drive back to Shinn Corners at what time, Mrs. Berry?"

"Mercy, *I* don't know. And you wouldn't either, if you had to unlock your car and pile that crew in and back out of a parkin' lot with a ten-year-old slappin' his six-year-old sister silly and the baby screamin' and tryin' to claw his way into your lap—"

"What time did you get home, Mrs. Berry?"

"Now how can I answer that? And why," demanded Emily Berry suddenly, "should I? Who's on trial here? What difference does it make where *I* was? Or when? It must have been some time after four o'clock, if you must know, but I think this is all a waste of time. When I got home the village was in an uproar over that horrible tramp beatin' Aunt Fanny to death—"

"Objection!"

"Well, he did, didn't he? Seems to me there's an awful lot of fuss bein' made here over what everybody *knows*. 'Course, I s'pose he's got to be tried and all that, but if you ask me it's a lot more than he deserves, he ought to be strung up the way folks used to do around here. My grandmother told me that her grandfather actually saw with his own eyes when he was a boy—"

The last remarks were somehow not stricken from the record. But Andy Webster prudently did not cross-examine, and Judge Shinn rapped with Aunt Fanny's darning egg and declared court adjourned until ten o'clock the next morning.

It seemed the only sure way, the Judge remarked afterward, to bring Em Berry's testimony to a close.

Josef Kowalczyk left the Adams house not so much gripped as gripping. He held on to Constable Hackett's arm tightly, hurrying Hackett along and looking back over his shoulder. Through it all his pale lips murmured, as if he had to keep saying something to himself over and over, something of considerable importance. Burney Hackett said it must have been Polish.

That night, after Millie Pangman had cleared away the dinner dishes and tidied up and run home, the Judge and his four guests sat around the study with brandy and cigars, chuckling over the trial's first day. Judge Shinn had compiled a list of breaches and errors covering many ruled yellow pages, and the lawyers studied them with a sort of guilty small-boy enjoyment. Usher Peague said that he had covered his quota of murder trials in his days as a reporter and feature writer in Boston and New York, but this was going down in his book as the greatest of them all, bar none.

"You gentlemen will be enshrined in the ivied annals of your noble but humorless profession," said the Cudbury editor with a wave of his brandy glass, "as the pioneers of a new branch of the law, to wit, the musical comedy murder trial, guaranteed to rate a smash hit in any dusty old lawbook lucky enough to house its collection of sure-fire yuks."

"It would be very funny indeed," said the Judge, "if not for two things, Ush."

"What?"

"Aunt Fanny and Josef Kowalczyk."

When they resumed the conversation, the note of amusement was missing.

"I want you to keep right on questioning everybody you get into that witness chair, Ferriss," said Judge Shinn, "on the subject of their movements Saturday. It's Johnny's idea, and it's a good one. It may give us something."

"But why, Judge?" asked Ferriss Adams. "Do you seriously suspect one of your own Shinn Corners people of having killed Aunt Fanny? In the face of the circumstantial case against Kowalczyk?"

"I don't suspect anybody. All we're doing is seizing the chance to check up on everyone in sight while we're going through the motions of this mock trial. It's exactly the kind of checkup that would have been made by the police and the state's attorney's office before an indictment."

"I think it's important as hell," said old Andy. "Because I don't believe Kowalczyk did it. And if he didn't, the odds are somebody in this God-forsaken neck of the woods did."

"Why do you say Kowalczyk didn't do it, Judge Webster?" complained Adams. "How can you say that?"

"Because," said the old man, "I happen to believe his story."

"But the evidence—"

"This won't get us anywhere," said Judge Shinn. "Johnny, you haven't opened your mouth. What do you think?"

"Curious pattern's developing," said Johnny with a frown. "If it keeps up—"

"What d'ye mean, curious?" demanded Peague.

"Well, seven people testified today, four Shinn Cornerites and three outsiders. Of the seven, six couldn't possibly have murdered Fanny Adams. Take the three non-residents first. Dr. Cushman of Comfort—"

"You don't suspect old Doc Cushman," snorted Peague. "Why, he's about as big a menace to Shinn Corners as Dr. Dafoe was to Callander, Northern Ontario!"

"Suspicion isn't the word," said Johnny. "It's a math problem. A certain number of factors have to be canceled out. They're not suspects; they're simply factors.

"According to Dr. Cushman's testimony, he was in his office Saturday seeing patients from about one o'clock till after five. After we broke up today, I phoned his nurse. Pretended to be a patient who'd driven up to Cushman's office in Comfort Saturday at a quarter past two but hadn't gone in, 'thinking' the office was closed. His nurse told me indignantly that it was *not* closed at a quarter past two Saturday, that she was there and Dr. Cushman was there—in fact, she said, Cushman's car was parked right out front, hadn't I seen it?—And a great deal more of the same, but I had what I wanted. At two-thirteen Saturday, when Fanny Adams was killed, Dr. Cushman was in Comfort. So cross him off.

"Second non-resident," said Johnny, "myself—"

"You?" exclaimed Ferriss Adams.

"Why not? Especially since I've got a hell of an alibi," grinned Johnny, "Judge Lewis Shinn of the Superior Court. At two-thirteen Saturday I was sloshing along with said eminent jurist in a minor flood between Peepers Pond and Holy Hill. We couldn't have been more than three-fifths of a mile from the pond, which means we were almost two and a half miles from Shinn Corners at the moment the poker came crashing down."

"Thank God for Emily Berry," said Adams, "verbal diarrhea notwithstanding!"

"Yes, Emily Berry corroborates your testimony that at two-thirty Saturday you were finding her note under your office door, calling her from your phone, and setting out for Shinn Corners. So you couldn't have been here, twenty-eight miles away, a mere seventeen minutes earlier.

"Now," said Johnny, "the residents who testified today.

"Burney Hackett: At two o'clock Saturday, Hackett said, he was leaving Lyman Hinchley's office in Cudbury. At two-thirteen, he calculated, he must still have been some nineteen miles from Shinn Corners. I phoned Hinchley's office, and he confirms—Hackett left his office, Hinchley says, just about two o'clock Saturday. So Hackett can't have murdered Fanny Adams, either.

"Judge Shinn. Judge Shinn is my alibi, which makes me his. Of course, we could have bashed Aunt Fanny's head in together and rigged the alibi; but even that cockeyed theory can be disproved. Kowalczyk himself passed us on the road as we were headed for Shinn Corners, and we were still a mile and three-quarters away.

"Emily Berry: You confirmed her whereabouts as having been in Dr. Kaplan's office in Cudbury, Adams, when you phoned her there at two-thirty, and I've checked with Kaplan's office, too.

"Samuel Sheare . . . His testimony today was restricted to the cinnamon jar and the money, so technically he's still to be eliminated." Johnny smiled. "But somehow, I'm not much worried about Mr. Sheare."

"In other words," said the Judge, "out of Shinn Corners's total population of thirty-five—and that includes Merritt Pangman, off somewhere in the Pacific—seven are eliminated by today's testimony and your checkups, Johnny: Burney Hackett, myself, and Emily Berry and her four youngsters."

"Leaving," murmured Johnny, "a mere twenty-eight to go." He stretched, yawning. "Saving our way of life is exhausting," he said. "Who's for a little poker?"

The first witness Tuesday morning was Peter Berry.

The fat storekeeper, looking more like William Jennings Bryan than ever, took the oath and sat down in the witness chair trying to keep his smily-jowly face from getting out of control. Berry was surprisingly nervous, Johnny thought. As if the ordeal of facing his customers in a public interrogation presented certain disagreeable possibilities. He kept clearing his throat and mopping his face.

After his wife had left with the children in the sedan Saturday for the dentist's office, Peter Berry said, he had worked in the store. At about a quarter of two the store emptied and he had stepped out to his garage next door with Calvin Waters to see what was the matter with his new delivery truck.

"Calvin'd come back from makin' deliveries for me in the mornin', and when he went to start her up again she wouldn't," Peter Berry said. "He was kind of anxious about it, Calvin was, thinkin' I'd blame him for the trouble. Fact of the matter is, I *was* put out with him. He'd not only done somethin' to the truck, he'd parked it in the garage in a place where it boxed in my wrecker, so that if somebody'd called up about an auto accident or somethin' I might have been held up so long tryin' to get the wrecker out they'd call Frank Emerson's garage in Comfort."

"Mr. Berry—"

"Anyway, Calvin hung around to see what was what. We hadn't been in the garage tinkerin' ten minutes—"

"You say," interrupted Ferriss Adams, "that you entered your garage at one forty-five, Mr. Berry, with Calvin Waters. Did you notice defendant walking along Shinn Road?"

"Nope," said Berry regretfully. "We were *in* the garage, and we both had our backs to the road. Otherwise I'd 'a' seen him sure. Anyway, in about ten minutes I heard my store bell jingle—"

"The bell over your screen door, that rings when the door is opened and closed?"

"Aya."

"This was at five minutes to two you heard the first jingle?"

"That's it. So we went back into my store—"

"Calvin Waters, too?"

"Well, yes." Berry glanced over at Juror Number Eleven —balefully, Johnny thought. The odorous town handyman thought so, too; he squirmed under the Berry glance like a worm that has been prodded. "Calvin don't mean nothin' by it, but if ye leave him alone round machin'ry, he starts to fussin' and tinkerin' like he knew what was what, which he don't. Don't know how much damage he's done that way. So I never leave him in the garage by himself if I can help it."

"We understand. Go on, Mr. Berry."

"Well, once we got back in the store I was kept hoppin'. Bell kept a-jinglin'—"

"Between five minutes to two," said Ferriss Adams, "and, say, half-past two, how many customers came into the store, Mr. Berry? How many times did the bell jingle?"

Berry thought, his facial curves shifting and overlapping wonderfully. "Six!"

"Six customers?"

"Six jingles. Three comin' in, three goin' out. The same three."

"Oh, I see. Who was the first, the one who came in at five minutes of two?"

"Hosey Lemmon. I was kind of surprised, 'cause I'd thought old man Lemmon was hired out over at the Scotts', helpin' Drakeley. But he said he'd just up and quit and he wanted to buy some beans and flour and such, he was headed back up Holy Hill to his shack." Berry shook his massive head. "Can't never tell about Hosey."

Mathilda Scott, in seat number four of the front row, nodded unconsciously, and Johnny heard her sigh.

"And the second customer?"

"Prue Plummer, just about two minutes after Hosey'd come in."

In the jury box in seat number ten, Prue Plummer smiled violently. She nudged the occupant of seat number nine, Emily Berry, who replied with a withering look and a haughty shoulder.

"Two minutes? You mean Miss Plummer arrived at one fifty-seven? Three minutes of two?"

"Must have been. Hadn't yet started to rain. I remember she was in the store a couple minutes before the rain started."

"How long were Hosey Lemmon and Miss Plummer in your store?"

"A spell. They were still there when Hube Hemus came in for some quotations on a new harrow, and for some time after that."

"Can you remember what time Mr. Hemus came in?"

"Few minutes after Prue. I'd say about two-four, two-five. Rain was comin' down hard. He had to run from his car, even though he'd parked it right in front of the store."

"What happened then?"

"I'd told Hosey Lemmon to wait, and Prue was pokin' through the frozen foods case while Hube and I went through some catalogues—"

"And Calvin Waters was still there?"

"Yep. The five of us."

"How long, Mr. Berry," asked Adams casually—and Judge Shinn, Webster, Peague and Johnny all leaned forward, "how long were the five of you together in the store?"

"Till two-nineteen. Hube was the first to leave, and that's when he left."

"How can you recall the time so exactly, Mr. Berry?"

" 'Cause just before Hube left he took out his watch and set it by my store clock. My clock said two-nineteen. Prue Plummer said her watch made it only two-eighteen, but I told her my clock ain't missed a minute in ten years —best on the market. She was wrong, and she knew it." (Prue Plummer's lips retracted, bringing her nose down in a power dive.) "Then Hube run out to his car and drove off, I waited on Mis' Plummer and *she* left, must have been a few minutes later, and then I finished up with old man Lemmon. Fact is," said Peter Berry, "I wasn't too sure Hosey had any money. Naturally I don't ever charge any of *his* purchases. . . . Well, he'd been paid off in cash at the Scotts'. Must say I was surprised, seein' that . . ." Peter Berry stopped, glancing quickly at Judge Shinn. "I mean," said Berry with a cough, "Hosey left a few minutes after Mis' Plummer, and then Calvin and me went back to the garage."

Ferriss Adams turned the witness over to Andrew Webster.

"Mr. Berry," said the old jurist, "you say that between a few minutes past two o'clock Saturday and two-nineteen you and the other people you mentioned were in the store together. Did you happen to notice, or did one of your customers happen to mention noticing, anyone passing on Shinn Road during that period? Going either toward the Adams house, or away from it?"

"No, sir."

"You didn't see the defendant at all?"

"Nope. Couldn't have, anyways. Can't see the Adams house from my store 'less you stand in the doorway or climb up on the mrechandise in my display window on the Shinn Road side."

"Thank you, that's all."

Ferriss Adams called a conference with Andy Webster before Juge Shinn's table. They discussed in low tones the advisability of calling Calvin Waters. Finally they decided against it; the time period would be covered by other witnesses, and to try to get anything coherent out of Laughing Waters, as the Judge said, would be just about a feasible as throttling Emily Berry.

"We've got his half-wittedness on the record, anyway," whispered Judge Webster.

So Adams called as his next witness Prue Plummer.

* * *

Prue Plummer was a lawyer's nightmare; or, in Peague's version during the noon recess, a gypsy tartar. She had dressed in her artiest skirt-and-blouse combination. The skirt was felt, with felt abstractions appliquéd on it in screaming oranges, pinks, and greens; the blouse was a handpainted, offshoulder cotton at which the other women had been glancing disapprovingly all morning; and she had put on her dangliest earrings and bound her head in a purple silk scarf to complete the illusion.

She literally ran away with Ferriss Adams's questions. As Adams said later, it would have taken Roy Rogers on a fast horse to catch her.

"*Certainly* I remember Saturday's events, Mr. Adams. Every last, bloodcurdling detail! At one forty-five there was a knock on my back door and I opened it to find a dirty, *filthy* man standing there, with a dark foreign skin and eyes that burned *holes* through me, a murderer if I ever saw one—that monster there!"

"Miss Plummer—" began Ferriss Adams.

"Objection!" howled Andy Webster simultaneously.

"Sustained!" said Judge Shinn. "Miss Plummer, you will please stick to what happended. No opinions, please." (But he did not order the answer struck.)

"Well, he did!" rasped Prue Plummer. "I don't *care*, a fact's a fact and that's a fact. You can tell a great deal from a human face, at least I can, not that his face is human . . . *Yes*, Judge . . . I mean your honor . . . Yes, sir . . . Well, he had the colossal *gall* to beg for something to eat and you can bet I lost no time telling him what I thought of beggars and sending him packing! I'm not feeding any stray off the roads who looks like a killer in *my* house when I'm alone. . . . But he does, your honor! . . . Yes, your honor.

"Anyway, I followed him to my gate and watched him walk up Shinn Road and cross the intersection diagonally to the horse trough and go past the church to Aunt Fanny Adams's house. He kind of hesitated at her gate, then he sort of looked around—*furtively*—"

"*Objection!*" roared Judge Webster for the fifth time.

"—as if he wanted to be sure no one was seeing him, and he sneaked around the side of the house toward Aunt Fanny's kitchen door—"

"What time would that have been, Miss Plummer?" asked Adams despairingly.

"Ten minutes of two. Then I went back into my house and began locking doors and windows—"

"Why did you do that?" asked Adams, in spite of himself.

"You don't think I'd leave my house wide open with all my valuable antiques and things in it, while a *murderer* was loose in the village!"

"Please," said Andrew Webster feebly.

"And anyway I had to go to the store. I needed something for my dinner."

"You walked over, of course, Miss Plummer."

"Walked over? Certainly I walked over! Don't be ridiculous, Mr. Adams. I'm no cripple. Though if I'd known it was going to rain, I *would* have driven over, only I couldn't have because my car's at 'Lias Wurley's garage in Cudbury being overhauled, as Peter Berry can tell you himself—he saw Mr. Wurley's mechanic drive it away." She sniffed at Peter Berry—repayment, no doubt, thought Johnny, for Berry's slur at the unreliability of her timepiece. "I'm supposed to leave next week for a motor trip to Cape Cod. To visit some friends, famous artists—"

"Yes, Miss Plummer. What time was it when you entered the Berry store?"

"Peter Berry told you. It was just one fifty-seven—"

Adams finally caught up with her testimony about the episode of the Berry store, although he was a little out of breath by the time he brought it down. Her story corroborated Berry's in every detail except the time Hubert Hemus had left the store—"It was two-*eighteen*. By *my* watch, anyway!"

The balance of Prue Plummer's testimony concerning her overhearing of Burney Hackett's phone call at three-fifteen to Judge Shinn—"I did *not* eavesdrop, as alleged. It was an innocent mistake, but of course when I heard Aunt Fanny had been murdered and remembered that foul *tramp* over there . . ."—and her very busy time afterward calling Burney Hackett and broadcasting the news to everyone she could think of. She had yelled out her back door to Orville Pangman, who was out at his barn with his son Eddie and young Joel Hackett; and she had dashed over to the Hacketts' next door to shout into Selina Hackett's ear; but the rest had been phone calls. . . .

Andy Webster, mercifully, made no attempt to cross-examine.

*   *   *

Hubert Hemus's testimony had to be mined out of him. He answered as if every word were a precious stone to be weighed to the last grain.

It soon became apparent that he was suspicious of the kind of questions Ferriss Adams was asking, and Adams wisely shifted his tactics and left the legal improprieties to Webster's cross-examination.

He and his twin boys, Hemus said, had been plowing and harrowing a field all morning, preparing it for a late corn planting. The harrow had broken down shortly after lunch, and he had driven into the village to see Peter Berry about ordering a new one. On his return, he and the twins worked in the barn, the rain holding up the planting. They were in the barn when Rebecca Hemus came out screaming that Prue Plummer had just called to say Aunt Fanny Adams had been murdered. Hemus had run ahead, jumping into the car and driving back to the village; Tommy, Dave, their mother, their sister had followed in the only other available vehicle, the farm truck. The three Hemus men had then joined the posse. . . .

Andy Webster said: "About your visit to Peter Berry's store, Mr. Hemus. Who was there when you came in?"

"Peter, Calvin, Hosey Lemmon, Prue Plummer."

"What time did you leave the store?"

"Peter said. Two-nineteen."

"Between the time you went in and the time you came out, Mr. Hemus, did anyone in the store leave? Step out for a few minutes, maybe?"

"No." Hube Hemus shifted squarely in the witness chair, challenging Judge Shinn. "Your honor, I want to ask a question."

"As a witness, Mr. Hemus—" began the Judge.

"I'm askin' as a juror. Juror's got a right to ask questions, ain't he?"

"All right, Hube," said the Judge in a friendly way, but fast.

"What I want to know is, why's everybody bein' asked where *they* were round the time of the murder? Who's on trial here, like Em Berry asked—this furrin tramp, or Shinn Corners?"

Talk fast, Mr. Moto, thought Johnny, grinning to himself. It had been too good to last, anyway. He wondered what the Judge was going to say, feeling a hearty gratitude that it was the Judge who had to say it.

Johnny thought the Judge, who had grown the merest bit ruddy about the ears, did a remarkable job of improvisation.

"Hube, how much do you know about trials?"

Hemus kept looking at him. "Not much."

"Think I know anything about trials?"

"Expect you do, Judge."

"What's the purpose of a trial, Hube?"

"Prove a man guilty."

"How is a man proved guilty in a court of law?"

"Through evidence and testimony."

"Is all evidence the same, Hube?" Hemus frowned; as he frowned, his jaws began to grind. "No," the Judge answered himself. "There are two kinds of evidence, direct and indirect. What evidence would prove most directly in this case that Josef Kowalczyk did in fact strike Fanny Adams on the head with that poker until she fell dead?"

Hemus thought that over. Finally he said, "Guess if somebody'd seen him do it."

Judge Shinn beamed. "Exactly. Did you see him do it, Hube?"

"No. I was in Peter's store . . ."

"How could the attorneys responsible for the proper conduct of this trial know that you were in Peter's store at the time of the murder, Hube, and therefore didn't see the defendant do it . . . unless they *asked* you?"

Bong! said Johnny to himself.

Hube Hemus's jaws ground away furiously.

"How could they find out who *did* see him do it, if anybody did," the Judge went on with terrible eloquence, "unless they asked everybody where they were?"

Hemus's back drooped. "Didn't think to see it that way, Judge. But," he added quickly, "that's not the only way to prove a man guilty—"

"Course not, Hube," said Judge Shinn indulgently. "Trial is a complicated business. All sorts of angles to it. This case may very well be decided solely on circumstantial evidence—most murder cases are. But I think you'd be the first to stand up and say, Hube, that everyone in Shinn Corners wants to do this right. So now if Judge Webster is through with his cross-examination, let's get on with the trial, shall we?"

And Judge Webster was through. Judge Webster, in fact,

was taken with a coughing fit that doubled his frail old carcass over.

"No more questions," he spluttered, waving helplessly.

Although it was early, Judge Shinn recessed for lunch.

Court reconvened for the afternoon session with all participants under control, although through varying disciplines. The forces of law and order, who had come into the room in the well-being of danger bypassed and easy going ahead, soon glanced at one another doubtfully. The jury and the bailiff were too quiet, their never-loose mouths jammed shut.

The defendant sat down wearily, watching like an animal. He had sensed the hardening at once. There was a smear of egg at one corner of his mouth, a clue to Elizabeth Sheare's complicity.

Rebecca Hemus's great buttocks squeezed between the rungs of the witness chair in long rolls, like sausages. She kept sucking at her teeth and moving her lower jaw from side to side in a bovine continuity. Her stare disconcerted Judge Shinn, and he kept glancing elsewhere.

That's it, thought Johnny. They've talked over the Judge's doubletalk and they've spotted it for what it was. He felt rather sorry for the Judge.

Rebecca's testimony confirmed her husband's. Hube and the boys had worked in the field all Saturday morning while she and Abbie were in the truck garden weeding and thinning. When the harrow broke down and Hube left for Peter Berry's, the twins came over and cultivated in the rows till the rain began. They all ran back to the house and the boys fixed a separator that needed doing. When Hube got back he and the twins went out to the barn. Then about twenty or twenty-five minutes past three Prue Plummer phoned the terrible news, Hube got into the car, she and Abbie and the boys got into the truck . . .

"In other words, Mrs. Hemus," said Adams, "at two-thirteen Saturday afternoon you, your daughter, and Tommy and Dave were in your house within sight of one another?"

"We were," said Rebecca Hemus accusingly.

Andrew Webster waived cross-examination, and Mrs. Hemus was excused."

"I recall to the stand," said Adams, "Reverend Samuel Sheare."

The minister was poorly today. His movements were slow and his bloodshot eyes suggested that there had been little rest for the spirit. He took his seat with the stiffness of a man who has been too long on his knees.

Adams came to the point at once: "Mr. Sheare, where exactly were you at two-thirteen Saturday afternoon?"

"I was in the parsonage."

"Alone?"

"Mrs. Sheare was with me."

"In the same room, Mr. Sheare?"

"Yes. I was workin' on my sermon for Sunday. I began directly after lunch, which was at noon, and I was still hard at it when the fire siren went off. Mrs. Sheare and I were never out of sight of each other."

Adams was embarrassed. "Of course, Mr. Sheare. Er . . . you didn't happen to see anyone pass the north corner —let's say from a window of the parsonage overlooking Shinn Road—between a quarter to two and a quarter after?"

"We were in my study, Mr. Adams. My study is at the opposite side of the parsonage, facin' the cemetery."

"Judge Webster?"

"No questions."

"You may stand down, Mr. Sheare," said Judge Shinn. But Mr. Sheare sat there. He was looking at Josef Kowalczyk, and Josef Kowalczyk was looking back at him with the unclouded trust of a mortally injured dog.

"Mr. Sheare?" said the Judge again."

The minister started. "Pa'don. I know this is probably out of order, Judge Shinn, but may I take this opportunity to make a request of the court?"

"Yes?"

"When I took Josef the lunch tray my wife prepared for him today, he asked me to do somethin' for him. I should very much like to do it. But I realize that under the circumstances it's necessary to get permission."

Andrew Webster shot a glance at the prisoner. But the man had eyes only for Samuel Sheare.

"What is it the defendant wants, Mr. Sheare?"

"His faith forbids him to accept spiritual consolation from a clergyman not of his church. He would like to see a priest. I ask permission to call Father Girard of the Church of the Holy Ascension in Cudbury."

Judge Shinn was silent.

"He's very much in need, Judge," said Mr. Sheare urgently. "We must realize that he's goin' through tremendous anxiety not only because of his predicament but also 'cause he's bein' held in a Protestant church. Surely—"

"Mr. Sheare." The Judge leaned forward in a sort of colic. "This is a request which shouldn't even have to be made. But you know the peculiar . . . restrictions of our circumstances here. To bring in an outsider now, even a man of the cloth, might give rise to complications we simply couldn't cope with. I'm dreadfully sorry. In a few days, yes. But not now, Mr. Sheare. Do you think you can make the defendant understand?"

"I doubt it."

Samuel Sheare gathered himself and went back to his chair, where he folded his hands and closed his eyes.

"Elizabeth Sheare," said Ferriss Adams.

Then followed the spectacle of the court stenographer exchanging her notebook for the witness chair, and the ancient defense attorney, who claimed to have perfected a shorthand system of his own almost two generations before, temporarily taking over her duties.

Her tenure was short. The stout wife of the pastor testified in a soft and troubled voice, seeking the eyes of her husband frequently—they opened as soon as she took the stand—and answering without hesitation.

Yes, she had joined her husband in his study immediately after doing the lunch dishes Saturday. No, she had not helped him with his sermon; Mr. Sheare always prepared his sermons unaided. She had planned to go to Cudbury with Emily Berry and the Berry children to do some shopping—

"Oh, you don't have a car, Mrs. Sheare?"

She flushed. "Well, we don't really need one, Mr. Adams. This is a very small parish, and when Mr. Sheare goes parish-calling he walks. . . ."

But she had changed her mind about going to Cudbury; Johnny gathered that some stern Congregational discipline had had to be exercised. The school year had ended on Friday, June the twenty-seventh, and in the week before Independence Day she had been busy cleaning up the schoolroom, taking inventory of school property, putting textbooks and supplies away, filing students' records, and the like; on Thursday, the day before the holiday, she had

finished and locked the school for the summer. But she had
one further duty to perform, and it was this that had dis-
suaded her from going into Cudbury with Emily Berry on
Saturday. She spent the afternoon at work beside her
husband preparing her annual report to the school board,
summarizing the year just ended, attendance records, a fi-
nancial statement, the probable enrollment for the fall
term, and so on. Yes, they had worked steadily without
leaving the house until the alarm sent them rushing outdoors to learn of Aunt Fanny Adams's shocking death.

Andrew Webster had only one question: "Mrs. Sheare,
when you got home Friday from Mrs. Adams's get-
together, or perhaps after the Fourth of July exercises on
the green, did your husband give you any money?"

"Yes," answered Elizabeth Sheare in a low voice, "twenty-five dollars, two tens and a five, with which he told
me to buy a dress. That's why I wanted to go to Cudbury
Saturday with Emily Berry. Mr. Sheare didn't say where
he'd got the money, but I knew. The bills smelled of
cinnamon."

Orville Pangman raised his enormous hand, took the
oath, and lowered his body into the witness chair.

At one-thirty Saturday afternoon, he testified, he and
his son Eddie and Joel Hackett, who was "helpin' out,"
began work on the roof of his barn, which needed re-
shingling. At one forty-five they had noticed the tramp—
Orville Pangman jerked his head toward Kowalczyk—at
Prue Plummer's back door; they had remarked about him.
They had seen Prue turn the tramp away, the tramp leave,
and Prue follow him to the road and stare after him for a
few minutes before going indoors again.

They had worked right through until about half-past
three, Eddie ripping up the old shingles on the roof, Joel
handing up the new ones from the farm truck, and he,
Orville, nailing them into place. Yes, right through the
rain and all. With half the rotten shingles ripped off the
roof and the rain looking as if it were going to keep up
indefinitely, they had to keep going or flood the barn.
"We grabbed some slickers hangin' in the barn and kept
goin'. Got wet some, but we finished the job." Pangman
had just nailed the last shingle into place when Prue Plummer came running to her back door screaming the news
that Aunt Fanny had been murdered. The three of them

had immediately jumped into the truck—"Car was in the garage and I didn't want to waste time backin' her out"—and driven over to the Adams house to join the posse. No, Millie wasn't home at two-thirteen. She'd gone over to the Judge's and got back about half-past two.

Millie Pangman's honest face was set in iron curves as she took the oath. She sat down and made two fists menacingly, glaring at Kowalczyk through her goldrimmed eyeglasses.

She certainly did know where she'd been at two-thirteen on Saturday. Fool question, seeing that her husband Orville had just said where she'd been, but if they wanted her to say it, too, she'd just as soon. She was over in Judge Shinn's kitchen, that's where she was. She'd gone over there just before the rain started with a meat pie she'd got ready at home, and she put it in the oven on low heat and prepared some vegetables for the Judge's supper, and then she went back home, figuring to drop in a few times during the afternoon to keep an eye on the meat pie. Only with what happened, it burned and the Judge and Mr. Shinn had to eat out of cans Saturday night. Yes, she left the Judge's house about two-thirty. No, she wasn't alone. She had Deborah in tow, to keep the child out of mischief. Debbie got into more mischief than any six-year-old in Cudbury County; she'd be mighty glad when fall rolled around and the child started school. . . .

Andy Webster asked Millie Pangman a question that puzzled her: "Mrs. Pangman, when did you last hear from your son Merritt?"

"From Merritt? Well, I declare . . . Just Monday mornin'. Yesterday. Got an airmail letter from Japan. Merritt's on some kind of special Navy duty there. What on earth—"

Mathilda Scott had dressed with care for the great event in what must once have been an expensive dress and a hat that had been in fashion during the war. Her beautiful eyes did not look up during her testimony. Her ravaged face with its dark hollows was apprehensive; she kept twisting her work-crippled hands. It was as if she were concealing not only a sorrow but a shame.

It was just another proof of the rottenness of fate,

Johnny reflected, that her neighbor in the jury box was Peter Berry.

At two-thirteen on Saturday, she said, she had been in the bedroom of her husband and father-in-law—because of the work involved in caring for two invalids, she had found it more convenient to keep them in the same room. She was sure of the time because she had had to give Earl his medicine at two o'clock—he took it every four hours during the day, and was always careful to give it to him on the dot. And from that time until Prue Plummer called about twenty-five minutes or so after three, she remained in the bedroom . . . she, her husband, her father-in-law, and her daughter Judy. Earl was kind of jumpy, and Judy was reading to him, a Western magazine, he loved cowboy stories, even old Seth Scott seemed to enjoy them, though she doubted if he really understood. . . . She? She was cleaning the room.

"There's a mess of cleaning up has to be done around two helpless men," Mathilda Scott murmured. "My father-in-law especially."

"When you heard the news from Prue Plummer, Mrs. Scott, you went immediately to the Adams house?"

"Well, I didn't want to, I mean I didn't want to leave my husband, but Earl said Judy could take care of them—as she's doing now—and I was to drive right over with Drakeley and find out what had happened. So Drakeley and I jumped into the jeep—he'd put the car into the garage out of the rain, the jeep was standing out front all day and had got wet anyway, and we don't have a truck any more—anyway, we came on over."

"Was Drakeley working around the place all that time you and the rest of your family were in the house, Mrs. Scott?"

"Well . . . not all the time."

"Oh, Drakeley wasn't home for a while?" asked Ferriss Adams.

"No." The twisting hands twisted faster.

"Where'd your son been, Mrs. Scott?"

"He . . . he'd had to go somewhere for his father."

"I see. What time did Drakeley leave the house?"

"Well, he worked all morning. . . . He left about half-past one."

"In the family car?"

"Yes."

"What time did he get back?"

"About a quarter of three. Talked to his father some, changed his clothes, then went on out back to work. I called him in when I heard the news about Aunt Fanny."

"Where did Drakeley have to go, Mrs. Scott?"

Mathilda Scott looked stricken, and Johnny sat forward. Was this the break?

But guilt has many faces. There was nothing in Mathilda Scott's story of her son's actions Saturday that to the insensitive called for twisting hands and a public agony. It was a familiar story, Johnny felt sure, to everyone there with the possible exception of the Berry's. Drakeley had simply gone over to Comfort to try to borrow money from Henry Worthington, president of the Comfort bank. The bank being closed on Saturdays, Drakeley had made a two o'clock appointment to see Worthington at his Comfort home. The boy had dressed in his best clothes and driven off at one-thirty. He had come back at a quarter to three, empty-handed. That was all. But it was apparently enough to make Mathilda Scott act like a criminal.

Judge Shinn adjourned court until Wednesday morning.

"I don't know what there is about this thing that interests me," Johnny said that night in the Judge's study, "unless it's the puzzle in it. Like one of those jigsaws. You have to keep looking for the missing pieces."

"You'll find 'em all," predicted Ferriss Adams comfortably. "And when you do, you'll have the picture on the cover—our Polish friend."

Andy Webster sucked on his cigar and glared at Adams. "I hear enough of you during the day, Adams," he said querulously. "Shut up and let the boy speak."

Adams grinned.

"Both of you shut up," snapped Judge Shinn. "How do we stand as of close of business tonight, Johnny?"

"Well, statistically speaking, we're moving along," said Johnny. "Nine people testified today. But they add up to a lot more.

"At the opening of court this morning we had twenty-eight people in Shinn Corners to account for.

"At two-thirteen Saturday Peter Berry, Prue Plummer, Hube Hemus, Hosey Lemmon, and Calvin Waters were all in Berry's store. That's five eliminated. Five from twenty-eight leaves twenty-three.

"Rebecca Hemus: She, her daughter, and the troglodyte twins were all in the Hemus house at two-thirteen. I've questioned Tommy and Dave separately this evening, even took a whack at Abbie, who made eyes at me. They alibi one another. Four more out. Four from twenty-three leaves nineteen.

"Nineteen to go, and we have the Sheares in the parsonage study. They alibi each other. Leaving seventeen.

"Orville Pangman's testimony: He, his son Eddie, and young Joel Hackett were fixing the Pangmans' barn roof at the crucial moment. Eddie and Joel agree—I've talked to them, too. Three more out, leaving fourteen.

"Millie Pangman: She and little Debbie were in this house preparing to burn a meat pie—"

"Hold it," said Usher Peague. "Unconfirmed."

"Confirmed," said Johnny.

"Now see here! I'll buy most anything in this fairy tale, but I draw the line at time corroboration by a six-year-old, who wouldn't know two-thirteen P.M. Saturday the fifth from the date the first flying saucer was sighted."

Johnny smiled. "I was lucky. Elizabeth Sheare tells me she was working on her school board report at the one study window in the parsonage that overlooks Four Corners Road. From that window, she says, she had a clear view of the west corner of the intersection and of this house. She says she saw Millie and Deborah arrive, and she saw them leave, at about the times Mrs. Pangman testified to. And she says she's sure that if Millie Pangman had left the house at any time during that period, she'd have noticed. So Millie gets her alibi sans benefit of little Missie Deborah. Two from fourteen leaves twelve.

"Mathilda Scott: She, her husband Earl, her father-in-law Seth Scott, Judy—all in the same room in the Scott house at two-thirteen Saturday. Confirmation through Judy, a very intelligent young lady. Four from twelve leaves eight."

Judge Shinn was drumming on his desk. The sound made him stop and reach for his brandy.

"Go on," he growled.

"Drakeley Scott: Left at one-thirty to see a hardhearted Yankee banker about a farm loan. I have called said hard-hearted banker and, regardless of the degree of his cardiac petrifaction, he's done young Drakeley a good turn. Mr. Henry Worthington states that at two-thirteen P.M. Saturday Drakeley Scott was seated opposite him in the Worthington library being told that his father owed the Comfort bank enough money already, and to go peddle his dairy prospects elsewhere.

"Leaving seven.

"And still we're not finished. I left out Merritt Pangman. His mother's testimony about the airmail letter arriving from Japan yesterday morning pretty well covers Seaman Pangman, notwithstanding the clever theories to the contrary that could be worked up by old mystery story hands."

"Leaving, as of this moment, six."

There was silence for some time.

"Well," said Ferriss Adams at last, "tomorrow morning ought to see *this* nonsense cleaned up."

Nobody replied.

Wednesday began with a bang. They heard the shot at the breakfast table and it brought them up like one man in a rush for the door.

A dusty convertible was hauled up at the intersection. The Hemus twins flanked it; smoke still drifted from Tommy Hemus's gun. A pale elegant man in a pale elegant suit of gabardine and a pearl gray Homburg sat behind the wheel, sputtering.

As they ran into the road, Burney Hackett came streaking from his house on the south corner. They joined forces at the car.

"What's ailing these thugs?" cried the stranger. His voice was fussily cultivated, falsetto with outrage. "These armed hoodlums jumped in front of my car and had the effrontery to order me to go back where I came from! When I refused, they fired a shot in the air and informed me in the most callous way imaginable that the next shot would be right at me!"

"You want to learn not to argue with a gun, mister," said Tommy Hemus, "you'll live longer. We wouldn't 'a' shot him, Judge."

"I'm glad to hear that," said Judge Shinn.

"Maybe put a hole through his beautiful hat," said Dave Hemus. "I bet that lid cost more'n ten bucks."

"Nearer thirty-five," murmured Usher Peague.

"I told you boys not to mess with people passin' through!" scolded Burney Hackett. "Now, didn't I?"

"Sure you did, Burney," drawled Tommy Hemus. "But this character ain't passin' through. He's bound for Aunt Fanny's house."

"What is this?" shrieked the elegant man. "Isn't this a public thoroughfare? I wasn't speeding, was I, breaking any of your piddling hick laws? Will someone please explain!"

"Calm down, sir," said the Judge. "May I ask who you are and why you want to visit Fanny Adams?"

"Ask anything you ruddy well please, I don't have to answer you. Damned if I will!"

"Of course, you don't have to answer, sir. But it would simplify matters if you did."

"The name will mean nothing to you, I'm sure," the man said shortly. "I'm Roger Casavant—"

"The art critic?" said Johnny.

"Well! There's a fellow with at least a primeval culture—"

"Holy smoke," said Ferriss Adams. "I'm responsible for this, Judge. Mr. Casavant phoned last night. I meant to tell you about it this morning. He asked for Aunt Fanny. Naturally—"

"Naturally," said the Judge. "Mr. Casavant, you have an apology coming. Been driving all night?"

"Most of it!"

"Then perhaps you'll join us in a bite of breakfast. No, leave the car here. The boys," and Judge Shinn glanced at the twins, "will take very good care of it, you may be sure. It's all right, Burney. . . ."

It turned out that Roger Casavant had telephoned the night before to ask Fanny Adams if he might not drive up to see her.

"I suppose you might call me," the art critic said, a little mollified by Millie Pangman's ham and eggs, "the world's leading authority on the painter Fanny Adams. I recognized her genius long before the others and I flatter myself that I've had a little something to do with the burgeoning of her career. A great artist, gentlemen! One of the greatest of the modern primitives. As a matter of fact, I'm her biographer. I conceived the idea over a year ago of doing her life and a definitive critique of her place in modern art, and she's been gracious enough to give her consent and cooperation. She made only one condition about my book, that she have final say as to its factual content. I phoned last night to tell her that the first draft of the manuscript was finished. I meant to ask her permission to bring it up so that we could discuss any changes she wanted. Instead," and Casavant glared at Ferriss Adams, "some furtive-sounding pinhead refused to call her to the phone and gave me such a slimy line of jabberwocky that I became seriously concerned. After all, I said to myself, she's a very old lady and she does live alone. I was so alarmed I decided to drive right up . . . only to find my worst fears realized!"

"I'm afraid they're even worse than that, Mr. Casavant," said Judge Shinn. "Fanny Adams was murdered last Saturday afternoon."

It took them some time to restore Roger Casavant's aplomb. He wept real tears and wrung his beautiful hands as he delivered tragic periods to her memory.

"Saturday afternoon, you say? What an irony! Exactly when? . . . No, that's *too* much. Lay another crime at the feet of television! I'd fully intended to come up here Friday evening for the weekend. But last Wednesday I was asked to join a Saturday round table TV program emanating from Chicago—on a discussion of modern art—so I flew out there instead on Friday evening. And there I was, in a wretchedly humid Chicago studio on Saturday afternoon between one and one-thirty, breaking lances against the impenetrable density of two so-called university professors, when but for that stupid waste of time I might have been here saving the life of Fanny Adams!"

Casavant seemed barely able to assimilate the vigilante situation in the village. He kept saying dazedly that he hadn't seen a word of it in the papers.

"That magnificent, that God-given talent," he kept repeating. "A trial, you say? Then you've run the animal to earth. Good, good! Why didn't the newspapers—"

Far from bridling at the warning that he might not be permitted to leave Shinn Corners for a day or two, Casavant tilted his delicate chin and said that a legion of ruffians could not drive him from the village now. There was so much to do. He had to catch up on Fanny Adams's recent paintings; this was his first visit since the previous August. He must see the one they said she was working on when she died—the last, the very last paint-

ing from that inspired brush. . . . In the end, to be rid
of him, Judge Shinn asked Ferriss Adams to take Casavant
over to the Adams house and turn him loose among the
paintings in the cabinets.

"Will it take you long, Mr. Casavant?"

"Oh, days and days. I'll be making copious notes—"

"Well," the Judge sighed, "as long as you stay out from
underfoot. . ."

The first witness Wednesday morning was Selina Hackett, the constable's mother. ("Long as we're engaged in a
mathematics problem," said the Judge, "we may as well
cancel out old Selina, too!")

Each question had to be shouted in the old woman's ear,
and half the time her responses made no sense. But
finally they got out of her a reasonable picture of her
Saturday. Burney had left the Hackett house, she said,
well before noon to drive to Cudbury. She had given her
grandchildren their lunch at about a quarter past twelve—
Joel had to run over from the Pangmans' and run right
back—and after lunch she had made Cynthy and Jimmy
go out with her to the small vegetable garden Burney
had put in behind the garage to hoe and weed the carrots
and onions and lettuce and beans. The rain at two o'clock
had driven them back indoors, and there they had remained, through her son's return from Cudbury and after,
until Prue Plummer came running over to tell her about
Aunt Fanny's murder.

"Fine thing!" shouted Selina Hackett bitterly. "Fine thing
when a body's own child can't tell his mother *first*, but I
have to hear it from a neighbor!"

She still was glaring at her constabulary son when Ferriss Adams helped her out of the witness chair.

Judge Shinn called a short recess while Constable Hackett took his mother across the road to Shinn Free School,
where the children were segregated, and brought back
Sarah Isbel.

Merton Isbel got half out his campchair when his
daughter came in. But Orville Pangman seized the old
man's arm, Hube Hemus leaned over, both said something
insistent to him, and he sank back, mumbling.

The Isbel woman spoke in whispers while the jury
looked at the paintings on the walls, at the ceiling, at the
hands in their laps.

Nobody looked at Merton Isbel.

Sarah had been in her workroom at the Isbel farm with her child Saturday from lunch time on, she said, sewing and fitting a dress; neither of them had set foot out of the house. The workroom was at the back of the house; it had been the smokeroom of the original farmhouse; her mother—this was almost inaudible—her mother had changed it over. Until the rain began her father was visible to her and Mary-Ann through the window. He was plowing behind Smoky, the old gray. The rain had brought him in; he had stabled Smoky. He had his smithy in a corner of the horse barn and she had heard the clang of his hammer on the anvil on and off until Prue Plummer phoned. When the news came, her father hitched Smoky and Ralph to the farm wagon—they had no car— and they drove into the village at a gallop.

When Andrew Webster signified that he had no questions, Sarah Isbel fled.

Ferriss Adams called Merton Isbel to the stand.

The old farmer began quietly enough. When the rain drove him into the barn, he had taken the opportunity to reshoe the two horses. No, he had not left the barn. . . . He dropped to a mutter. The Swedish iron that he used to use for the nails . . . Johnny could not make out whether the Swedish horseshoe nails were no longer available or Isbel could no longer afford them. . . . The lined face, full of pits, a face of weathered granite, came alive in the most curious way. Muscles and nerves began to move, so that the stone seemed turning to a lava, heating more and more from below, until the whole rocky structure was in motion.

And then, with a roar, Mert Isbel erupted.

"Whoreson! Seducer! Antichrist!"

He was on his feet in a crouch, left arm dangling, right arm leveled, chin and nose thrust forward in total accusation.

He was addressing Josef Kowalczyk.

Kowalczyk pressed back in his chair like a man flattening before a hurricane. Andrew Webster's bony little bottom lifted itself clear of his seat as he grasped the edge of the pine table.

"Merton," said Judge Shinn in a shocked voice.

"Mr. Isbel—" began Adams.

"Mert!" Burney Hackett reached.

But Merton Isbel roared again, and as he roared the people held their breath. For this was not the outburst of a sane man heated to anger; it was the explosion of sanity itself. Mert Isbel was hallucinated. For the moment he thought Josef Kowalczyk was the traveling man who had destroyed his daughter Sarah a decade before. And he damned the destroyer and praised God for delivering him into his hands.

"Robber—despoiler of virgins—father of bastards—furrin scum!"

Before their immobilized eyes the old farmer lunged across the pine table and pulled the stupefied prisoner from the chair, his powerful hands about the man's throat.

"Ten years I've waited—ten years—ten years . . ."

Kowalczyk's skin turned from gray to gray-violet. His eyes popped. He made strangling noises. . . .

It took six men to drag Mert Isbel off the prisoner. They held him down on Fanny Adams's trestle table, pinning his arms, hanging onto his thrashing legs. Gradually his struggles subsided, the madness went out of his eyes. They got him to his feet and took him upstairs to one of the bedrooms.

Judge Shinn surveyed the wreckage wildly.

"We'll recess, we'll recess," he kept saying. "Will you people please help clean up this mess!"

Lunch was solitary. Each man chewed away at Millie Pangman's sandwiches tastelessly.

It was only when Ferriss Adams rose to return to the Adams house that Judge Shinn remarked, "Better polish it off, Ferriss. We're going nowhere with extreme rapidity. Were you intending to rest?"

Adams said, "I was, but Casavant said something this morning when I took him over to Aunt Fanny's that I think ought to come out."

"That earbender?" The Judge frowned. "What can he possibly contribute?"

"It's about the painting on the easel."

"Oh?" Andy Webster looked up, interested. "What about the painting on the easel?"

"Never mind," said the Judge. "All right, Ferriss, put Casavant on and wind up. Does it matter what he has to say, Andy? Or what you have to say? What have you

to say, by the way? You'll have to make some gesture
at a defense."

"We have no defense," grunted the old man. "Truth is
our defense, only nobody'll believe it. I can only put
Kowalczyk on the stand and let it go at that."

"You may not be so sure Kowalczyk's telling the truth,
Judge Webster," said Adams slyly, "when you hear what
Casavant says."

"Oh?" said old Andy again.

Adams left, whistling.

Usher Peague glanced curiously at Johnny. "Judge
Shinn's been telling me some fabulous stories about you.
What are you doing, son, preparing to serve us a hasen-
pfeffer from that rabbit you've got up your sleeve?"

"No rabbits," said Johnny. "Or anything else up my
sleeve. You heard the testimony this morning. Old Selina
and the Hackett kids, the three Isbels—that's six more
whose alibis eliminate them, and since those were the only
six left to eliminate . . ."

"Zero," said Peague thoughtfully.

"Yep," said Johnny. "By the trickiest kind of luck everybody in town has an alibi. Everybody, that is, but one.
And that's the one who was tagged for it from the start."

"Well," said Andy Webster, slamming down his napkin,
"that's that!"

Judge Shinn was massaging his head.

"There's always," said the Cudbury editor brightly, "the
man from Mars."

"Oh, sure," said Johnny. "If Kowalczyk didn't kill her,
someone else did. And since everybody's whereabouts for
the time of the murder is confirmed as having been elsewhere, that provisional somebody is an unknown. The
only thing is, I've queried and requeried everyone in sight,
with special attention to the kids, and nobody saw the
slightest sign of one. There just wasn't any stranger in
Shinn Corners Saturday but Josef Kowalczyk." Johnny
shrugged. "Therefore Kowalczyk it's got to be. It's got
to be Kowalczyk if only because—always excepting the
man from Mars—there's just no one else it could have
been."

The Judge looked at his watch. "Andy," he said, "why
do you believe Kowalczyk's story?"

The old lawyer stirred. "You, of all people, Lewis!"
he exclaimed. "How can you ask me a question like that?

As a matter of fact, don't you believe him? You know you do."

"Well," said the Judge uneasily.

"I've even," murmured Johnny, "given myself a hayride in a daydream. You know—you start thinking things. Especially when you have my type of mind . . ."

"What things?" demanded the Judge.

"Well, I see some three dozen people in this daymare of mine, last inhabitants of a decrepit community called Shinn Corners, getting together in a secret hate session and conspiring to alibi one another so that the furriner's guilt will be unassailable. Fact! That's what I've been thinking. Why? Don't ask me why. I suppose when you get right down to it, I don't believe Kowalczyk's guilty, either. Or, to put it more correctly, I don't *want* Kowalczyk to be guilty. I still have enough romanticism left to get a smug bang out of seeing right triumph and evil get kicked in the prat. That's my trouble, really. . . . A conspiracy of thirty-five people, not excluding tender kiddies! Oh, and Pastor Sheare as well. Of such fanciful nastinesses is sentimentality made. All to avoid seeing my nose.

"Let's face it, friends," said Johnny, "we're making passes at a non-existent animule. I'm sorry, Judge, but if that Gilbert and Sullivan jury you finagled me into were to take a vote right this minute. I'd have to vote our suffering Josef guilty."

"Before you start with your witness, Mr. Adams," said Judge Shinn, "Juror Number Three will please rise!"

"That's you, Mert," whispered Hube Hemus. "Get up."

Merton Isbel got to his feet. He was haggard, but the wildness had gone out of his eyes and he looked like what he was, a sagging old man.

"Mert, you and I have known each other since we were boys hooking apples out of old man Urie's orchard back beyond the Hollow," said the Judge softly. "Have you ever known me to lie to you?"

Mert Isbel stared.

"So I tell you now: If you so much as lay one fingernail again on the defendant in this case, Mert, I will swear out a warrant for your arrest and personally see to it that you're prosecuted to the full extent of the law. Do you understand what I'm saying?"

The big old head slowly nodded.

"And what I have just told Merton Isbel," said the Judge to the jury, "applies to every mother's son and daughter in and out of this room who's in any way involved in this case." He rapped with Aunt Fanny's darning egg so suddenly that Prue Plummer jumped. "Proceed with your witness, Mr. Adams!"

As Casavant was sworn in by Burney Hackett, and Ferriss Adams went to work eliciting from him his background and long association with Fanny Adams and her work, Johnny watched Josef Kowalczyk resentfully. The man both puzzled him and wrung his heart. He was either the world's greatest actor or something was incredibly wrong. It grew increasingly hard to be cynical about him, and Johnny wanted above all to maintain his neutrality in a world of warring self-interests. . . . Where before the Polish refugee had been frozen in terror, now he seemed frozen in peace. It was as if the clutch of Mert Isbel's frenzied hands on his neck had been, in its dark taste of death, the fate he had dreaded from the beginning, the execution, the consummated dealing out of his punishment . . . as if he had been hanged, and the rope had snapped, and he was saved to face hanging all over again. No man could feel that fear twice. The knobby hands unconsciously—or consciously?—caressed the swollen throat. The welts, the pain, were—or made to appear?—a reassurance.

Kowalczk's beard was quite heavy now. Put a gold ring on a stick over his head, Johnny thought, and get him into a nightgown, and he'd look like a medieval painting of Jesus Christ. Born to suffer for the redemption of mankind. But mankind was in this room, a bunch of ignorant idiots breathing hell's fire down a scared killer's neck. Unredeemed trash in a dirty old pawnshop. The lot of them.

Kowalczyk closed his eyes and his lips began moving soundlessly, as they did so often now. The sonofabitch was pretending to pray.

Johnny could have kicked him. Or himself.

He struggled go pay attention to Casavant.

"Now Mr. Casavant," Ferriss Adams was saying, "I show you the painting on this easel, the same painting on the same easel found in Fanny Adams's studio beside her body. During the course of your examination of the

Adams canvases this morning did you examine this canvas also?"

"I did."

"Exhibit E, your honor." When the painting had been marked, Adams continued: "Mr. Casavant, is this a genuine Fanny Adams painting?"

"Very much so," smiled Roger Casavant. "If you'd like, I shall be happy to go into details of style, technique, color, brushwork——"

"That won't be necessary, Mr. Casavant," said Judge Shinn hastily. "There's no question here of your qualifications. Go on, Mr. Adams."

"Mr. Casavant. Will you tell the court and the jury whether this painting is finished or unfinished?"

"It is finished," said the expert.

"There's no question in your mind about that?"

"I have said, Mr. Adams, that the painting is finished. Naturally there is no question in my mind, or I should not have said it."

"I see. Of course," said Ferriss Adams humbly. "But our knowledge is not on the level of yours, Mr. Casavant——"

"Please note," interrupted Casavant, "that when I say 'the painting is finished' I verbally italicize the word *painting*. By that I mean that the creative process of applying paint to canvas is over; I do not mean that no work remains to be done. There are mechanistic aspects to art: for example, when the canvas is dry, the artist usually applies a thin lacquer retouch varnish, which not only protects the surface from dust and the deteriorative action of the air—especially where inferior pigments have been used—but also to bring out the darks. The retouch varnish has the further advantage of allowing the artist to paint over it if he wishes to make changes. On the other hand——"

"Mr. Casavant."

"On the other hand, this thin lacquer is a temporary expedient only. Most artists allow anywhere from three to twelve months to elapse, and then they will apply a permanent varnish made from dammar resin. At this point one might say that not only is the *painting* finished, but its mechanistic aspects also."

"But Mr. Casavant——"

"I might interpolate," said Roger Casavant, "in the

aforementioned connection, that Fanny Adams had strong-
ly individualistic work habits. For example, she did not
believe in applying a preliminary retouch varnish; she
never used it. She claimed that it had a slightly yellowing
effect—a moot point among artists. Of course, she used
only the finest pigments, what we know as permanent
colors, which are remarkably resistant to the action of
air. She did use dammar varnish, but never sooner than
ten to twelve months after she completed the painting.
So you will find no varnish on this canvas—"

"Mr. *Casavant*," said Ferriss Adams. "What we want
to find out is: What are your reasons for making the
positive assertion that this is a finished painting?"

"My *reasons?*" Casavant glanced at Adams as if he had
said a dirty word. He placed his joined hands to his lips
and studied Fanny Adams's ceiling, seeking there the ele-
mentary language necessary to convey his meaning to the
brute ears about him. "The work of Fanny Adams is
above all characterized by an impression of realism,
absolute realism achieved through authentic detail. The
secret of her power as an artist lies precisely there . . . in
what I might call her primitive scrupulosity to life and
life-objects."

"Please, Mr. Casavant—"

"In her quaint way, Fanny Adams expressed it thusly:
'I paint,' she would say, 'what I see.' Now, of course,
regarded superficially, that's an ingenuous statement.
Every painter paints what he *sees*. The esthetic variety
of artistic experience comes about because two painters
looking at the same object see it in two different *ways*
—one as a disoriented basic form, perhaps, the other as
an arrangement of symbols. The point is that when
Fanny Adams said, 'I paint what I see,' *she meant it
literally!*" Casavant glared triumphantly at Ferriss Adams.
"It is one of the great charms of her painting style.
She never—I repeat, *never*—painted from imagination,
and she never—I repeat, *never*—painted from memory.
If she painted a tree, it was not any old tree, it was not
the tree as she remembered having seen it in her girl-
hood, or even yesterday, it was *the* tree, the particular
tree she was looking at, the particular tree she was
looking at *now*, at that precise moment in time; in all
its nowness, as it were. If Fanny Adams painted a sky,

it was the sky of the instant. If she painted a barn, you may be sure it was the very barn before her eyes—"

"Excuse me for interrupting, Mr. Casavant," said Ferriss Adams with a sigh, "but I thought you told me this morning . . . I mean, how do you know this painting is *finished?*"

"My dear sir," said Casavant with a kindly smile, "one cannot answer a question like that in a phrase. Now you will recall that a moment ago I referred to Fanny Adams's work habits. They had one further oddity. Just as she never deviated a hair's breadth from the now-object, so she never deviated a hair's breadth from her work habits. I call your attention to the *F.A.* in the lower lefthand corner of this canvas, which is the manner in which she invariably signed her works; and I repeat for the information of the court and jury that never in the case of any canvas from Fanny Adams's brush, in the course of her entire career, did she stroke in that *F.A.* until the *painting* part of the picture was consummated. Never! However, that's a childishly oversimplified reason. When we deal with an artist we deal with a living, pulsing personality, not a lifeless thing under a microscope. There are esthetic reasons, there are emotional reasons if you will, for pronouncing this painting utterly, irrevocably, perfectly finished."

"I think the oversimplified reason you've already given, Mr. Casavant," murmured Judge Shinn, "will suffice."

Ferriss Adams flung the Judge a look of sheer worship. "Now, Mr. Casavant, an analysis of the defendant's movements indicates that he must have quit these premises at approximately the time Aunt Fanny Adams was assaulted and murdered. Also, there is a statement, now part of the court record, made by defendant on the night of his arrest. We're interested in testing defendant's statement for truthfulness—"

Andrew Webster opened his mouth, but he shut it again at a sign from Judge Shinn.

"—for if in any particular it can be shown that his statement lies, there will be a strong presumption that his denial of guilt is a lie, too."

Old Andy struggled, and won.

"In his statement defendant claims, Mr. Casavant, that a moment before leaving this house he pushed the swinging door from the kitchen open a crack and looked into the studio. He says he saw Aunt Fanny at her easel, her back to him, *still working on this painting*. Since that was just about the time she was murdered, and since you have pronounced the painting *finished*, wouldn't you say that the defendant, then, is lying when he maintains that the painting was still being worked on?"

"My God, my God," mumbled Andy Webster.

"My dear sir," said Roger Casavant with an elegant whimsicality, "I can't tell who saw what or when, or who was lying or telling the truth. I can only tell you that the painting on this easel is finished. For the rest, you'll have to work out your personal conclusions."

"Thank you, Mr. Casavant." Ferriss Adams wiped his streaming cheeks. "Your witness."

Judge Webster strode up to the witness chair so determinedly that the witness recoiled slightly.

"As you've no doubt gathered, Mr. Casavant," began the old lawyer, "this is a rather unusual trial. We're allowing ourselves more latitude—to say the least—than is customary. Let's take this in detail. A study of the relative times and certain other factors shows that the defendant must have left the Adams house at approximately the time Mrs. Adams was murdered, as Mr. Adams has stated —within two or three minutes, at most. The time of the murder is fixed as having taken place at exactly two-thirteen P.M. I ask you, sir: Isn't it possible for the defendant to have left this house at, let us say, two-ten, and at two-ten Mrs. Fanny Adams was still working on this painting?"

"I beg pardon?"

"Let me put it another way: Isn't it possible that in the three minutes between two-ten and two-thirteen Fanny Adams finished this painting—the last brush stroke, the initials of the signature, or whatever it was?"

"Well, naturally," said Casavant in an annoyed tone. "There comes a moment—one might say *the* moment— when a painting, any painting, is definitely and finally completed. Whether that moment came *before* the defendant looked in, or *as* he looked in, or *after* he looked in, is not, sir, within my competence."

"How right you are," muttered Andy Webster; but Johnny heard him. "No, just another minute, Mr. Casavant. You have asserted that Fanny Adams painted only what she saw. Tell me, did she paint everything she saw?"

"What's that, what's that?"

"Well! Suppose she was painting the barn and cornfield as seen through her window. Suppose there was a pile of firewood in the lean-to within her view. Would she include the firewood in her painting?"

"Oh, I see what you mean," said Casavant languidly. "No, she did not paint *everything* she saw. That would be an absurdity."

"Then she might decide to include the firewood or she might decide *not* to include the firewood?"

"Exactly. Every painter must be selective. Obviously. By the simplest laws of composition. However, what she did include in a plainting was at least a *part* of the scene she was painting."

"But it is true that the wood might have been stacked in the lean-to, in plain sight, and still she might *not* have included the wood in the picture?"

"That is true."

"That's all, thank you!"

"Mr. Casavant!" Ferriss Adams jumped to his feet. "You say that even if the firewood was in the lean-to, Aunt Fanny might have chosen not to include it in this painting?"

"Yes."

"But isn't it just as true that the fact that she *didn't* paint in any firewood doesn't mean it *was* there?"

Casavant blinked. "Would you mind repeating that, please?"

"Well," said Adams, "if the firewood *was* included in the painting, then—on the basis of your familiarity with Fanny Adams's painting habits and so forth—you'd be positive the firewood was in the lean-to. She painted only what she actually saw, you said."

"That is correct. If there were firewood in this painted lean-to before us, I can say without equivocation that there would have been firewood in the real lean-to."

"But there *is* no firewood in this painted lean-to!" said Adams triumphantly. "That's a fact! An absolute, undeniable fact! Isn't it more likely, then, that since there is no firewood in the painting there was no firewood in the lean-to? And if there was no firewood in the lean-to, the defendant lied?"

"Why, that's sophistry!" shouted Andy Webster. "That doesn't follow at all! It's going around in circles!"

Roger Casavant glanced helplessly at Judge Shinn. "I can only repeat, gentlemen, this painting is finished."

The Judge looked at Andy Webster, and Andy Webster looked at the Judge, and both men looked at the jury. Their faces were a whitewashed wall, unsmudged by comprehension.

"Are you finished with the witness, gentlemen?" asked Judge Shinn.

"Yes, your honor," said Ferriss Adams. "And as far as the People are concerned, we're through—"

"Just a minute."

Everyone in the room turned. It was the juror in the last seat of the second row, Juror Number Twelve. He was scribbling rapidly on the back of an envelope.

"What is it, Mr. Shinn?" asked the Judge, leaning forward.

Johnny folded the envelope. "Mind passing this to his honor, Constable?"

Burney Hackett took the folded envelope gingerly and gave it to Judge Shinn.

The Judge unfolded it.

It read: *Eureka!!!! Call a recess. I think I've got something.*

Five

❖◈━◈━◈━◈━◈━◈━◈━◈━◈━◈━❖

Johnny was excited. It was like playing a slot machine to kick away an hour and suddenly you hit the jackpot. You didn't believe it, but there it was.

There was something else, too. A kind of small wriggling hope, like a newborn baby. You didn't believe that, either, but there it was, too.

It was for laughs, because what after all did it mean? That a nobody hanging in limbo, faceless and unloved, could be cut down and restored to some reasonable imitation of life. The Judge's "one man" notwithstanding, how important could a thing like that be? The nobody still had to face the world as it was. Cut the rope, and you only delayed the execution.

Still, Johnny was stirred. That was almost an end in itself, knowing you could be excited by something good again. It was, as the Judge would have said, progress. The first step in the miracle cure of an incurable disease.

There I go again, Johnny grinned to himself. The eternally springing hope of the human rubber ball. Well, he thought, it proves I still belong to the species.

He took Judge Shinn, Andrew Webster, and Adams, Casavant, and Peague into Fanny Adams's studio with the easel and the painting and he told Peague to put his broad back against the door. They kept staring from Johnny to Exhibit E and back again. Behind everything was the comfortless buzz of the courtroom. There was a restless bass note in it.

"What is it, Johnny?" demanded the Judge.

"Why, simply this," said Johnny. "The painting is all wrong."

They turned back to the painting again, baffled.

"I assure you, Mr. Shinn," said Roger Casavant, "you're entirely mistaken. From every standpoint—and I speak with some claim to authority—this painting is all *right*."

"Not from every standpoint, Mr. Casavant. From every esthetic standpoint maybe. But it's all wrong as far as this case is concerned."

"As to that," said Casavant exquisitely, "I am not qualified to joust with you."

"*What's* wrong?" asked Andy Webster.

"Mr. Casavant has said that Fanny Adams invariably painted only what she saw," said Johnny. "As a matter of fact, she told me substantially the same thing Friday morning herself. The trouble is, I didn't take her literally."

"Can the buildup," said Usher Peague coarsely. "Lay it on the line."

"It's too lovely," grinned Johnny. "Because look. On Saturday, fifth July, Aunt Fanny was standing where I'm standing now and she was looking out this picture window and painting—Mr. Casavant says—what she saw. So let's do the same thing. It's the ninth of July, only four days have passed. Let's look at the cornstalks she saw in Merton Isbel's field there. Anything queer-looking about that corn?"

"Not to me," said Ush Peague.

"It's corn," said Ferriss Adams.

"Yes, Mr. Adams," said Johnny, "It's corn—corn as the good Lord intended corn to look on the ninth day of July. The plants stand a little better than knee-high; like all early July corn, they're young and green. But now I ask you," and Johnny suddenly pointed to the stalks in the painted cornfield on the canvas, "to observe the corn in her picture. Mr. Casavant, did Fanny Adams— who always painted exactly what she saw—see tall withered cornstalks where nature placed small green ones?"

Casavant turned a beautiful rose color. "By George," he mumbled. "It's autumn corn!"

"So this can't be the painting Fanny Adams was working on when she was murdered. But if you want to argue, I can nail it down. This is a finished painting, according to Mr. Casavant. It's a painting of the scene visible from this window, with the addition of a rainstorm. Again, if we're to accept Mr. Casavant's expert knowledge, Aunt Fanny wouldn't have painted in a rainstorm unless rain were actually falling—that is, if this were the painting she was working on Saturday, she must have started it as a scene without rain, but as she was working the rain began to come down and so she painted it into her picture.

"But on Saturday," said Johnny, "the rain didn't start until two o'clock. So she couldn't have begun to paint the rain in until two. Yet thirteen minutes later, the time of her death, the painting's supposed to be finished! I think Mr. Casavant will agree that, no matter how fast a worker Fanny Adams was, she could hardly have painted in this rainstorm in its present finished form in a mere thirteen minutes."

"No, no." Casavant nibbled his perfect fingernails.

"So I repeat, this is the wrong painting."

They studied the canvas.

"But what's it mean?" asked Andy Webster, bewildered.

Johnny shrugged. "I don't know, beyond the obvious fact that somebody switched paintings on the easel. Removed the picture she was actually working on and substituted this one. The question is, what happened to the other painting? Seems to me we ought to look for it."

But he did know. Or thought he knew. Johnny was a hunch player. In a world in which the odds went crazy it seemed as reasonable a way of life as any. He wondered if he would be proved right.

They were banging the slide-doors of the cabinets and beginning to haul out canvases when Roger Casavant smacked his pale forehead with his palm. "Wait! She kept a master list in here . . . she'd assign a number and title to a picture when she started one. Didn't she keep it—? On the top shelf somewhere!"

"One side, slow boy," grunted Usher Peague. "Found!" It was a sheaf of plain yellow papers clipped together. They crowded around the newspaperman.

"God bless her practical old soul," said Johnny, "if she didn't even check off the ones she'd sold! . . . Wait, wait. Number 259, *not* marked sold. September-something. What is that?"

"*September Corn in the Rain*," read Judge Shinn.

"That's it!" Johnny was at the easel turning the painting over. "Ought to be a number on it somewhere . . . There was! But it's been scraped off. See this paper shred still stuck to the frame?" He turned the painting face up again. "Any doubts? This is *September Corn in the Rain*. And now I remember something, Judge. Orville Pangman's crack Friday morning about the rains last September coming too late to save the crop—he lost practically his whole stand of corn because of the drought! September corn isn't normally this dried-up-looking, is it?"

"No," muttered Judge Shinn. "You're right, Johnny. Last September's corn grew to a good height, but it went completely to pot one night between sunset and dawn."

"Here's a notation of the one she *was* painting," cried old Andrew Webster. "The last entry on the last sheet."

"Let's see!" said Johnny. "Number 291, *July Corn* . . . Search the backs of the canvases for a Number 291!"

They found it midway in the rack, where it had been thrust apparently at random.

"Easy! Gently! This has unique value," snarled Roger Casavant. He turned *July Corn* to the light. Then he removed the canvas that was on the easel, propped it against the window, and put the new canvas in its place.

The differences from *September Corn in the Rain* were evident even to a layman's eyes.

"No *F.A.* on it," said Judge Shinn. "So she didn't get to finish it—"

"Not nearly finished," said Casavant impatiently. "It's the same scene painted in the same perspective and from the same vantage point. But observe her treatment of the rain. She'd hardly begun to paint it in. She hadn't even got around to making the stones of the fence look wet, or the foreground or barn roof. And the leaves of the young corn are still vigorously erect, not beaten down as they would have to be if she'd begun the painting as corn in a rainstorm.

"What happened, of course," said Casavant, "was that she had begun to paint the picture as a dry scene. She did considerable work on it before the storm came up. When the rain started, she had the choice of either stopping work and waiting for another rainless day, or incorporating the rainstorm into the picture. Every other artist I know of would have stopped and waited. But I suppose something in the changed conditions piqued her. This was an experiment of a most unusual sort—a sort of overleaf reflection of nature, rain attacking a world that was dry to begin with. Of course, the sky must have been dark and threatening all day, so that the mood of the picture as far as she'd gone was in harmony with the suddenly altered conditions. If only she'd had time to finish this!"

Pay-off, thought Johnny. My man comes in at—what?— thirty-five to one? He felt a glow whose warmth surprised him.

"She did have time to do one thing," smiled Johnny, "and for that Joe Kowalczyk can light a candle to her memory."

"What's that?" demanded Casavant.

"Aunt Fanny added something else that hadn't been there when she started the picture. Look at the interior of the lean-to."

On the floor of the lean-to in the unfinished painting a pile of firewood had been painted in. The individual sticks had merely been sketched; she had not even had time to give the wood grain or character. But it was recognizable as a woodpile.

"Just for the hell of it, and to make the acid test of your claim, Mr. Casavant, that when Fanny Adams did paint what she saw she painted it exactly as it was," murmured Johnny, "suppose you count the pieces of wood she sketched in."

Casavant produced a lens. He went close to *July Corn*

and peered at the lean-to. "One, two, three four . . ." He kept counting until he reached twenty-four.

Then he stopped.

"Twenty-four," said Johnny softly. "And what's Kowalczyk kept saying? *That he split six lengths of log into quarters and stacked them in the lean-to.* What price reliability now, Mr. Adams? Was Pal Joey telling the truth?"

"I'll be jiggered," said Adams in a feeble way.

"You've done it," chortled Andy Webster. "By God, that Army training has something to recommend it after all. Let's get back in there!"

"Yes, who knows?" echoed Peague. "Even into those sunless mentalities some light of doubt may fall."

"Only thing is," said Johnny with a frown, "what does it lead to? Seems as if it ought to give us a lot. But I just can't put my finger on it."

"Never mind that now," said Judge Shinn grimly. "I want to see their faces when this is brought out."

They hurried back to the courtroom.

They had to wait before they could spring the big surprise. First Adams rested his "case." Then there was some legalistic hocus-pocus, and Andrew Webster opened the "defense." He put Josef Kowalczyk on the stand as his first witness, and a long struggle began with the prisoner's monosyllabic English. Through all of this Johnny was conscious of a restlessness about him, a feel of pressures building up. When Ferriss Adams sharply cross-examined, while Adams and Webster wrangled, the tension mounted in the room. About him Johnny could hear the stealthy creak of campchairs as bottoms tightened. *They know something's due to pop here and they're worried stupid,* Johnny thought with enjoyment as he kept chasing the artful dodger in his head: *Keep dodging, I'll corner you in time, there's plenty of that, these poor benighted Hindus aren't going anywhere, wriggle, you bastards. You'll soon be wriggling like worms on a hook.*

He did not really pay attention until Andy Webster put Roger Casavant on the stand as a witness—this time! —for the defense.

Johnny admired the way the old man handled Casavant and *July Corn.* Cudbury's dean of the bar had been a great angler in his day. Now he pulled his fish in on a long taut line, little by little, giving it sea room, never letting it break the surface, until the jury were pulling with him, straining to catch a glimpse of what was moment by moment becoming more obviously a big one. And just when he had them at the snapping point, Judge Webster yanked.

"Will you count the pieces of firewood in Exhibit F —the painting *July Corn*—for the benefit of the jury, Mr. Casavant?"

And Casavant whipped out his lens, stooped over the paint, said, "One, two, three, four," and kept counting until he reached the number twenty-four.

"Mr. Casavant, you have just heard the defendant, in confirmation of his original statement on his arrest, testify that he split six logs into quarters at Mrs. Adams's request and stacked them in the lean-to. Six logs quartered make how many pieces of firewood?"

"Twenty-four."

"And you have just counted how many pieces of firewood in the picture Mrs. Adams was painting when she was stopped by death?"

"Twenty-four."

"In other words, friends of Shinn Corners," cried old Andy, wheeling on the jury as if he had never heard of the rules of evidence, "the defendant, Josef Kowalczyk, is *not* the criminal liar the state's attorney has made him out to be. This man told the truth. The exact, the literal truth. He told the truth about the money, and he told the truth about the firewood!"

Ferriss Adams could no longer contain himself. He jumped up with a shout. "Your honor, counsel is concluding!"

"You will save your conclusions, Judge Webster, for your summation. . . ."

The two lawyers summed up bitterly. No mock battle now. They were using live ammunition as they whanged away.

But Johnny was no longer on the battlefield except in body. The spirit was elsewhere, back on the sidelines. Fight for what? The stupid look on Calvin Waters's face?

He did not really wake up to a sense of time and place until he found himself upstairs in Fanny Adams's bedroom with his eleven co-jurors. The women were chittering away on the four-poster, the men milled about, grumbling. The door was locked and through its aged panels came the sound of Burney Hackett's nasal breathing. It was a small hot room and it was filled with Prue Plummer's strong perfume and the sweetish odors of the barn.

Johnny slouched in a corner, suffering.

A dud, a big loud nothing. They might have been listening down there to an abstruse passage from *Das Kapital* in the original German for all the conviction it had carried. "I want to see their faces," the Judge had said with happy grimness. Well, so he had seen them. Even Lewis Shinn had been fooled. How we want the truth to be what we believe!

Johnny was sore. Suckered by the same old catchwords! "Truth . . ." The world was lousy with sentiments about truth, how it must prevail, how it shines in the dark, how it is simple, tough, knowledge, supreme, open to all men. But who was it had said, "What I tell you three times is true?" Lewis Carroll or somebody. *That* was the truth. Nothing else. Hitler had known it. The Kremlin gang knew it. McCarthy knew it. The good guys kept kidding themselves that they were using yardsticks of eternal adamant, when all the time the damned stuff in the hands of the bad guys was made of goo. . . .

Hube Hemus was saying, "Anybody want to ask questions?"

"Questions about what?" yipped Emily Berry. "There's nothin' to ask, Hube Hemus. We all know he did it."

"Now, Em," said Hemus. "We got to do this right."

"Take a vote," said Merton Isbel heavily. "Take a vote and let's git this abomination over with."

Johnny caught himself preparing to make a speech. He fought with it, he tried to pin it down and throttle it.

But there it was, coming out of his mouth like a demon. "Wait, wait, I'd like to say this. Can anyone here look me in the eye and say he feels no *doubt* about Kowalczyk's guilt? No shadow of doubt?"

They could look him in the eye. He was surrounded by eyes looking him in the eye. Eyes and eyes and eyes.

"How can you be *sure?*" Johnny was outraged to hear himself pleading. "In view of the fact that nobody saw him? No blood was found on him? There's no fingerprint evidence on the poker?"

"The money," Mathilda Scott said passionately. "The

money, Mr. Shinn. He did steal Aunt Fanny's money.
A man who'd steal money—"

What was the use? Reason would make about as big
a noise here as a pinfall in a shooting gallery.

"He got skeered," growled Orville Pangman. "Lost his
head. Maybe she caught him at the cin'mon jar with his
fingers in it—"

"She was killed in the studio, Mr. Pangman, not the
kitchen!" His voice was actually getting up into the
Casavant regions. That was going to help, that was.

"Well, maybe he chased her back into the paintin'
room. Any one of a dozen things could 'a' happened,
Mr. Shinn—"

"Yes, Mr. Pangman. And maybe he didn't chase her
back into the studio, too. Maybe she *didn't* catch him
stealing. Maybe it all happened just the way he says it did.
Show me one thing that proves his testimony false. In the
only two particulars in which his story could be checked
—the stealing of the money and the splitting of the
firewood—he's proved to have told the truth! You folks
are supposed to remember what the law says about the
burden of proof being on the prosecution. You show
me proof—*proof*—that Josef Kowalczyk murdered Aunt
Fanny Adams!"

He had not intended to go that far at all. It was all so
silly and pointless. Hell, it was no trial, anyway. Kowalczyk would get his deserts somewhere else, later. What did
it matter what these yokels did and what they didn't do?

And yet, somehow, it seemed to matter. It seemed
suddenly of tremendous importance that these people see
it right, see it without prejudice, see it . . . Whoa, Johnny-
boy. You're falling into old Lewis Shinn's trap.

He stood at bay, hemmed in by their stupid anger.

"If this furriner didn't murder Aunt Fanny," Peter
Berry shouted, "you tell me who did. Who could have!"

"Take a vote!" roared Merton Isbel.

"He was there," shrilled Millie Pangman.

"The *only* one there," said Prue Plummer triumphantly.

"Was he?" cried Johnny. "Then who switched those
two paintings? *That* proves someone else was there,
doesn't it? Why in God's name would Kowalczyk do a
thing like that? Don't you see what happened? We know
Kowalczyk split that wood and left it in the lean-to—we
know that because Aunt Fanny painted it. We also know

that the wood wasn't there when Burney Hackett found the body. So somebody took the wood away—took it away for the same reason that the paintings were switched: *to make Kowalczyk out a liar!* And if Kowalczyk could be made to look like a liar on a little thing like did he split wood · or didn't he, then who'd believe him on a big thing like did he kill Aunt Fanny and him saying no? *Kowalczyk's been framed, my fellow Americans!*"

"By who?" said a quiet voice.

"What?"

"By who, Mr. Shinn?" It was Hube Hemus.

"How should I know? Do I have to produce a killer for you before you'll let an innocent man go?"

"You have to show us somebody could have been there," said the First Selectman. "But you can't. 'Cause nobody was. There ain't a livin' soul in this town hasn't got an alibi, Mr. Shinn . . . if what ye're drivin' at is one of *us*. Even you outsiders got alibis. Maybe we ain't sma't enough to figger out all that stuff about the paintin' —like you educated folks—but we're sma't enough to know this: Had to be *somebody* bring that poker down on Aunt Fanny's poor old head, and the only one there was who could have is that tramp furriner, Mr. Shinn."

"Take a vote!" snarled Mert Isbel again, making a fist.

Johnny turned to the wall.

Okay, brethren. I'm through.

"Neighbors!" It was Samuel Sheare's voice. Johnny turned around, surprised. He had forgotten all about Samuel Sheare. "Neighbors, before we take a vote . . . As you would that men should do to you, do you also to them likewise. . . . Be you merciful, even as your Father is merciful. And judge not, and you shall not be judged; and condemn not, and · you shall not be condemned; release, and you shall be released. Isn't there one here for whom these words mean somethin'? Don't you understand them? Don't they touch you? Neighbors, will you pray with me?"

Now we can both be happy in the discharge of our duty as we saw it, Johnny thought. Reason and the mercy that comes from faith. We've tried them both, Reverend.

And we're both in the wrong pew.

"Pray for his whoreson's soul," grated Mert Isbel. *"Take a vote."*

"We take a vote," nodded Hubert Hemus. "Peter?"

Peter Berry passed out new pencils and small pads of fresh white paper. The pencils had sharp, sharp points.

"Write your verdicts," directed Hemus.

And for a few seconds there was nothing in the air of Fanny Adams's bedroom but the whisper of pencils.

Then the First Selectman collected the papers.

When he came to Calvin Waters, he said, "Why, Calvin, you ain't wrote nothin'."

Laughing Waters looked up in an agony of intellectual effort. "How do ye write 'guilty'?"

They stood ten to two for conviction.

Two hours later Johnny and Reverend Sheare were backed against a highboy before a three-quarter circle of angry men and women.

"Ye think to deadlock us?" rumbled old Isbel. "Ye think to balk the will of the majority? Vote guilty!"

"Are you threatenin' me, Merton Isbel?" asked Samuel Sheare. "Are you so far gone in hatred and passion that you'd force me to cast my lot with yours?"

"We'll stay here till the cows dry up," rasped Orville Pangman. "And then some!"

"It's a conspiracy, that's what it is," spat Rebecca Hemus. "Puttin' a minister on a jury!"

"And an out-and-out stranger," said Emily Berry. "Ought to run *him* out o' town!"

"And me," sighed Mr. Sheare.

They were shouting and waving their arms. All but Hube Hemus. Hemus leaned against the chintz-hung window, jaws grinding, eyes on Johnny.

"Excuse me," said Johnny in a tired voice. "It's very close in here, good people. I'd like to go over to that corner and sit down."

"Vote guilty!"

"Make him stand!"

"Throw him out!"

"Let him," said Hemus.

They made way.

Johnny sank into the aged pine captain's chair by the four-poster, wiping his face. Thinking came hard in this airless, supercharged room. What idiots they had been to think at all, to "plan" a "campaign." This sort of mindless tenacity, he thought, can't be argued or wheedled or prayed into letting go. It was a blind force, as manageable as the winds. It only went to prove what he had known for a long time now, that man was a chaos, without rhyme or reason; that he blundered about like a maddened animal in the delicate balance of the world, smashing and disrupting, eager only for his own destruction. Compared with the vast and plunging mob, how many beings of wisdom and order and creativeness stood out? A miserable few, working wonders, but always against mind-shattering odds, and doomed in the end to go down with their works, cities and prophets, appliances and arts. The first men to set foot on Mars would find, not goggled-eyed pinheads with antennae, or supermen, but lifeless fused deserts still radiating death. In the evolution of life there was no gene of the spirit; God, Who provided for all things, had left the most important thing out. . . .

"Mr. Shinn."

"Yes?" Johnny looked up. It was Samuel Sheare. The room was suddenly quiet. Hube Hemus was surrounded by his pliable neighbors, and he was whispering to them.

"I think," said Mr. Sheare in a low voice, "somethin' very bad is goin' to happen."

"Sure," said Johnny. "And as far as I'm concerned, the sooner the better."

"Are you one of them, too?" cried the minister.

"What?" Johnny was surprised.

"Givin' in? Givin' up?"

"I didn't give up, padre. But what do you expect me to do?"

"Fight error and evil!"

"Even unto death? All right, Mr. Sheare, I was a chronic neck-sticker-outer in my day. But what does it accomplish? How does that change anything?"

"It does, it does," said Mr. Sheare, wringing his hands. "We mustn't despair, above all we mustn't despair . . ." He bent over Johnny, whispering. "Mr. Shinn, there's no time for talk. They're confused, they're poor and sick, and in their extremity they're plottin' somethin' wicked. If you can get out of here and downstairs to warn the others, I'll stay and try to distract their attention—"

"The door is locked and Burney Hackett's on the other side, Mr. Sheare." Johnny squeezed the little man's hand. "Look. I know this goes down hard with a man like you, padre. There's one way to lick this—for a while, anyway."

"How?"

"By pretending we're won over."

"Won over?"

"If you and I vote guilty, they'll be satisfied. That will get Kowalczyk a reprieve—"

Mr. Sheare straightened. "No," he said coldly. "You're makin' fun of me, Mr. Shinn."

"But I'm not!" Johnny felt anger rising. "Isn't the object to save Kowalczyk? That may do it. This trial doesn't mean anything, Mr. Sheare. The whole thing is a ruse— was from the beginning! It's not the real thing."

"Who knows," asked Mr. Sheare oddly, "what's the real thing and what's not? I won't, I can't, do what I know to be wrong, Mr. Shinn. Nor can you."

"You think so?" Johnny smiled with violence. "A man can do anything. I've seen good Joes, firstclass soldiers, pining away for their loved ones, staunch patriots, faithful churchgoers, who were made to deny and betray their buddies, their wives, their children, their country, their God—every last thing they believed in. They didn't want to do it, Mr. Sheare, but they did."

"And you've also seen men who did not," cried the minister scornfully, "but you choose not to remember those! Mr. Shinn, if you don't stand up now and do what you can, you're worse than Hube Hemus and Mert Isbel and Peter Berry—you're worse than the lot of 'em put together! Wrong as they are, they're at least doin' what they're doin' 'cause they believe in it. But the man who knows what's right and won't stick by it—he's a lost man, Mr. Shinn, and the world's lost with him."

Samuel Sheare darted to the door. They key was in the lock. He turned it with trembling fingers and yanked the door open. Constable Hackett faced about.

"Reached a verdict?" he yawned. " 'Bout time."

Mr. Sheare dashed by him. But before the minister could take two steps in the hall, Hube Hemus was upon him.

"No, Mr. Sheare," Hemus panted. *"No."*

Then the others were there, and before Hackett's unbelieving eyes they dragged their pastor back into the bedroom. Johnny was half out of his chair, staring.

"Set your back against that door, Burney," rapped

Hemus. His expressionless glance was on Johnny. "Orville, watch *him*."

Johnny felt his arm clutched and paralyzed. Orville Pangman said in a low voice, "Don't try nothin', Mr. Shinn, and ye won't git hurt."

And Samuel Sheare's eyes were on him, too. And a great roaring came into Johnny's ears, and he felt for the back of the chair.

"We're givin' ye one last chance," said Hube Hemus. "Mr. Sheare, will ye change your vote?"

"No," said Samuel Sheare.

Johnny struggled to get away from those eyes. But they bored through his lids, burning.

"Mr. Shinn, will you?"

Johnny said, "No."

"Then we know where we stand," said the First Selectman. "Ye tricked us. I think I saw it comin' a long time ago. It's our own fault for lettin' Judge Shinn talk us into this, for lettin' you sit in with us, Mr. Sheare, for lettin' this stranger from New York take his place amongst us like he belongs. We had our trial. We had it in our minds when we caught that murderin' furriner. Ye're only tryin' to take him away from us, like Joe Gonzoli was taken away from us."

The only thing left was the Governor and the National Guard . . .

"He ain't escapin' us through a hung jury. That's what you want, ain't it? But you're not takin' this killer tramp away from us. Are they, neighbors?"

A growl answered him.

Those twenty-four sticks of fresh-cut firewood, Johnny thought wildly. All of a sudden they were running through his head like a fence. What was there about that wood . . .

"Come on!"

But Constable Hackett was in the doorway, licking his lips.

"Hube—" began Hackett uncertainly.

"You, too?" shouted Hemus. "One side!"

And Burney Hackett fell back, and the mob swept by him and out through Fanny Adams's bedroom door, dragging Samuel Sheare and Johnny Shinn with them. They thundered down the stairs and into the astounded room where Judge Shinn waited over coffee with Andrew Webster and Ferriss Adams and Roger Casavant and Usher

Peague, while Josef Kowalczyk sat at the pine table with his face on his outspread arms and the Hemus twins standing over him.

The damned firewood. What was it again? *Oh, yes, what had happened to them. What had happened to them . . .*

And suddenly there was nothing to be heard in the room, nothing at all. The men at the table slowly turned, and the prisoner raised his head, and they remained that way.

"Hube," said Judge Shinn.

But he knew. They all knew.

"This trial," said Hube Hemus, "is over. The verdict is guilty. The punishment—"

Josef Kowalczyk dropped out of his chair and to the floor like a snake. On all fours he slithered along under the table until he reached Lewis Shinn's place. There he entwined himself around the Judge's legs.

The twins jumped. Tommy Hemus flung the table aside. His brother dropped on the clinging man.

The Judge shrieked, "Stop, stop!"

What had happened to them . . .

Tommy Hemus brought his left arm up. It caught Judge Shinn full across the throat. The old man gagged. He staggered back, and the twin clawed at the prisoner in his brother's clutch.

Something happened to Johnny Shinn. Something devastating, like the clap of the last Judgment.

There was no warning. Suddenly, there it was.

The answer.

The answer!

The room was a hell of shouting, plunging people and crashing furniture. Constable Hackett fell against the corner cupboard; the glass shattered and Fanny Adams's old silver tumbled out. Mathilda Scott was down, screaming as Peter Berry's heavy shoes trampled her. Elizabeth Sheare crouched in a corner like an animal. Her husband was trying vainly to reach her, his lips moving in frantic soundlessness.

"String 'im up!" Merton Isbel roared.

Old Andy Webster, Peague, Casavant, Adams were struggling in the grip of frenzied men and women. Eddie Pangman and Drakeley Scott were suddenly there, in the thick of it.

Johnny found himself fighting through the wreckage. It was like an episode in one of his recurring dreams, in which fists struck him, nails tore his skin, knees doubled him up, and all the while there was no pain, no feeling of any kind, just the cool remoteness of a bodiless mind, as if all the rest of him were dead but the spirit and will to think. And somehow, he never knew how, or even why, he was on the table kicking at reaching arms, stamping and shouting and screaming and pleading. "Wait! Wait! If you'll hold it—if you'll give me a chance—I'll hang Kowalczyk for you with my own hands if I'm wrong . . . *I'll give you your damned proof!*"

"Funny thing," Johnny was saying, "funny and grim. Simplest thing in the world . . . But it had to be got to. It was camouflaged. Hidden under a mess of people. And people had nothing to do with it. That's what's funny. Dead wood and people. And it's the people who turn out to be the dead wood."

He was feeling lightheaded. With the dusk had come fireflies and mosquitoes, and they were winking and buzzing everywhere, impervious to slaughter, dancing the humid evening. The road was as airless as Fanny Adams's bedroom had been. The lights of the cars lined alongside the bushes showed up the vacuum dance of tiny wings, and the sounds of what was going on where the people were came hollowly to the two men leaning against Peter Berry's delivery truck.

"What?" said Judge Shinn. He was fingering his throat.

"The alibis," said Johnny. "Three days of alibis for mere people. And all the time the important ones were being set."

"Important what, Johnny?"

"Alibis."

"Alibis for whom?"

"Alibis for *what,*" Johnny corrected. "Why, for cars."

"For cars?" The Judge stared. "Is that—"

"Yes," said Johnny. "Remember Burney Hackett? 'I parked my car in the garage.' And 'it's only a one-car garage.' Burney Hackett owns one automotive vehicle. Fair enough?"

"Fair enough," said the Judge, "because it's true."

"And where was Hackett's only car at two-thirteen P.M. Saturday? It was some nineteen miles from Fanny

Adams's house, being driven back by Hackett from Lyman Hinchley's office in Cudbury.

"And the Berrys," said Johnny, murdering a mosquito. "A passenger car, a delivery truck, and a wrecker from the public garage. At two-thirteen P.M. Saturday the passenger car was locked in a parking lot in Cudbury while Emily Berry and her children sat in Dr. Kaplan's office. At two-thirteen Saturday the delivery truck was standing in Berry's garage, where it had stood since at least ten minutes of two, when Berry began tinkering with it to find out why it didn't start. And what's more, the truck was boxing in his wrecker, as he complained on the stand. Three vehicles, all accounted for.

"Hosey Lemmon?" Johnny shook his head. "No conveyance of any kind. You told me that yourself.

"Prue Plummer's car? She said on the stand it was at Wurley's garage in Cudbury being overhauled for a trip. She said Peter Berry saw Wurley's mechanic take it away. A statement she'd hardly have made in Berry's hearing if it weren't true. Out.

"The Hemuses. Two available vehicles, according to Hube's testimony: the passenger car he drove to the village, and the farm truck his family took to follow. At two-thirteen Saturday the car was parked before Berry's store in plain sight. At the same time his truck had to be on the Hemus place, because no one else in his family left the farm till the news of the murder came.

"The Sheares, no car at all.

"Pangman." Johnny slapped himself in the face. "Same as the Hemuses—one passenger car, one truck. The truck was parked below the barn roof all Saturday afternoon while Joel Hackett handed up shingles to Orville. And the car, Pangman, said, was in his garage.

"Scott. Again two vehicles, a car and a jeep. The car was with Drakeley in Comfort at two-thirteen waiting for a banker to say no. The jeep, according to Mathilda, stood out front on the Scott place all day.

"Calvin Waters. Like Hosey Lemmon, no vehicle of any kind, you said.

"The Isbels. One farm wagon, period. So it shares the alibis of old Mert and Sarah Isbel.

"That cleans out Shinn Corners," said Johnny, "except for you and Dr. Cushman. And you had Russ Bailey drive that decrepit hack of yours back to Cudbury when he dropped us here a week ago, and I established through Dr. Cushman's nurse that at two-thirteen Saturday the doctor's car was parked outside his office in Comfort.

"Hell, you can even eliminate Judge Webster, if you've got that type of mind. His car didn't get to Shinn Corners until the day after the murder."

"And that," said Johnny, "covers the alibi of every vehicle involved with anyone in the case. Except one, the one that's brought us here. And by the way, how did I pull it off? I don't remember."

"Neither do I." Judge Shinn shivered.

There were shouts now on the still night air, peculiar sucking sounds, clanks and creaks and the muffled straining of an engine.

"But how do you connect the two parts of the argument?" asked the Judge. "Because that's what they're going to want to know."

"No, they won't," said Johnny. "They won't want to know anything after this. All they'll want to do is go home and milk their lousy cows. Till the next time."

"Johnny, Johnny," said the Judge with a sigh. "The world does move. You've just moved it a little. . . . If you won't tell them, will you tell me?"

"It was the wood, the firewood." Johnny listened; it seemed to him from the confused sounds that it must soon be over. "What happened to Aunt Fanny's firewood? It was always the sixty-four dollar question, but we were too stupid to ask it. . . .

"The wood was in that lean-to, where Kowalczyk had stacked it at two o'clock. Aunt Fanny painted it before she died at two-thirteen. After she died, after two-thirteen —gone. Taken away.

"Because taken away it was—off the property, an act of total removal, not just a transfer from one place to another. I searched for those twenty-four pieces of wood myself and didn't find them.

"Aunt Fanny was struck down dead and her striker-downer picked up twenty-four lengths of split log—and did what?" smiled Johnny. "Carried them off by hand? With a fresh corpse a few yards away and the possibility of interruption and discovery any minute? It would have taken four or five trips—he could hardly have carried more than five or six pieces of wood in one armful. . . . The likely answer was a vehicle of some sort. A car, or a wagon. Took the mental stature of a foetus to figure out! Disgusting.

"If the wood was carted off in a car or a wagon, and only one vehicle has no alibi—or rather, a faulty alibi . . ." Johnny shrugged.

"I hope," said the Judge. "I hope you're proved right."

Johnny lounged against the truck, waiting. How *had* he done it? Not through sheer lung power—Mert Isbel had outroared him by many decibels. Yet, somehow, in that pandemonium, he had arrested their frenzy, caught their ears, seized their minds, such as they were. He had no faintest memory of what he had said to them. Maybe —the thought came out of nowhere—maybe they *wanted* to be stopped. Could that be it? Like kids in a tantrum, begging for their little world to be set right again. Johnny laughed, and the Judge looked at him sharply.

"They've got it out!"

It was Usher Peague, bursting out of the blackness of the swamp with his red hair flying like a banner, arms whirling in triumph.

They rushed with Peague up the old wagon road through the marsh, each with a flashlight scribbling nonsense on the dark, the sounds of the people and the machinery suddenly stilled.

They came to the end of the road. Flares had been set up, and they cast a cheap pink light over the scene. The derrick of Peter Berry's wrecker was dangling the corpse of Ferriss Adams's bogged coupé from its teeth like a dog. The wrecker was slowly pulling away from the quagmire. Men with two-by-fours and pulleys were maneuvering the car clear of the bog as the wrecker dragged it off. The women of Shinn Corners stood about in silence, watchfully.

"Set it down!" shouted Judge Shinn. "Never mind how! Just so we can get at the trunk!"

The coupé came down with a crash.

Men leaped from every direction.

In a moment the trunk compartment was open. . . .

It was full of firewood.

Ferriss Adams sagged. He would have fallen if not for the Hemus twins.

"One, two, three, four, five—" Johnny kept flinging the sticks to the ground as he counted aloud.

Kowalczyk was there, too, beside Burney Hackett. His

hands were still tied with a rope. He was gaping at the
wood, his eyes glaring in the pink light.

"Fifteen, sixteen, seventeen—"

Samuel Sheare's lips were moving.

"Twenty, twenty-one . . ."

Hubert Hemus stepped back. There was a look of
enormous uncertainty on his gaunt face. He was blinking,
grinding.

"Twenty-four," said Johnny. "And that's the last, good
friends and kindly neighbors."

Burney Hackett untied Josef Kowalczyk's wrists. He
took the rope over to Ferriss Adams and the Hemus
twins jammed Adams's wrists together and Hackett tied
them.

Hube Hemus turned away.

Slowly the people followed.

The peepers and chugarums were really going at it in
the Hollow. A calf bawled in Orville Pangman's cow
barn; the Scotts' dog was howling faintly at the moon.
The street light above Berry's Variety Store on the east
corner lit up the deserted intersection.

Judge Shinn puffed a smoke screen from his cigar and
complained: "I really ought to screen this porch. Promise
myself to do it every summer, but I never seem to get
around to it." He waved his arms at the insects.

"Quiet tonight," said Johnny.

"Enjoy it while you can, my boy. With dawn's early
light come the reporters."

The Hackett house, Prue Plummer's, the Pangman
farmhouse were dark. One window of the parsonage
glowed.

They smoked peacefully, reviewing the noisy aftermath
of the swamp . . . the arrival of the state police, the
magical reappearance of Sheriff Mothless and Coroner
Barnwell, Ferriss Adams's twitching face in the studio
as he re-enacted his crime, his hysterical confession, the
silent villagers looking on and then melting away, Hube
Hemus the last to leave, as if defying Captain Frisbee to
arrest him for the wounding of the trooper. . . . They
were all gone now, the police and the officials and
Adams and Peague and Casavant and Andrew Webster.
Only Josef Kowalczyk remained; Samuel and Elizabeth

Sheare had taken him into the parsonage, where they insisted he spend the night.

"Hard to believe it's all past," remarked the Judge.

Johnny nodded in the darkness. He was feeling empty and restless. "The stupidity is still with us," he said.

"Always," said the Judge. "But so are perception and the right."

"But late," grinned Johnny. "Anyway, I was referring to myself."

"Your stupidity? Johnny—"

"For letting that trick alibi of his take me in."

"What should I say?" growled the Judge. "I didn't see it at all. Still don't, entirely."

"Oh, you were on the phone with the Governor when Adams told all." Johnny flipped his cigaret into the dark garden. "His trick was so simple it was clever. Adams's alibi was that he'd left his office in Cudbury just before one o'clock Saturday afternoon and got back to his office 'about two-thirty' to find Emily Berry's note saying that she was at the dentist's office and he was to phone her there, she had a message for him from his aunt. So, Adams said, he used his office phone to call Mrs. Berry and she gave him his aunt's message to go right over to Shinn Corners and he did—arriving here, he said, at three-thirty, over an hour and a quarter after her murder. Emily Berry confirmed the note business, Adams's phone call at two-thirty; we ourselves saw him get to the Adams house at three-thirty. . . . Complete. A rounded picture of his innocent afternoon.

"Only," said Johnny, "we'd been conned. In all that mess of testimony and confirmation we lost sight of the only important fact in it: *that Emily Berry had merely, Adams's word for it that when he phoned her at Dr. Kaplan's at two-thirty he was calling from his office phone in Cudbury.* The vital part of his alibi was completely without substantiation. A phone call can be made from anywhere. He might have been calling from New York— or Shinn Corners.

"So at two-thirty Saturday afternoon Ferriss Adams wasn't necessarily in Cudbury, twenty-eight miles from the scene of the two-thirteen crime. And if Adams wasn't necessarily in Cudbury at that time, neither was Adams's car. In other words, neither Adams nor his car had a real alibi for the time of the murder; and that's why I staked everything on my proposal to dig that coupé out of the muck."

"The firewood," murmured the Judge. He shook his head in the darkness. "And you say there's no justice, Johnny? He's going to roast in hell over that firewood."

Johnny said nothing.

The Judge's cigar glowed brightly.

"Tell me," said the Judge at last, "about his confession. He found Em Berry's note earlier Saturday, I take it?"

"Yes. He got back from lunch not at two-thirty but about twenty after one—he'd grabbed a sandwich at a diner. The note mentioned that there was a message from his Aunt Fanny. Instead of phoning Emily Berry at the dentist's, Adams phoned his aunt direct . . . at one-twenty, from his office. And what Fanny Adams told him over the phone at that time sealed her fate."

"What did she say to him? Why in God's name did he kill her?"

"Nothing epic," said Johnny. "He's been scrabbling along with his law practice, barely making a living, and as Fanny Adams's only relative he'd always expected to inherit from her when she died. She told him over the phone that she'd decided to make a will leaving her entire estate in trust to Shinn Corners—a permanent fund to be administered by the town elders for school maintenance, making up budget deficits, loans to needy villagers, and so on. She wanted him to draw the will for her . . . What you might call killed by kindness."

"Johnny," said the Judge.

"Well, wasn't she?" Johnny was silent. Then he said, "He got his car and drove to Shinn Corners. It was just about two-ten when he drove down the hill into the village and saw a tramp running out of his aunt's house stuffing something into a pocket. Adams parked in the driveway and went in. His aunt was painting away in her studio . . . At this point," said Johnny, "our big bad killer starts whining. He had no intention of killing her, he says. He'd just come to plead his cause—the blood tie, his need, his hopes, the rest of his piddling concerns. But she cut him short and said he was still young and the town was old and in need. So he went blind-mad, he says, and the next thing he knew he found himself over her dead body, the bloody poker in his hand."

Judge Shinn stirred. "The legal mind. He's already setting up a plea of unpremediated murder."

"The whole thing, he says, took no more than two or three minutes. Right away his brain cleared—it's wonderful how these attacks of temporary insanity go away as suddenly as they come! He needed an alibi and a fall guy, he says. Luck seemed to be with him. The tramp who'd been running away . . . Adams found the empty cinnamon jar and realized that the tramp had robbed the old lady. Made to order. He must be headed for Cudbury—the road went nowhere else—and going on foot he'd be a sitting duck any time that afternoon Adams chose to sick the hunters on him.

"As for the alibi, Adams says he had to use what means he had. He simply picked up his aunt's phone in the kitchen at two-thirty and phoned Emily Berry at Dr. Kaplan's office in Cudbury, telling her he was calling from his own office. The record of that call, by the way, ought to be a strong link in the evidence against him. It's a toll call and will be in the phone company's records."

"So will the call from his office to Aunt Fanny's at one-twenty," said the Judge grimly. "And the firewood business?"

Johnny struck a match and held it to a fresh cigaret. "That's where friend Adams began to get clever. He decided to make the case against the tramp look even blacker. He'd noticed the freshly split firewood stacked in the lean-to. Obviously his aunt at ninety-one hadn't been splitting wood; therefore, he reasoned, it must have been the tramp's work, payment for the half-eaten meal on the kitchen table. Adams went outdoors, threw the twenty-four sticks into his coupé trunk, removed the evidences of Kowalczyk's axwork behind the barn. That would make the tramp out a liar. . . . Adams still thinks it was an inspiration."

"Then he noticed the painting on the easel," said Judge Shinn. "I see, I see. She'd already sketched the firewood into the picture—"

"Yes, and he realized that he either had to replace the wood or get rid of the painting. To put the wood back in the lean-to meant wasting time and running the further risk of being seen. And he couldn't bring himself to destroy the painting—even intestate, her estate came to him and her paintings constituted the valuable part of it.

So he began rummaging in the closet for a possible sub-stitute picture which showed the lean-to empty. He found *September Corn in the Rain*. He put that one on the easel and stowed the unfinished picture away in the cab-inet. He figured that by the time it was dug out again the paint would be dry and it would simply be dismissed as a picture she'd once started and never completed. The seasonal differences between the two canvases just never occurred to him, Adams says.

"And then all he had to do," Johnny yawned, "was drive up the hill and off the road, and park. He waited in the woods till he judged he could safely make his ap-pearance as Horrified Nephew, and then he did just that."

"Lucky," muttered the Judge. "Lucky throughout. Not being seen. The heavy rains. Kowalczyk's pushing his car into the bog—"

"And there he snafued himself," Johnny said, grinning. "He'd completely forgotten the wood in the trunk of his coupé—just went clean out of his mind, he says, other-wise he'd have dumped the twenty-four sticks in the woods somewhere before going back. When he saw his car sinking into the muck late that afternoon it all came back to him with a thud. Of course he pretended to be riled, but you'll recall he also gave us some cogent reasons on the trip back to the village after Kowalczyk's capture why he wasn't going to 'bother' salvaging the car. He simply can't explain why he forgot about the firewood till it was too late for him to do anything about it."

"Mr. Sheare could probably explain it," remarked Judge Shinn, "citing chapter and verse to boot. There goes the light in the parsonage. I imagine Josef Kowalczyk will sleep soundly tonight."

"More likely have nightmares." Johnny stared over at the little dark house of the Sheares. "By the way, what happens to Kowalczyk?"

"Well, I called Talbot Tucker in Cudbury last night—he owns the tanning factory. Talbot said to send Kowal-czyk to him, and that's where Kowalczyk's headed to-morrow morning. With a visit first to Father Girard of the Catholic Church. I talked to Father about Kowalczyk, and he's finding him a place to live, get him settled, and so on."

"I didn't mean that. He still has a theft rap hanging over his head."

"Oh, that." Judge Shinn dropped his cigar neatly over the porch railing, and rose. "Who's going to press the charge—Ferriss Adams?"

Samuel Sheare held open the door of the parsonage. Josef Kowalczyk stepped into the early sunlight, blinking.

Most of Shinn Corners was gathered on the parsonage lawn, the men in their sweaty work clothes, the women in their house dresses, the children in dusty jeans and shorts.

They faced him silently.

Kowalczyk's eyes rolled toward the minister. He took a jerky backward step, his gray skin darkening.

His trousers and tweed jacket looked almost spruce this morning. He wore a tie and shirt of Mr. Sheare's, and he carried an old black felt hat from the same source. A tin lunch box was clutched to his ribs.

He had not shaved, and his hair was still long. "He was anxious," Mr. Sheare explained later, "to get away." His beard was very thick now, its ends beginning to curl. A blond beard with gray in it. It gave him a curiously dignified appearance.

Mr. Sheare put a hand on his arm and murmured.

Josef Kowalczyk let his breath go; he even smiled. But the smile was nervous and perfunctory, a polite flickering of the muscles about his mouth.

His eyes remained wary.

Now Hubert Hemus stepped out of the crowd, one hand out of sight behind his back. He was almost as gray-skinned this morning as Kowalczyk; his eyes were inflamed, as if he had not slept.

He wet his lips several times.

"Mr. Kowalczyk," he began.

Kowalczyk's eyes widened.

"Mr. Kowalczyk," Hube Hemus began a second time. "As First Selectman of Shinn Corners, I'm speakin' for the whole community." He swallowed. Then he went on in a rush. "I expect, Mr. Kowalczyk, we used you hard. Made a mistake." Hemus's jaws ground futilely. "Bad mistake," he acknowledged.

And he stopped again.

Kowalczyk said nothing.

Hemus cried suddenly, "We're a law-abidin' community! Don't ever think we ain't! Town's got a right to protect itself. That's how we figgered." Then his narrow

shoulders slumped. "But I guess we went off half-cocked
. . . went about it the wrong way. Seemed so open and
shut . . ."

Hube Hemus stopped once more, bitterly.

Kowalczyk's lips tightened.

"I go Cudb'ry," he said.

"Wait!" Hemus sounded panicky. He brought his con-
cealed hand around and thrust it at Kowalczyk. It held a
purple-stained pint berry basket. "We're askin' you to
accept this, Mr. Kowalczyk," he said rapidly. "Here."

Josef Kowalczyk stared in the basket. It was full of
bills and coins.

"Here," Hube Hemus said again, urgently.

Kowalczyk took it.

And Hemus turned away at once, and as he turned
away the people of the town turned away, too. Men,
women, and children went quickly back into the road,
and some climbed into cars, and the Isbels climbed
into the wagon behind the horses tethered at the trough,
and some walked across the intersection, and soon they
were all gone.

"I'll give you your text for your sermon Sunday, Mr.
Sheare," said Judge Shinn dryly. " 'The wicked flee when
no man pursueth.' "

Samuel Sheare shook his head, smiling. "Josef, don't
stand here gawpin' at it. It's their way of makin' amends.
A conscience offerin'."

But Kowalczyk eyed the money sullenly.

"It's all right, Joe," said Johnny. "It's an old American
custom. Kick a man between the legs and then get up a
collection to buy him a truss."

A grin spread over the bearded face. Kowalczyk pressed
the basket into Mr. Sheare's astonished hand.

"You take," he said.

And he turned and shuffled rapidly down the parsonage
walk as if he were afraid the minister might come
running after. He hurried up Four Corners Road and
around the horse trough into Shinn Road, putting on Mr.
Sheare's hat with a sort of fussy enjoyment as he went.

"Now that's nice," said the minister slowly, looking
down at the basket. "That's real nice."

They went to the intersection. Kowalczyk was already
passing Fanny Adams's house. He did not glance at it,
but they noticed his steps quicken.

He began the long climb up the sun-drenched hill.

"What am I thinking of? Kowalczyk, wait!" shouted Judge Shinn. "Don't you want me to get somebody to drive you to Cudbury?"

But Josef Kowalczyk only walked the faster. They watched him until he was a speck against the blazing eastern sky.

As he topped the rise and disappeared over Holy Hill, two cars came rushing past him and bore down the hill toward the village. They were taxicabs from Cudbury.

"What did I tell you?" chuckled the Judge. "Out-of-town reporters, and they never even looked his way."

"What's a tramp?" said Johnny.

"Indeed, indeed," said the Judge absently. "Well, Mr. Sheare. Who was it remarked that only the poor know the luxury of giving?"

"A wise man," Mr. Sheare murmured, "I'm sure. I think—yes!—I'll use this money to keep fresh flowers on Fanny Adams's grave. She was real fond of flowers."

And the minister hurried smiling back across the parsonage lawn to tell his wife.

The Judge and Johnny sauntered over to the Shinn lawn and up the porch steps. They sat down in the rockers to wait for the newsmen.

"Ah, me," said the Judge. "Fine, fine day in the making, Johnny."

Johnny looked at the houses and the roads and the fields and the blue blue sky, and he breathed in with real pleasure.

"I've seen worse," conceded Johnny Shinn.